FIRE STORM

KAELY QUINN PROFILER

—— BOOK TWO ——

NANCY MEHL

BETHANYHOUSE

a division of Baker Publishing Group
Minneapolis, Minnesota

© 2019 by Nancy Mehl

Published by Bethany House Publishers
11400 Hampshire Avenue South
Bloomington, Minnesota 55438
www.bethanyhouse.com

Bethany House Publishers is a division of
Baker Publishing Group, Grand Rapids, Michigan

Printed in the United States of America

Library of Congress Cataloging-in-Publication Data
Names: Mehl, Nancy, author.
Title: Fire storm / Nancy Mehl.
Other titles: Mind Games
Description: Bloomington, Minnesota : Bethany House Publishers, [2019] | Series:
    Kaely Quinn profiler ; 2
Identifiers: LCCN 2019003721 | ISBN 9780764231858 (trade paper) | ISBN
    9780764234095 (hardcover) | ISBN 9781493418671 (e-book)
Subjects: | GSAFD: Mystery fiction. | Suspense fiction.
Classification: LCC PS3613.E4254 F57 2019 | DDC 813/.6—dc23
LC record available at https://lccn.loc.gov/2019003721

Cover design by Faceout Studio
Cover photography by Ebru Sidar/Arcangel

Author is represented by The Steve Laube Agency.

19 20 21 22 23 24 25   7 6 5 4 3 2 1

To my brother, Danny.
When we were kids, I usually walked ahead of you,
but this time you took the lead.
I love you so much.
See you soon.

PROLOGUE

He waits, hidden in the shadows of the tall, stately trees that line the street. He is the only one who knows that hell has just opened its door. Houses stand as monuments to the families sleeping peacefully inside, unaware that this day will be like no other. A day that will be seared into their psyches for the rest of their lives.

First comes the smoke, the deadly stench overcoming the scent of flowers from gardens dotting the neighborhood. A thick plume of black slips up into the early morning air.

Suddenly there is a whoosh that seems to suck all the air out of the world. Like a silent storm. Grasping fingers of flames reach out, clutching hungrily for anything they can utterly destroy.

The sleepy neighborhood begins to wake up. People run outside to stare at the monstrosity rising to life down the street, horrified by what they see and ashamed to be grateful it isn't happening to them.

The silence of the morning explodes with the high wail of fire trucks, confirming that the façade of safety residents had trusted to keep them from this moment has literally gone up in smoke.

This is judgment. This is righteousness.

A familiar old verse slips from his lips. "'Jack be nimble, Jack be quick, Jack jump over the candlestick. Jack jump high, Jack jump low, Jack jumped over and burned his toe.'"

He laughs and slowly walks away, not garnering any attention. All eyes are on the great red-and-yellow beast devouring 319 Harbor Lane.

ONE

Kaely turned the heat up in her recently purchased SUV. She spent most of her time in government-owned cars. Having her own vehicle gave her a sense of control. Helped her feel a little more independent.

She checked her GPS. It was set for Darkwater, Nebraska, a small, nondescript Midwestern town in flyover country.

Kaely hadn't planned to visit her mother, but a call from her brother, Jason, changed everything. *"Jessie,"* he'd said, using her given name. *"Mom is sick. Really sick. The doctors thought they got all the cancer, but it seems to have surged back with a vengeance. It's stage three. She's on some kind of experimental treatment, but the doctor says there's no guarantee it'll work. I think you need to see her before . . . well, just come, sis. Please."*

Finding out about her mother's condition at this late stage irritated Kaely, but that's the way communicating with Marcie had been for years. After Kaely's dad was revealed as the notorious Raggedy Man, a serial killer who terrorized Des Moines, the relationship between Marcie and her children shattered. Although Marcie took care of their physical needs, she closed off emotionally. It seemed that every time she looked at Kaely and Jason, all she could see was the husband she hated.

After their lives completely imploded, her mother moved Kaely and her brother to Lincoln, Nebraska. They had no friends left in Des Moines, and it was clear the entire city wanted

9

them gone, hoping that if the monster's family left, the stench of evil might fade away too.

Several years after Kaely and Jason moved out, their mother married again and relocated to Grand Island. It seemed life had given her a second chance. Then, about six months ago, her second marriage fell apart. Marcie promptly packed up and moved to Darkwater. Kaely had no idea why, but she suspected her mother wanted a place where she could disappear. Darkwater sounded like the perfect place to achieve that goal.

Although Kaely called Marcie occasionally, the length of time between calls had begun to stretch out further and further. Complicating the situation was Marcie's revulsion toward Kaely's work with the FBI, where she sought to put away people just like her father. Kaely couldn't really blame her mother for how she felt. She had observed a psychopathic serial killer firsthand. That was enough for any human being in one lifetime.

Kaely had taken two weeks off work—packed on Saturday, left on Sunday, and was arriving on Monday. She still wasn't sure just what she could do for her mother. *"Just let her know you care about her,"* Jason had said. *"Mom has a lot of regrets. If she doesn't get better . . . I mean, are you happy with the way things are now?"*

Of course she wasn't. She knew she had to try to fix things with her mother. Give God a chance to heal their broken relationship.

She was looking forward to seeing Jason again. He owned a successful vintage auto body shop in Colorado. He'd left it in the hands of his staff and traveled to Darkwater to care for their mother. He'd even put off his upcoming wedding. He'd given up everything to be at his mother's side during her illness. There was no way Kaely could turn down his request. So now, here she was, driving through Nebraska, trying to find Darkwater.

"Don't let her manipulate you. She'll try, you know."

Kaely sighed at Georgie's admonishment. "Maybe she's changed." She glanced over at her friend, whose direct stare made Kaely uncomfortable.

"If she'd changed, she would have called you herself to let you know she was sick. Not have Jason do it."

"Look, I'm going in there with a good attitude. My expectations are . . . low. But God can fix what people aren't able to. I can't shut the door entirely, can I?" She arched her eyebrow at Georgie, who smiled, her brown curls bouncing as she shook her head.

"You want me to tell you to have hope." Georgie sighed. "Just be careful. I don't want to see you hurt."

Kaely laughed lightly. "You mean I don't want to see myself get hurt."

"Well, I am you, right?"

"You keep showing up out of the blue. You're not supposed to come unless I call you."

"And yet I'm here."

"And yet you're here . . ." Kaely repeated slowly.

The real Georgie had been her best friend in junior high. When her dad was arrested, Georgie's parents refused to let the girls get together. Losing that friendship had been devastating. This version of Georgie was someone Kaely created a few years ago when she needed someone to talk to about feelings she couldn't share with anyone else. Now Georgie was a debate device, a way to balance her emotions against her common sense. Maybe she'd become a crutch, but Kaely needed her.

"You don't want me to leave," Georgie stated firmly.

"No, I don't. I just . . . well, I'd rather you stop popping up on your own. I feel like . . ." Kaely took a deep breath. "I feel like I'm losing control."

Georgie was silent for a moment. "You haven't recovered from what happened in St. Louis, you know."

"I don't want to talk about that," Kaely snapped.

"It's been three months. You'll have to face it sooner or later. You're aware of it. If you weren't, I wouldn't be warning you."

Kaely waved her free hand toward Georgie. "Go. Right now." When she glanced over at the passenger seat, it was empty.

Kaely couldn't think about what had happened in St. Louis and her mother at the same time. Once she was home, when she was ready, she'd try to make sense of it. Her boss, Special Agent in Charge Solomon Slattery, had insisted she talk to a therapist the Bureau used from time to time. She'd tried to open up to him, but she just couldn't. She'd prayed about it. Asked God for help. So far there had been only silence, but she was confident He was listening. That He was there for her. He'd healed her from so much already. Unfortunately, she still had a long way to go.

Trusting anyone was tough for Kaely. Her father's betrayal still haunted her. Until she could banish his ghost, she couldn't risk getting too close to anyone. She kept men at arm's length, and the past had proven she was right to do so.

She was beginning to depend on Noah Hunter, an agent she'd worked with several times, but she didn't trust him enough to tell him about Georgie—or a lot of other things. Still, she had a feeling about him. That they would end up being close friends. But for now, she liked their relationship as it was.

She smiled to herself as she remembered there was someone else she could talk to. Someone real. Of course, he didn't actually talk back. Well, he did, but not in a way she could always understand.

A month ago she'd acquired a cat, a large Maine coon she'd named Mr. Hoover. Before adopting him from a local rescue organization, she'd spent a few months pretending she had a cat just to prove to herself she could actually care for a living creature. When she was sufficiently certain a pet could survive in her home, Mr. Hoover moved in. He'd previously been named Sampson and had been left behind in an apartment when his family moved out. Kaely's blood had boiled when she'd heard his story.

At first, Mr. Hoover was distrustful and anxious. But he'd finally settled down. A week after moving in with Kaely, he started jumping up on her bed at night and curling up next to her. One night Kaely heard him purr for the first time. As silly as it sounded, she cried for joy.

Then the call came from Jason. She hadn't expected to have to leave Mr. Hoover so soon. She rarely traveled now, but someday that could change, as her dream was to go back to Quantico. If that happened, she would have to travel when the Behavioral Analysis Unit was called on for assistance. She would receive a per diem that would allow her to rent a hotel room or apartment, and she'd be able to take Mr. Hoover with her. If she wasn't certain she could care for him if she moved back to Virginia, she wouldn't have taken him in. Mr. Hoover wouldn't be abandoned again.

Thankfully, her boss's wife offered to take the cat while Kaely was gone. She felt comfortable with Solomon and Joyce, and she was confident they would take good care of Mr. Hoover. But Kaely could still see the look on Mr. Hoover's face when she walked out of the Slatterys' house. Was he wondering if she would come back for him? Just thinking about it brought tears to her eyes.

Kaely probably trusted Solomon more than anyone she knew. He had always supported her. When Quantico forced her to leave when the truth about her father became public, Solomon took her in willingly. He even knew about her peculiar profiling methods and not only accepted them but made her feel they were beneficial. Valuable.

Kaely checked her GPS one more time. She'd need to turn off the highway in about three miles. She glanced at the clock on her dash. A little after four in the afternoon. Maybe she could have supper with her mother and brother and then scoot off to the B&B where she'd made a reservation. She'd spent ten hours in the car yesterday. Today she didn't get on the road until almost ten o'clock, but she'd driven almost five hours. She kept finding excuses to stop along the way. Probably because she wasn't in a hurry to arrive in Darkwater. Her stomach clenched at the thought of confronting her mother. Here she was, a one-time behavioral analyst with the FBI, someone trained to hunt down the most evil people on the planet, and she was afraid to face her own mother. She sighed and tightened her grip on the steering wheel.

"You really need to be careful," Georgie whispered from the back seat this time. "You could walk into another trap. Like you did in St. Louis."

"Hush," Kaely said sharply. "I mean it."

She didn't need any extra pressure right now. This trip was stressing her enough.

She took the turn toward Darkwater. Up ahead, she saw a convenience store. Although she still had half a tank of gas, she pulled in. Better to get gas now since she had no idea what to expect in the small town. Of course, there were over seven thousand people living there. They had to have a gas station. She shook her head as she got out of the car. She was stalling.

Kaely filled her car with gas and then went inside the store to get a candy bar. She grabbed several PayDays, her favorite. She paid for the candy and was headed for the door when she noticed a pile of newspapers on the counter. She caught the cashier's eye and pointed at them.

"How much?" she asked.

The cashier shrugged. "Free."

Kaely thanked her and grabbed a paper. *The Darkwater Digest*. Creative. She went out to her SUV and tossed the paper in the passenger seat. After taking a drink from the coffee in her thermos, she opened one of the PayDays. Early February temperatures in Nebraska had plummeted below their usual frigidness, and snow was in the forecast. Kaely was prepared. She had special tires put on her car. She had no plans to get trapped in Darkwater, Nebraska. She'd drive in over ten inches of snow and ice if she had to. Whatever it took to get home.

As she munched on her candy bar, she decided to check out the *Digest*. Maybe she could learn something about the town her mother had chosen to fade into. On the front page, the big story seemed to involve several house fires. The fire chief was railing against the use of space heaters during cold weather. *"Many of them are cheaply made,"* he'd said to the *Digest*'s reporter. *"People think they can save money by turning down the heat at night and using a space heater. But losing your house, your belongings, and maybe even your life is much more costly."*

"Boy, this guy really hates space heaters," Kaely muttered.

He went on to say that the fire department would be repeating a safety class about the use of space heaters and encouraged residents to attend.

Kaely had to admit she was impressed. He seemed dedicated to keeping his community protected. She took another bite of her candy bar and squinted at the grainy photo of the chief. Nice looking but intense.

There was also a quote from the local sheriff. This picture was a little clearer. A good-looking man with blond hair who also encouraged residents to take safety precautions during cold weather. The end of the article mentioned that Sheriff Brotton had lost an election in November. It seemed he was filling in for the new sheriff who couldn't take office until March due to illness in his family.

She turned the page and found a list of recent fires in Darkwater. In the past two months, there had been three. One death. An older woman living with her family had died of smoke inhalation. *Three fires in two months for a town this size is unusual*, Kaely thought. A rather crudely drawn map showed the various locations where the fires had started. A note under the map indicated where the lone death had occurred.

As she looked at the map, Kaely took a deep breath. She carefully studied it again to make certain her initial impression was right. A second look only confirmed her suspicion. She didn't like the locations of the fires. Her training told her that the fires in Darkwater might not be random accidents. Was it possible Darkwater was being targeted by a serial arsonist?

TWO

The town of Darkwater appeared to be a haven for the middle class. Neat, orderly, well-maintained houses and businesses without much imagination. Those with money lived in large houses outside of the city limits while the rest of the population existed in small homes with tiny lawns and fences designed to keep dogs and children safely contained.

It didn't take long to find her mother's house. It was an unimpressive brick ranch situated in a row of similar houses. Kaely wondered what her mother's other house looked like—the one she'd shared with the husband who'd deserted her.

Kaely didn't know much about him. Her mother had only mentioned him once, right after they got married. According to Marcie, Rod was the antithesis of her father. Supposedly, his kindness and love had healed her. Until it didn't.

Jason explained what he could, but his information was filtered through Marcie's bitterness, so it was hard to know if they were hearing the whole truth. According to Marcie, when she got sick, Rod took off. His first wife had died of cancer, and Rod's explanation was that "he couldn't go through that again." If Marcie was telling the truth, it seemed good ol' Rod's wedding vow about sickness and health had been conditional. The jig was up should his wife actually become ill. What a jerk.

Since her first husband's arrest, Kaely's mom had become extremely negative toward everything and everyone. Her anger brought with it myriad physical complaints. Kaely knew they were not much more than a cry for attention. However, now that she was really sick, Kaely wondered how it would affect her mother's personality. Whatever she encountered, Kaely hoped she was ready for it. She was determined to treat her mother with compassion. Still, a part of her wanted to back the car out of the driveway and race back to St. Louis before anyone knew she was here. She could feel a surge of adrenaline urging her to flee. But all choices faded as the front door of the house opened and Jason stepped out on the porch. As he waved at her, a big smile on his face, she felt embarrassed about her momentary panic.

She grabbed her purse and got out of the car. "Hey, bro!"

Jason came bounding down the steps like an excited puppy. She marveled again at how much they looked alike. Although there was more blond in his hair than in Kaely's auburn locks, they had the same dark eyes. Considering how he'd wanted nothing to do with his family when he left home, the difference in her brother over the past few months was nothing if not miraculous. She credited his newfound faith for most of the changes she saw in him.

As soon as he reached her, he wrapped his arms around her. "I'm so glad you came," he said. "I've missed you."

The time they'd spent together in St. Louis had been brief, but Kaely had really enjoyed it. Truthfully, she had to admit she'd missed him too.

"Back atcha," she said, suddenly feeling emotional. She blinked back tears she hadn't expected.

"Ah, sis. Don't start or you'll get me goin'." He let her go and took a step back. "Where are your bags?"

"I . . . I'm not staying here, Jason," she said. "I've got a room at a B-and-B a couple of miles down the road."

Jason crossed his arms over his chest. A defensive move. "I'm sorry. I thought I made it clear that Mom needs someone with her all the time now. I've been taking care of her for the past month, but I need a break. I'd hoped you could stay here for now while I get some time to myself. Frankly, I'm exhausted."

Kaely took a quick breath, pulling in icy air that made her cough. She struggled to regain her voice. "You didn't say you wanted me to move in with Marcie. I can't do it. I just can't." A thought popped into her head. "Besides, I already paid for the first few nights, Jason. It's too late to cancel." Surely that would get her off the hook. As soon as she said it, she realized how lame it sounded. If Jason really needed a rest, Kaely had to find a way to help him. This was *their* mother. Not just his. "Can't I stay with her during the day? Help her get ready for bed and then go to the B-and-B?"

"No, Jessie. Mom is really weak. She might need help getting to the bathroom in the middle of the night."

"Surely Marcie's insurance covers home health care. If not, I can pitch in financially."

Rather than answer her, Jason just stared down at the ground.

"She won't let anyone in the house she doesn't know." Kaely stated it matter-of-factly. She'd forgotten. That was Marcie. Ever since Des Moines, she wouldn't allow strangers in her home. "If we need to get help, Jason, we will. We can't let her call all the shots. This isn't just about her. We may have to override any objections."

"I agree, but right now is not the time to confront her, Jessie."

"All right, but at some point we'll have to broach the subject." It looked like Kaely was going to have to give in to her mother's demands. She didn't have a choice. *You win again, Marcie.*

"Okay, look. I'll make you a deal. You quit calling me Jessie, and I'll stay with Marcie."

"She hates it that you call her by her first name, you know."

Kaely shook her head. "She hasn't really been my mother for a long time. I'm more comfortable dealing with her as one adult to another. I'm not trying to be cruel. It helps me to keep a balanced attitude."

"And what about how it makes her feel?"

"Oh, come on, Jason. She hasn't shown any interest in me for years. Maybe someday I'll be able to call her Mom again. But that day hasn't arrived yet." Kaely endeavored to switch the subject. "When are you going back to Colorado?"

"I don't know. Mom's too sick. I can't leave yet."

"You've stayed at the house all this time?"

"Yeah." He sighed, and Kaely saw the weariness in his face. "Look, I don't expect you to stay with her twenty-four hours a day. I'll come back in the evenings to cook supper, and if you need a night off, I'll come over. But maybe not for a couple of days?"

"You might as well take my reservation at the B-and-B. On-line it looks like a really nice place. You should enjoy it."

A smile spread across his face, reminding Kaely of a slow-moving sunrise.

"Thanks," he said. "You have no idea how great that sounds." He laughed lightly. "I guess I can call you Kaely, but then you might have to call me Joe. Joe Tucker. That's the name I used so no one would know who I really was."

"But you've gone back to Jason Oliphant. Why?"

"Because it's been a long time since Dad got locked up. People forget, Jess . . . I mean, Kaely. Have you thought about taking back your name too?"

20

"I'm an FBI agent, Jason. Trust me, no one's forgotten Dad's name in the Bureau. Can we get inside before I die of hypothermia and it doesn't matter what my name is?"

Jason laughed. "Okay. Suitcases?"

Kaely turned and reached inside her car, flipping the switch that unlocked the back of the SUV. "Suitcase," she said. "I know how to travel light. Comes in handy when we have a case out of town."

Jason grinned. "So being an FBI agent is really all about learning to pack efficiently?"

Kaely nodded. "It's the most important part. We go through weeks of training at Quantico."

Jason burst out laughing. "Okay, okay. I'll get your suitcase. Let's get inside. I think I've lost the feeling in my feet and hands."

Kaely waited until he had her suitcase, then she grabbed her purse and her "Go Bag." That bag went everywhere with her. It held what she would need if she were called into an unplanned situation that required her to work. The bag contained a couple of changes of clothing, should a case require her to stay overnight or go undercover. In addition, there were a few other items she could use to hide her identity: sunglasses, hats, and a couple of wigs. It also held eye protection, hearing protection, an extra magazine pouch, additional magazines, handcuffs, a bulletproof vest, and her FBI raid jacket.

Inside the larger bag, she also had a smaller tote that contained several files. She was investigating some ongoing cases on her own. Although she wasn't officially allowed to work up profiles since she wasn't with Quantico anymore, Solomon had a few SACs he was close to who contacted him from time to time, asking for Kaely's help. But that was on the down-low. All field offices were supposed to work with the Behavioral Analysis Unit at Quantico, however some of Kaely's anonymous tips had brought closure to crimes that had stumped the police. She couldn't help working profiles. It was who she was.

She followed Jason to the front door of the house. Kaely's heart pounded in her chest. What was it with parents? They brought out reactions no one else could. If Kaely could only see her mother as someone she could analyze without emotion, life would be much simpler. But somehow being around Marcie made Kaely feel as if she were the one being profiled—and the results weren't flattering.

Jason opened the door and ushered Kaely into a cozy living room with comfortable furniture and a fireplace. Thankfully, someone had started a fire. Kaely put her purse on the floor near the couch and hurried over to the welcome heat. She began to thaw a little, but she couldn't stop shaking . . . and lack of heat wasn't the main reason she trembled. Kaely hated being afraid. It made her angry, and she could feel her irritation growing.

"Hello, Jessie."

At the sound of her mother's voice, Kaely spun around, determined to stand her ground. But what she saw made her resolve vanish. Her mother stood before her. Gaunt, thin, and sallow. A shadow of who she'd once been. It was obvious she was wearing a wig. Kaely's determination to confront her melted away. One thing was clear. No matter what, Kaely couldn't walk away now.

"See, I told you," Georgie whispered.

THREE

Hi, Marcie," Kaely said, mustering every ounce of control she could. She walked over to her mother and hugged her. She was shocked to feel Marcie's bones through her clothes. The embrace she received in return was perfunctory and quick. Exactly what Kaely had expected.

"I hope you had a pleasant trip," her mother said, wrestling herself out of her daughter's grasp. "I told Jason you didn't need to come, but he doesn't listen to me."

"You should have called me yourself," Kaely said gently. "Why didn't you tell me you were sick?"

Her mother frowned. "Why? You're not a doctor. What could you do?"

Kaely pushed down the frustration that bubbled up inside her. "Not the point. We're family, remember?"

One of her mother's carefully drawn eyebrows arched. "Yes, Jessie. I understand family. I'm not certain you do."

Kaely's sharp intake of breath was involuntary. She'd called and written so many times and never received a response in return.

"Let me show you to your room," Jason said, stopping Kaely from the sharp retort that almost slipped from her lips.

He picked up Kaely's suitcase and nudged her toward the hallway. She gulped down the bitter words she wanted to throw back at her mother, grabbed her purse and her bag, and silently followed him.

"Is she out of her mind?" she whispered to her brother when they were out of earshot. "Do you know how many times I've tried to reach out to her?"

Jason opened the door to the room where she would be staying. "I know. Mom has her own view of reality, sis. Especially now. When you face your own mortality, it can change the way you see things. I don't think she can deal with the knowledge that she turned her back on us after Dad was arrested, so she's simply changed the facts to suit her needs." He shook his head. "Trying to reason with her won't help. Just apologize."

Kaely's mouth dropped open. "Apologize? For what?"

Jason took her by the arm and pulled her into the bedroom, shutting the door behind them. "Hush," he said sharply. "She's not doing well, Jess . . . I mean, Kaely. Can't you tell by looking at her? I didn't ask you to come here so you could find some kind of justice. I called you because our mother needs us." His dark eyes searched hers. "Why can't you let the past go after all this time? Forgive her? I did."

Jason's words were like a sharp blow. She had every right to be upset with Marcie. Jason's comments felt self-righteous. But, at the same time, they brought uncomfortable conviction. She'd tried to put the past behind her and was surprised at the resentment that slithered up from somewhere deep inside.

"Remember when I called her from St. Louis to tell her what happened to you at the hands of . . . that man?" Jason asked.

Kaely nodded.

"She was shocked. Really upset. I think she realized she could have lost you."

Kaely snorted. "So you said. But she wouldn't speak to me at the time, nor did she call me later. We've never even talked about it."

"Look, I think she was just overwhelmed. You know she can't handle confrontation or displays of emotion. But I told you then and I'll tell you now, she was devastated." He frowned at her. "How are you coping, by the way? When I was in St. Louis, I kept waiting for you to break down. Get emotional. You went through something traumatizing, but you really kept it together—too well, in my opinion."

"I'm fine, Jason. I really am." She shrugged. "I dealt with it in my own way. I moved on."

He stared at her in a way that made Kaely feel uncomfortable. Was Georgie right? Had she actually faced the situation or was she simply ignoring it? She sighed inwardly. She needed to keep her focus on the here and now. She had no choice but to keep the past where it belonged. In the past.

"I guess I need to work on my attitude," Kaely said. "Maybe there's just something between mothers and daughters." She sat down on the bed and tried to rub away the ache in the back of her neck. Another challenge. A new giant. "I can do this," she said, not sure she meant it. "I have to know I tried."

Jason nodded. "I feel the same way. Mom seems to accept me, but she still keeps me at arm's length. And then once in a while, she drops those 'mom bombs.'"

Kaely knew exactly what he meant. A few words linked together with animus, aimed at the heart. Marcie could cut her children down with incredible precision. Kaely constantly fought to keep those comments out of her mind.

"How will you ever find a boyfriend with that horrid red hair?"

"You need to find some kind of job where you don't need any special talents or abilities."

Kaely pushed the words back into the vault where she kept them, before she could feel the deep wounds her mother's criticism had caused. Kaely forced herself to concentrate on her brother. "You said the doctor is trying an experimental treatment?"

Jason nodded. "She wasn't responding to the chemo. I guess this treatment is producing some good results." He cleared his throat and looked away. "It's her last chance, Kaely."

Kaely had realized it was true when she'd hugged Marcie. There wasn't much of her left.

Jason sat down on a chair that matched a desk pushed against the wall. He flashed a quick smile. "I've missed you, you know."

"Sorry it's been so tough for you. You hadn't been home long from St. Louis when she called you, right?"

He nodded and exhaled slowly. "Yeah. A little over a month. I had to scramble to make arrangements to come here." He studied her for a moment. "I'm really happy you're here," he said quietly. "I keep saying that, don't I?"

She grinned at him. "Yeah, but that's okay. I like hearing it."

Kaely gazed around the room. It was plain, but nice. The bed felt comfortable, and she was thankful for the desk where she could work, if she had the time. Then she noticed a large bookcase on the other wall, near the bed. "Oh my goodness," she said in a half whisper, "my books." She got up and walked over to it. There were books she hadn't seen since she'd left home when she was eighteen. "Marcie told me she'd gotten rid of these," Kaely said, running her hand across the spines of beloved novels she'd thought were gone.

When Kaely was thirteen, she'd discovered Agatha Christie. She'd spent her entire allowance on every novel she could find. She also had the Sherlock Holmes series by Arthur Conan Doyle and the Father Brown mysteries written by G. K. Chesterton. Her father had given her the complete set of novels by Charles

Dickens. The characters were so rich. So memorable. They'd stayed with her all these years.

"I don't get it, Jason. She acts like she couldn't care less if she ever talks to me again, but she keeps my books." Kaely tilted her head. "Unless she just wanted them for herself."

Jason laughed. "She's not a reader, Kaely. You know that. She never was."

"I want to think she kept these because of me, but I . . . I just can't." She went over and sat back down on the bed. "Has she said any more about this Rod guy?"

"No, not much. She talked about it when it happened, but now she won't let me bring it up." He shook his head. "You two are more alike than you realize. You both have this talent for not dealing with things that are hurtful." He sought Kaely's eyes. "I worry what will happen if one day everything you're trying to avoid decides it doesn't want to be ignored anymore."

"Two husbands," Kaely said, tuning out Jason's admonition. "The first one turns out to be an infamous serial killer, and the second one walks out when she needs him the most."

"Yeah." Jason leaned back in his chair. "She's had it tough. I'm trying to cut her some slack. It isn't always easy, believe me."

"I'll do my best, Jason, but you may have to pull me back from the edge a few times while I'm here."

Her brother chuckled. "I'll do what I can, but I think that may work both ways."

"I'll only see you for supper?"

"For now. Let me recharge a bit, and we'll set up a schedule that will be fair for both of us. I'm gonna take your reservation at the B-and-B, but I suspect it's rather expensive. There's a decent motel not far from here. I can book a room for us. We can take turns staying there."

"You can't sleep here? I mean, after you're rested up?"

"This is the only spare bedroom, and crashing on the couch is out. Mom spends quite a bit of time there. Sometimes she sleeps on it when she's really hurting. It's firm and it seems to help her. But like I said, I'll show up every evening to make sure you two don't starve to death. It will give us a chance to be together. And if you need to work or just need time for yourself, call me. I'll come over." His lips thinned. "I don't intend to go home until she gets better or . . ."

"Don't finish that sentence," Kaely said. "I can't deal with that possibility yet."

"I'll try, sis, but at some point we may need to call in—"

"Hospice," Kaely said, her voice breaking. She was surprised by a sudden rush of emotion. The mental wall she'd built to protect herself from her mother seemed to be crumbling. "Jason, are you sure it's that bad? Marcie can be a martyr."

"You just said you didn't want to talk about it."

"I changed my mind. I need to know the truth."

"I can only tell you what the doctor said," Jason said softly. "He thinks she could go into remission. But . . ."

"But what?"

"He's concerned that she's given up. He said she needs to fight. If she doesn't, she probably won't make it."

For some reason Jason's words made her angry. "So if we don't give her a reason to live and she dies . . . it will be our fault?" She ran her hand through her unruly hair. "I can't do this. I won't be responsible—"

Jason stood up and grabbed her shoulders. "Stop it, Jessie. This isn't your fault. None of it is. If Mom gives up, that's on her. This isn't a time for faultfinding. It's a time for—"

"Healing," Kaely said with a sigh.

"Yeah." Jason let her go. "It's a time for healing. Let's do everything we can to see that happen. That's what Mom needs more than anything."

He was right. Kaely had to try to build a bridge before it was too late. If she couldn't, the guilt would be too great for her to bear.

FOUR

e has taken special preparations for his next unveiling. This one is special. He waits for the moment when his audience will gather once again. He thrills at the wonder he sees in their faces. And the fear that grips their souls.

That fear belongs to him. It is his strength. His manifesto. His reason for living.

Once Jason left the room, Kaely unpacked. Although she'd teased him about her ability to pack efficiently, there was actually a lot of truth to it. At Quantico, agents traveled quite a bit. She'd been forced to learn how to organize a suitcase. Blouses, jeans, slacks rolled tightly. The same for underwear. She grabbed some hangers from the closet and carefully hung up the clothes she planned to wear during her stay in Darkwater. She was satisfied with the results. A few wrinkles. Not many. The clothes in her Go Bag would stay where they were. They were for emergencies. For official assignments.

She contemplated her conversation with Jason. It was clear God was peeling away another layer of emotional fortification she'd created for her own protection. It was time to face her mother. Deal with their issues. Start to heal little by little. Bit by bit. In ways she could handle. It was painful, but every time He removed some of the false security she'd wrapped around herself, she became stronger. She'd read once that plants pull away when they're pruned. Kaely had no idea if that was true, but God's pruning in her own life was certainly uncomfortable. Still, she welcomed it. Knew she needed it.

She changed into a pair of dark brown slacks and a cream-colored sweater. Then she brushed her hair, trying to bring it into submission. She thought about gathering it into the bun she wore at work but decided against it. She needed a break from Special Agent Kaely Quinn, Behavioral Analyst for the FBI. Of course, that title wasn't recognized by the Bureau right now, but she didn't care. She knew who she was—with or without the approval of Quantico.

She used her hands to smooth out her slacks, took a deep breath, and left the bedroom, heading for the kitchen, where Jason was preparing supper.

As she came around the corner, she heard her mother say, "I told you not to call her. Why don't you ever listen to me?"

Kaely stopped and leaned up against the wall in the hallway where they couldn't see her.

"You're her mother. She cares about you. You should have called her when you got sick. You're the one who created this situation. I think you need to clean it up."

"What situation? I have no idea what you're talking about."

Marcie's voice became higher, a sure sign she was in defense mode. Kaely sometimes wished she wasn't trained to read people, but it was second nature to her now, not something she could turn on and off. It didn't work all the time, but her mother was easy to read. She didn't know how to hide her feelings, giving Kaely a distinct advantage.

"She doesn't want to be here," her mother hissed. "She only came because she felt she had to."

Kaely's first reaction to her mother's declaration was resentment. How could she be so ungrateful when Kaely had given up so much to come to Darkwater? But as soon as the thought popped into her head, another voice reminded her that her mother's assertions were true. Every word. Kaely hadn't wanted to come. She had done so out of a sense of duty.

Jason shushed his mother. "Look, she came. She could have said no, but she didn't. Why don't you give her a chance? You two need to find a way to mend fences. You're family. *We're* family. That's worth fighting for. Especially now."

"You mean because I'm at death's door?"

"No," Jason said with emphasis. "The new treatment has real possibilities. I have a good feeling about—"

"For crying out loud, it's a clinical trial, Jason. Because nothing else worked." Marcie grunted. "It's my last chance."

"But it *is* a chance, Mom," Jason said gently. "Other people have responded well to it. No reason you can't."

"Sure. Because I've had such good luck so far."

Kaely's stomach turned over at Marcie's propensity to feel sorry for herself. She understood her mother's problems, but she couldn't respect her refusal to fight. Kaely hated her tendency toward self-pity, but she planned to keep that to herself. Voicing it would be cruel.

She walked quietly back toward the bedroom. Then she slowly opened the door and pulled it shut with enough force so it could be heard. She turned and started toward the kitchen, this time stepping purposefully so the heels of her flats could be heard on the wood flooring. Conversation immediately ceased in the kitchen.

"Hey, something smells great," Kaely said when she entered the room. She smiled at her brother. "When did you learn how to cook? I don't remember you being handy in the kitchen."

"He wasn't," her mother said. "When he was a kid I couldn't even get him to pick up his dirty dishes and put them in the sink."

"Necessity is the mother of invention," Jason said with a smile. "Living alone meant I had to learn to cook. No one can live on fast food forever."

"What about your fiancée? What's her name again? Audrey?"

Jason nodded. "Audrey is an adequate cook but not as good as I am. She's perfectly happy handing over the chef duties to me after we're married."

Kaely plopped down on one of the stools next to the breakfast bar where her mother sat. Out of the corner of her eye she saw her mother slide over a bit on her own stool. She tried to ignore the quick rush of annoyance that surged through her. "When's the wedding, Jason?"

Her brother took a pot off the stove and turned around to face her. "We're planning for something in the spring."

"After I'm gone," their mother mumbled.

"No, Mom," Jason replied. Kaely could tell he was struggling to keep his tone level. Marcie was pushing all the buttons she could. "I already told you we both expect you to be there."

Jason took another pan off the stove and carried it over to the sink. He poured the noodles into a strainer, then added them to a large bowl. He grabbed the other pot and dumped the contents on top.

"What is it?" Kaely asked.

"Shrimp fettuccine," Jason said. "My specialty. Audrey says it's the best she's ever eaten." He winked at them. "It's my super-secret recipe."

Kaely smiled at him and fluttered her eyelashes dramatically. "But you'll share it with family, right?"

Jason laughed. "Never. And don't try any of that profiler voodoo on me. It won't work."

Kaely snorted. "Profiler voodoo? I don't do voodoo."

Jason carried the bowl of fettuccine over to the table. Then he grabbed the salad he'd already put together, along with some garlic bread he'd just taken out of the oven. Kaely had only eaten a PayDay since early that morning. Her stomach growled with delight.

"It sounds like you're ready to eat," Jason joked.

"Yeah. It's been a long day on the road."

"I'm sorry to put you out," Kaely's mother snapped. She slid off the barstool and took a seat at the table.

"You're not putting me out, Marcie," Kaely said. "I'm just saying I'm hungry and the food smells great."

Kaely glanced over at her brother, who rolled his eyes.

Once they were seated, Jason said a prayer. He didn't even ask. Kaely snuck a look at Marcie. She sat stone-faced, glaring at her son. Well, this promised to be a boatload of fun. Surely she could stick it out for two weeks. When she got home, she might just get down on her knees and kiss the ground. When Jason said, "Amen," Kaely quickly closed her eyes so he would think they'd been shut the entire time.

As he passed the fettuccine around, Kaely could swear she heard someone knocking at the door. But when no one else responded to the sound, she decided she was hearing things. Not unusual for her. Then a voice whispered softly to her. It sounded like Georgie. A familiar line from Shakespeare.

"'By the pricking of my thumbs, something wicked this way comes. Open, locks, whoever knocks!'"

The hairs on the back of her neck stood up.

FIVE

Special Agent Noah Hunter pulled his frozen dinner out of the microwave. When he grabbed the plastic covering and pulled it back, steam released and burned his fingers.

He spit out a curse word. The instructions had advised him to let the entrée sit for a couple of minutes before opening, but he wasn't in the mood to wait. He dropped the meal on his kitchen counter and went over to the sink. After he ran cold water on his offended digits for a couple of minutes, they felt a little better.

He turned off the water and went back to the plastic tray that held his supper. Small slices of beef drowning in lumpy gravy sat next to watery mashed potatoes. He stared at it for a few seconds before taking it over to the trash and tossing it in.

Noah pulled his phone out of his pocket and ordered a pizza. He'd gone through two pizzas last week and had had an urge for something different tonight. But that mess in the trash was not it. The smell made his stomach turn over.

He was bored at work, stuck working a wiretap, what the Bureau called a Title III. He was monitoring an import and export company doing business in South America and the United States. The FBI suspected they were bringing drugs into the country. Noah's job was to monitor the company's phone calls, listening for something that would give them a valid reason to raid the company's shipment, confident they would find the drugs. The last thing they wanted to do was move too quickly and tip them off. They would simply move their operation somewhere else and the FBI would throw away months of work. Unfortunately, he hadn't discovered anything unusual yet.

This kind of work ate up time like nothing else. He listened in all day, but anytime he picked up a conversation that had nothing to do with the court's specific guidelines, he had to stop. Eavesdropping on the administrative assistant chiding her daughter for staying out too late on a school night or overhearing someone calling in a lunch order wasn't allowed. But when the company talked about shipments coming in or going out, Noah stayed on the line. So far the company seemed squeaky clean and full of incredibly normal, dull people. Unfortunately, he was stuck on electronic surveillance through Friday. He had a feeling this was going to be one of the longest weeks of his life.

He pushed down a flood of frustration that rumbled inside him like a hunger. If he was honest with himself, he'd have to face the truth.

He hated that Kaely was in Nebraska.

Thinking about her made it hard to concentrate on anything. Even his job. He knew she had to go. Her mom was sick. But walking into the St. Louis FBI field office knowing she wasn't there left him unsettled. Ever since she'd come into his life, he'd felt like he was walking a tightrope over the Grand Canyon. He had to be careful. Be her friend, but don't care too much. It was frustrating, yet he couldn't walk away. After his wife died, every morning when the alarm clock went off he'd lie in bed and stare up at the ceiling, trying to find one good reason to get out of bed. But since meeting Kaely he couldn't wait to get to work.

Some of his old pals from the SWAT team liked to tease him about being teamed up with "Crazy Kaely." He tried to laugh it off, but it really wasn't funny. He stared at his silent TV like there was something on. *Was* she crazy?

She was definitely the most brilliant FBI agent he'd ever met. But he had concerns. Deep concerns. Kaely's old FBI partner had told Noah about Kaely's imaginary friend, Georgie. Made him swear not to tell Kaely that he'd breached her confidence. Noah was worried—not just about Georgie but also about an interviewing technique Kaely had created.

She'd take the facts from cases, sit down, and pretend to talk to these twisted unidentified subjects, or UNSUBS, as they called them. It helped her to "see" them, to profile them. She'd use the interview technique until she could get a clearer idea of who they were—until she could clearly *see* them sitting across the table from her. The procedure had been wildly successful. Kaely had given law enforcement the information they needed to catch quite a few dangerous people. But at what cost? The criminals who she imagined were now talking back to her. Kaely had admitted she was losing control.

Added to that, a recent traumatic incident involving someone close to her had shaken her deeply, but she wouldn't talk about it. Noah was concerned it was affecting her work and emotional stability. She kept dismissing what had happened, insisting she was okay. It was clear to Noah she wasn't. Was she turning to an imaginary Georgie instead of talking to a real person? He had no way to confront her about it. No way to help her. He felt trapped by the promise he'd made.

Now she was in Nebraska with her mother. He knew they had a tumultuous relationship at best. Would this emotional reunion set her back even more?

Kaely professed to be a Christian. She claimed she had faith in God, that He would see her through whatever she faced.

Would her faith sustain her? Noah wasn't certain. He wanted to believe the way Kaely did, but he just couldn't. Noah had turned his back on the idea of God when his wife died. He couldn't accept that a loving God could stand by and watch Tracy die. She'd been the best person he'd ever met—beautiful, talented, kind, loving. How could God allow her to suffer? At one point Noah had completely convinced himself God couldn't possibly exist. Yet when Kaely talked about Him . . . well, now Noah wasn't so sure.

Noah picked up the remote and pointed it at his TV, but he didn't turn it on. "Look, God. If you're really out there somewhere, and if you care anything about Kaely, you need to help her. Please."

He finally turned on the TV and found *The Letter* with Bette Davis, one of his favorite film noir movies. But as he tried to focus, his mind kept wandering back to a small woman with wild, curly red hair and eyes like deep black pools.

Kaely took a bite of her brother's shrimp fettuccine. Her eyebrows arched in surprise.

"Wow, Jason. This is delicious." She put her fork down. "You're a great cook."

Jason smiled. "It's how I wooed Audrey. I'd love to introduce you to her before the wedding. Maybe we could come to St. Louis sometime soon." He glanced over at Marcie. "After Mom gets well."

Kaely nodded enthusiastically. "That would be great. I can't wait to meet her."

"Well, at least your sister will get to see the woman you're going to marry," Marcie said.

"Mom, I told you Audrey is making plans to come here. You'll meet her before Kaely does."

Marcie grunted. "I won't count on it."

Jason sighed. "Well, you should, because I'm telling you the truth."

Hoping to get through supper without an argument, Kaely changed the subject. "I picked up a local paper at a gas station just outside of town. It had an article about some house fires in Darkwater. What's going on?"

Jason shrugged. "I heard space heaters were the cause. Guess a lot of people use them when it gets cold. You know, to save money. Seems they're pretty dangerous."

"The fire department believes *all* of these fires were started by faulty space heaters?" Kaely didn't say it, but that was almost statistically impossible.

"I'm not sure." Jason pointed his fork at Kaely. "You should talk to Mom's neighbor a couple of houses to the west. He's a firefighter with the local fire department. Nice guy. I think he said they suspected space heaters caused at least two of the fires." He looked at his mother. "Am I right, Mom? I can't quite remember."

Marcie sighed, as if answering Jason's question took all the patience she possessed. "Yes, that's right," she said. "But they were still investigating the third one. It takes a long time to go through all the evidence, I guess."

"Did he mention any suspicions he had?" Kaely asked.

Marcie's eyes narrowed. "For crying out loud, Jessica. I don't know. They're just fires. Fires happen. People are stupid, and they don't take precautions. Please don't try to see something nefarious in everything. It's boring."

Once again Kaely had to fight to stay quiet. After taking a

long, slow breath to calm herself, she said, "I'm sorry to annoy you, but something about the location of the fires bothers me." She got up and hurried back to the bedroom, where she found her purse. She took out the newspaper she'd picked up at the gas station, then carried it back to the table and unfolded it. She pushed it close to her brother and pointed at the marks displaying the addresses of the fires on the map.

"Look, Jason," she said, "this is a pattern. If these were all accidents, this pattern shouldn't be here." Kaely tapped her finger in the middle of the ring of fires. "This is probably where the UNSUB lives or works." She frowned at her brother. "Of course, it's just conjecture at this point. Maybe it's a coincidence, but my gut tells me there may be a problem. If I'm reading this right, the next fire will be here." She pointed to an area of the map just north of her mother's home.

Jason frowned at the map. "I see what you're saying, but if Sam doesn't think these fires were purposely set . . ."

"Sometimes we don't see things because we're not looking for them." Kaely slipped back into her chair. "Again, I'm not certain. I'm just saying I find it suspicious."

"I've had enough of this," Marcie snapped. She grabbed her plate and carried it over to the sink. "I'm going to my room."

Kaely started to call her back, but Jason grabbed her arm and shook his head. She waited until Marcie left before saying, "I didn't take time off work to come here and upset her."

Jason took a drink and then put his glass down. He frowned at her. "Just why *did* you come here, Kaely?"

Surprised by his question, Kaely stuttered, "I-I came be-because . . ."

"Because you felt you had to?"

She leaned toward her brother. "I came because you asked

me to. Because you needed me. And you're right. I honestly don't want to be here. Don't get me wrong, I want this to work out. But I have to wonder what good it's doing her to have me hanging around when she wishes I was back in St. Louis."

Jason sighed. "I know. I've had the same thoughts." He peered at her through narrowed eyes. "You're the expert. What's your analysis?"

"It's not you. Or me," Kaely said slowly. "She's building walls." She knew the psychology of trauma. Had studied it. Had lived it.

Correction. Was still living it.

"It's like I said before," Jason said. "I don't think she really wants to shut us out. Truthfully, I think her mind just can't cope with everything she's been through."

Kaely understood what her brother was saying. As a Christian she knew she should try to help her mother, but she wasn't sure she was capable of giving Marcie what she needed. Her heart was still full of animosity, and she had no idea how to get rid of it.

SIX

ook, let's put our dysfunction aside for a while," Kaely said. "Can we get back to the fires?"

Jason wasn't so easily swayed. "Kaely, do you think Mom knew about Dad? About what he was doing?"

She shook her head. "No. That's one thing I'm sure of. She had no idea. I still remember her face when the FBI stormed the house and arrested him."

"You know, even after all this time, it's still hard for me to believe none of us suspected him."

"Not a new story, I'm afraid," Kaely said. "Look at BTK. Dennis Rader was active in his church. By all accounts he was a loving husband and father. His wife and daughter had no clue. Psychopaths have a way of compartmentalizing everything. Their regular lives exist in one part of their personalities, and their other lives fit neatly somewhere else. If they keep them separate, they can justify the evil deeds they commit."

"What you do, Kaely, does it help you understand Dad?"

Kaely shrugged. "Yes and no. I understand the psychology, but there's a part of me that can't accept Dad would trade life with us for . . . that." She picked up her glass and stared at it as if there were answers floating inside. "I've been taught that people like Dad feel compelled. Drawn by something larger than themselves. Rader called it 'Factor X.' I'm sure our father would tell you he felt the same thing. He was tortured by a compulsion he couldn't control—or says he couldn't anyway."

"You don't believe that?"

Kaely leaned back in her chair and crossed her arms over her chest. "In some ways I do, but I have a problem with anyone who says they can't help themselves when they're able to hide what they're doing. Lie to protect themselves. Stop if the police get too close. That means they are able to exert some power over their actions."

"Do you believe in demons, Kaely?" Jason lowered his voice as if someone else was listening.

"You mean do I attribute Factor X to demonic influence?" Kaely hesitated. "Yes, of course, but that's something I keep to myself. Some people in the Bureau already think I'm insane. Telling them I think demons are speaking to some of these twisted killers could get me tossed out of the FBI for good." She frowned. "In the end, what I do has nothing to do with the spiritual condition of an UNSUB. I follow patterns. Statistical possibilities. No matter who the UNSUB is, they still need to fit the profiles I come up with. I simply try to help the authorities narrow the field. After these monsters are locked up, they'll get the chance to speak to ministers who do prison work. Several rather notorious serial killers have found God while behind bars."

Jason tapped his fingers on the tabletop, not looking at his sister. Something was bothering him. Kaely waited.

"Have . . . have you ever thought about visiting Dad?"

"No. Never." Kaely's words were hurled at her brother like bullets from an automatic weapon. She wanted nothing to do with their father. Had promised herself she would never see him again.

"But, Kaely, we both have God in our lives now. Shouldn't we try to witness to him?"

"Sorry, Jason, but I won't do it. I don't want that man in my head again. If you feel you need to go visit him, do it. I won't be upset. But I don't want to hear about it."

"As Christians don't we have the responsibility to tell him about God's forgiveness?"

"Like I said, there are ministries that work with prisoners. Let them deal with him."

"But—"

"I can't talk about this now, Jason." She started to stand up.

Jason took her arm and gently pulled her back down. "Stay. We don't have to talk about Dad anymore. We can focus on figuring out those fires." He stared at the map for several seconds. "I'm not sure I see what you do, but if you're right . . . I mean, what can we do?"

"Well, first of all, the local authorities need to consider that these fires could be more than unintentional incidents. They need to look closely for evidence that this is arson, but until they do and open an investigation, there's nothing that can be done." She paused for a moment. "You mentioned there was a firefighter who lived nearby? Sam?"

"Yeah. Sam Lucas. He lives a few doors down. He's been really kind to Mom ever since she moved here. Would you like to talk to him?"

Kaely nodded. "That would be great. But don't tell him I'm with the Bureau. In fact, please don't tell anyone. I have no authority to look into this in an official capacity."

"Okay. I'll give him a call in the morning."

Kaely picked up her glass of tea and took a few gulps. Her mouth was dry from talking so much. "Enjoy my room at the B-and-B."

Jason got up from his chair. "Oh, I will. Trust me. Here."

He reached into the pocket of his jeans, took out a key, and handed it to her.

"It's like I'm experiencing one of my nightmares," Kaely said as she slipped the key into her own pocket. She laughed, but there was a grain of truth in her comment. Living at home with her mother again. Kaely was slightly terrified, but she wasn't sure why. She swallowed back her fear and helped Jason clean up the kitchen.

As he drove away, she waved good-bye. Kaely locked the front door and headed down the hallway. Even though this wasn't the house where her family had lived, ghosts of the past whirled around her, trying to get her attention. It was getting harder and harder to push them away.

SEVEN

After taking a shower, Kaely stopped by her mother's room. The door was closed, so Kaely opened it slightly, wanting to make sure Marcie didn't need anything. She was lying in bed, snoring softly. Kaely left the door open a crack so she could hear if Marcie called for help during the night. Kaely had just crawled under the covers when Georgie appeared, sitting on the end of the bed.

"This isn't going well," she said. "You know that."

"I can keep my emotions in check," Kaely retorted.

Georgie's brown curls wiggled as she shook her head. "I'm not sure that's true, hon."

Kaely rolled over on her back and stared up at the ceiling. "I'm a Christian. I have to forgive. Why am I having such a hard time?"

"You think being a Christian means you're never allowed to be angry or hurt?"

"I don't know," Kaely said softly.

"No one can hide their feelings forever," Georgie said. "Sooner or later they're going to force their way out into the open. How you deal with them makes the difference."

"You think I should try to have an honest discussion with my mother?" Kaely shook her head. "That won't work. She won't talk to me."

"And why is that?"

Kaely sighed. "Because she's trying to hold it all inside too. And that's why she—"

Before she could finish her sentence, Georgie disappeared. It was too obvious to ignore. Kaely and her mother were going through the same thing—and reacting exactly alike. Maybe Kaely wasn't feeling sorry for herself the way Marcie was, but their similarities were disconcerting. They really needed to talk. But could Marcie do that? Kaely would hate it if her mother died with this animosity between them. Kaely closed her eyes and prayed, asking God to help them bridge the gap. To bring healing to their relationship.

She lay in bed a long time, thinking about the books on the shelves next to her. They brought back memories of climbing under her sheets with a flashlight, reading into the early morning hours.

She pulled up the covers, grateful for the nightlight stuck into an outlet on the wall. She wasn't usually afraid of the dark, but in this room, it was as if she could feel specters hiding in the shadows, ghosts of herself at different ages. She remembered the night she couldn't sleep with her favorite teddy bear because Mom had to wash it. When she finally got it back, Boo Bear seemed different somehow. It was years later before she found out that her old bear had come apart in the washing machine. Her parents had searched almost every store in Des Moines looking for the same bear. Her father finally found it in a small toy store on the edge of town. When he slipped it into Kaely's arms she didn't question the differences. She trusted it was Boo Bear because her father told her it was. The memory gurgled around inside her like molten lava. She threw off the covers and sat up in bed, determined not to allow the past to ensnare her.

She'd worn sweat pants and her FBI sweat shirt to bed. The sweat shirt hugged her like an old friend, reminding her who she was now—not a little girl who needed a stuffed bear to feel safe, but a trained FBI agent who didn't need anyone else to protect her.

She unzipped her suitcase and took out her laptop, then crossed the room to the desk. After grabbing another one of her PayDays, she pulled up the local newspaper online and began searching through past issues. The fires were all on the front page, which made sense in a town this small. She discovered a clearer picture of the local fire chief. He was a good-looking African-American man with intense eyes and a determined expression. Probably in his forties. That surprised her. For some reason she'd thought he'd be older. She got her notebook and wrote down his name. *Fire Chief Tuck Reynolds.*

In an article from about a month ago, the chief urged homeowners to make certain their space heaters were safe. There was a list of recommendations to ensure a good outcome. Kaely was surprised by the long list of safety rules. Her parents had used space heaters when she and Jason were young, and she was pretty sure they hadn't followed all these suggestions.

Never leave them unattended. Keep them three feet from everything, including drapes, clothing, and bedding. Make sure they're approved by an independent testing lab. Use near a smoke alarm. Make sure they're the right size for the room. Place on a hard, flat surface. Don't use with extension cords.

Kaely gulped at this one. Extension cords had been a source of pride for her father when she was young. The more things he plugged into one cord, the better. The article gave at least five other warnings. Maybe the fires weren't that suspicious. Frankly, after reading the article, Kaely was pretty sure she and Jason were only alive by the grace of God. Kaely closed the article while promising herself she would never, ever buy a space heater.

She opened her candy bar and took a big bite. Then she looked again at the map of the fires. Was she just seeing what she wanted to? Could she be manufacturing something to take her mind off being with her mother? Or was there actually an uncomfortable pattern here?

She searched online for a local TV news station to see if she could learn anything else. It took a while to find KMVP, a station out of Valentine, a city not too far from Darkwater. The words *Breaking News* flashed across her screen. Kaely clicked on them, and a female reporter appeared. Kaely turned up the volume on her laptop.

"We have a report of another fire in Darkwater. We've sent a crew and will report more details when we have them. All we know right now is that the fire department has been called to a home in the northern part of the city. Fire crews are on the scene. We'll update you when we can."

The north part of town. Her mom's house was on the north side. Kaely turned the volume down and listened. Sure enough, she could hear the whine of sirens outside. She quickly finished her candy bar, then pulled on her boots and grabbed her coat and purse. After putting on her coat, she walked carefully down the hallway toward the front door. First, she looked in on her mother once again. Still sound asleep.

She checked for the house key Jason had given her. After locating it, she slowly opened the front door and slipped out, closing it behind her. She double-checked, making sure it was locked. Then she got into her car and backed out of the driveway without headlights. When she was safely in the street, she flicked them on and headed toward the area of town where she was fairly sure the fire would be. The thought skirted through her mind that maybe she shouldn't have left her mother alone, but she wouldn't be gone long. Marcie probably wouldn't even know she'd left. It was probably better to let her sleep.

It wasn't hard to find the fire. All she had to do was follow the police cars rushing past her, lights and sirens blaring. When she arrived near the scene, she could see the flames dancing in the dark. The water from the firefighters' hoses caused the flames to sizzle and jump, as if trying to escape extinction.

Kaely parked her car on the street and walked down the sidewalk toward the fire. She could flash her creds here and try to get closer, but she was from another state and had no authority in Nebraska. Besides, unless the FBI was called in, the local fire and police departments would handle this on their own. Her credentials wouldn't help her tonight.

The location of the fire confirmed her suspicions. In her experience, arsonists picked sites away from their own homes, but still in their comfort zone. Places where they felt they could get in and out safely. Although reliable profiles were sketchy and prone to embellishment by those being interviewed, most serial arsonists were young white males. Almost eighty percent of them set fires before they were twenty-nine. Most of them had poor interpersonal relationships, along with a large number of previous arrests. Only one-third had regular jobs. Serial arsonists tended to have distant relationships with their parents and might even be aggressive toward them.

But the part of the study that had propelled Kaely outside on a freezing winter night was the fact that nearly a third of serial arsonists liked to show up at the scene and enjoy the fruit of their labor. She wasn't there to see the fire.

She was there to see the person who set the fire.

Anger is breath. Anger is life. Rage is everything. He watches the emergency vehicles descend upon the scene, their lights bouncing around the neighborhood like some crazed disco ball. Firefighters jump down from their engines, everyone with a job to do, working like a well-oiled machine. But it won't be enough.

As they inch closer and closer, the fire storm greedily laps up another home. Another special family. He laughs. He controls the fire. He controls everything.

And no one can stop him.

No one.

EIGHT

Kaely kept her distance from the looky-loos gathered to watch the drama unfolding in their neighborhood. Mothers stood clutching children, their coats thrown over pajamas, their feet shoved into shoes without socks. Husbands and fathers gathered together as close as they could get to the barrier set up by the police, who'd cordoned off the area and stood their ground, determined to enforce the perimeter.

Kaely could hear the men discussing their opinions about the fire. Most felt it was electrical and explained their theories based on their knowledge of faulty wiring and the way homes were built nowadays. The remaining men stood and listened, trying to look as if they understood every word being said. Kaely smiled to herself. She could tell which guys actually knew something about the subject and which ones were clueless. Of course, they nodded along, afraid to breach the bond of male superiority when it came to all things electrical.

Kaely found it interesting that no one brought up the possibility that a space heater might have started this fire. She assumed the men naturally felt this blaze had to have been caused by something else, since the probability was astronomical that a space heater had caused another fire. Without realizing it, they'd made it clear something was amiss in Darkwater. As the men talked, their warm breath created an effect akin to smoke. It almost looked as if they were on fire themselves.

But Kaely wasn't really concerned about them. They appeared to be neighbors who knew each other. Nor was she interested in the women and children. She was looking for a lone man. Someone who stood off from the rest of the crowd. Someone trying to stay in the shadows.

She walked the perimeter until she saw him. He wore dark pants and a baggy black coat with the hood pulled up.

Kaely slipped behind the trunk of a large tree in the front yard of a nearby house so she could observe him. The man didn't seem to notice her. She waited until he moved a little closer to the police line. He appeared to be entranced by the frantic flames. Being as quiet as possible, Kaely moved nearer. Still no response. She pulled her cell phone from her pocket and snapped a few pictures. She was having a tough time getting a shot of his face, so she took another step toward him. When he seemed to sense her presence, she lowered her phone and tucked it behind her folded arms, praying it was still pointed toward him. Finally, he turned her way, a questioning look on his face. She quickly snapped several more pictures, coughing to cover the clicks of her camera.

"Awful fire," she said to the man, trying to act like just another neighbor out to see the excitement.

"Yeah," he said. "Looks like it's spreading to the house next door. Hope everyone got out okay."

"Me too." Kaely slipped the phone into her pocket so he wouldn't get suspicious. "You live around here?"

He shook his head. "A few blocks away. Just came to see what was going on."

Kaely guessed he was in his late twenties or early thirties. He fit the profile. She stuck her hand out. "Kaely Quinn. I'm from St. Louis. Staying with my mom for a while."

He stared at her hand for a moment but then took it, although he seemed a little reluctant. "Rick Cramer."

He had a firm handshake. A sign of confidence. Not something she would have expected from a serial arsonist.

"Sure have been a lot of these lately," she said after letting go of his gloved hand. "Darkwater seems like a rather unlucky town."

He nodded. "We're near the Niobrara River. The name means Running Water. This town was founded in 1872 after a local man's children drowned in the river. That's why it's named Darkwater."

"Wow. Are you some kind of expert on the area?"

He finally smiled. "No. I teach history at the high school."

Even though he was outside the preferred profile, it didn't mean he wasn't the one behind the fires. Kaely intended to look him up. Make sure he was who he said he was.

She excused herself and walked back toward her car, her eyes darting around, looking for someone else. Another loner who could be the arsonist. But no one else sparked her interest.

As she approached her car, she heard people talking. She put her car keys back in her pocket and walked over to where they stood. A man and a woman stood near three kids with matching hats and wide eyes. They all stared at the houses being consumed. Next to them she noticed an older woman and a man who looked to be in his thirties. She could tell they were related by their similar features. The man seemed uncomfortable. Wouldn't meet her eyes.

"You folks know the people who live in that house?" Kaely asked. She quickly flashed her credentials, hoping they wouldn't look too closely. They didn't.

"Yeah, the Andersons," the man said. "Two parents and three kids. We're really concerned about them."

Kaely's heart fell. Although the firefighters were giving it everything they had, the blaze was still raging out of control.

"Do you know if they got out?" Kaely asked, afraid to hear the answer.

The older woman shook her head. "We were just talking about that. We have no idea." She looked at a young man standing next to her. "My son Devin tried to ask about them, but the police wouldn't give him any information. Just told him to stay back."

A vehicle roared up the street. As it approached the police line, its brakes screeched loudly. Kaely turned to see an old pickup truck pull up next to the police car blocking traffic. A teenager got out of the pickup and ran toward the police car.

"That's Brant Anderson," the younger woman with the children said. She called out, "Brant! Brant!" but the teenager ignored her. A police officer hurried over and pulled the boy back. Brant began to talk frantically to the officer, who listened and nodded. He took the young man's arm and led him inside the cordoned area. Kaely could only pray he wasn't going to get the worst news of his life. Hopefully, the rest of his family had made it out safely.

As the neighbors began to talk among themselves, Kaely decided to walk down the sidewalk, farther away from the action. She noticed a man focused on the growing inferno. He was tall with longish dark hair and a beard. Thick glasses magnified his brown eyes.

"Do you know the people who live in that house?" she asked.

He shook his head. "No. I don't know anyone around here. Just staying at my mom's place for a while. She lives down the street. She had a stroke and can't get back to town for a few weeks. She was worried about leaving her home unprotected and asked me to stay until she makes it back. Thankfully, my sister's with her."

"That's nice of you. I'd get fired if I took off work that long."

He smiled. "I'm a graphic designer, so I can work from anywhere. All I really need is my computer. The sacrifice isn't as much as you might think." He held out his hand. "I'm Aaron Pollard. My mom's name is Sally. Do you know her?"

Kaely noticed his solid handshake and the way he gazed right into her eyes. Again, not what she would expect from an arsonist. He spoke with a soft southern twang, confirming his assertion that he didn't live in Nebraska. "No," she said. "I don't. I'm a couple miles south. Just checking out the fire."

He nodded. "Hard to stay away. I'm praying everyone made it out."

"Me too." She smiled at him. "Nice to meet you, Aaron."

"Same here."

She said good-bye and walked back to her car. Before she took off, she wrote down the names of Rick Cramer, Devin, and Aaron Pollard's mom. She also wrote down the address of the houses near the spot where the neighbors had gathered. She should be able to figure out where Devin lived and discover his last name. Kaely would look up the other addresses later. They all lived pretty close to the fire. Usually arsonists kept a more comfortable distance from their crimes, but she'd seen it before. A firebug who wanted to watch the neighbors burn. It could mean he was evolving. Getting braver.

She'd been gone longer than she planned, so she quickly drove back to her mother's house. As she passed a large oak tree in the middle of a nearby yard, she thought she saw some movement behind the tree. She backed up but couldn't see anyone. Just in case, she made a note of the address and then drove off.

The massive beast grows and grows, its eyes of flame searching for its creator. For him. When they finally find him, he smiles to himself. The creature knows him. Appreciates him. As it sucks life into its belly, it swells. It will take a while for firefighters to kill it. And when they finally do, it will only be temporary. His creation will rise again until its destiny is fulfilled.

He continues to appreciate his handiwork.

He and the beast are one.

When Kaely pulled into her mother's driveway, she noticed the light on in the kitchen. Had she left it on? She didn't think so. Her stomach clenched. Her mother was up. Had she needed help and found Kaely gone?

Worried, Kaely jumped out of the car and jogged up to the front door. She quickly slid the key into the lock and stepped inside the house. Then she gasped when she saw her mother's body lying on the living room floor.

NINE

Kaely felt as if all the air had been sucked out of the room as she struggled to catch her breath. She was an FBI agent. She'd seen bodies before. But not her mother's.

She dropped her purse on the floor and ran to Marcie's side. She put her fingers on her mother's neck and found a slight but steady pulse. Kaely gently cradled Marcie's head in her lap. Then she realized she should have brought her purse with her so she could call for an ambulance. She knew better. She wasn't thinking clearly. It was as if all her training had sprouted wings and flown away.

She breathed deeply several times in an effort to calm her trembling body. She'd decided to gently lower her mother's head and get her phone when Marcie's eyes fluttered open. Her eyes appeared to have problems focusing for a few seconds, then she looked up into Kaely's face.

"Jessie?" she mumbled. "Is that you?"

"Yeah, it's me, Mom. I'm here. I'm going to call for an ambulance."

"Oh, for crying out loud," her mother said, her voice shaky. "I don't need an ambulance. It's the chemo. It makes me dizzy sometimes. Just help me to my feet."

"Are you sure, Mom?" Kaely asked. "We need to make certain you didn't break anything."

Her mother struggled to sit up. "I didn't actually fall. I felt the dizziness coming on and lay down on the floor so I *wouldn't* fall. I've gone through this before." She took a deep breath and let it out slowly. "Would you please quit talking and help me to the couch?"

"Okay, Mom." Kaely wasn't sure she was doing the right thing, but there was something convincing about a parent telling you what to do. Maybe the automatic kid response never really went away.

Kaely slowly lifted her mother until she was on her feet. She couldn't believe how light Marcie felt. They walked slowly over to the large flowered couch, and Kaely helped her sit down. She could feel her mother's body tremble beneath her robe. Once Marcie was seated, she tried to push herself back against a pillow positioned against the arm of the couch. Kaely gently lifted her mother's legs until she could lean back on the pillow. Marcie collapsed into it with a deep sigh.

"Could you get me that throw?" Marcie asked, pointing a bony finger at the other end of the couch.

Kaely picked up the colorful afghan her mother indicated. She unfolded it and gently covered her mother's body.

"Can I get you anything, Mom?" Kaely asked. "Are you hungry? Thirsty?"

"You realize you're calling me *Mom*, right?"

Kaely hadn't been aware of it, and the revelation shook her. It also made her feel ashamed for making a big deal out of calling her mother by her first name. She suddenly felt incredibly childish.

"I . . . I'm going to make you a cup of that chamomile tea you like. I'll be right back." She fled into the kitchen. She'd seen the tea in the cabinet during supper, and Jason had mentioned their mother liked a cup now and then. As she found the cups and took one down, she noticed her hands were shaking.

What was wrong with her? She'd helped bring down psychopaths and some of the most evil people on the planet. She understood them as much as they could be understood. But here she was with her mother and her emotions were jumping all over the place.

Kaely recognized the cup and saucer she'd pulled from the cabinet. She'd given them to her mother one Christmas many years ago. Her father had taken her to a popular Des Moines department store, and Kaely had picked out a beautiful tea set. Although it cost too much, her father didn't say a word. Just took out his wallet. She could still remember her mother's face when she opened it on Christmas.

"Oh, Jessie," she'd said. *"It's so beautiful. Thank you."* And she'd smiled at her husband because she knew he'd actually paid for it.

Even though Kaely understood her father and could explain why he'd done the things he did, it was still difficult for her to accept the dichotomy of his thoughtful gestures while he was filled with so much malevolence. Her head understood him, but in her heart, a fourteen-year-old girl was still bewildered by his horrific actions.

Her mother had a water dispenser with hot water so Kaely used it to make the tea. After adding a little sweetener, she carried the cup into the living room.

"Thank you," her mother said.

Kaely put the cup down on the coffee table near Marcie. Then she sat down on a chair next to the couch. She wanted to escape to the bedroom so she could make notes about the fire and the men she'd talked to, but she couldn't leave Marcie alone until she was certain she was okay.

"Where did you go, Jessie?"

Kaely was relieved to hear her voice had grown stronger. "I went to check out a fire a few miles away, Mom."

Her mother sighed loudly and picked up her cup of tea. She took a sip and then set it down. The china made a ringing sound as it touched the surface of the saucer. "So you think these fires are suspicious?"

Kaely was surprised by her mother's question. "I'm not sure. But there's a pattern. And there shouldn't be."

Her mother appeared to study her. "You believe someone is purposely trying to kill people? Someone like your father?"

Although arsonists were a different kind of animal than the beast her father was, she nodded. Men like her father lived to enjoy the kill up close, while arsonists watched their destruction from a safe distance. But in the end, murderers were murderers.

"What can you do to stop this?"

"Not much. I'm out of my jurisdiction. The Omaha field office is in charge of the state. I might try to talk to the fire chief. Maybe I can get him to look a little more closely at these fires." She gazed at her mother, who actually appeared interested in what she was saying. "If there are many more incidences, the mayor or city council might become concerned. The chief answers to them."

"I haven't lived here long, Jessie, but I don't think the city council is very proactive. They seem to spend more time arguing with each other than doing anything constructive. I wouldn't count on them for help."

Marcie stared at her for several seconds, making Kaely feel uneasy. She got to her feet. "I think I need to get some sleep. I'm exhausted."

"Maybe you'd be more rested if you weren't running around town in the middle of the night."

There it was. Her mother's attempt at a normal conversation flew out the window.

"Let's get you to bed, Mom."

"I'd like to stay out here for now."

"But what if you need to get up during the night? If I'm asleep—"

"Thank you, Jessie, but I'm a grown woman. If I decide to sleep out here on my couch in my own home, I'll do it. Now go to bed."

Kaely stood there, not knowing what to do. If her mother got dizzy and really fell this time . . .

"If it's going to upset you this much," Marcie spat out, "help me back to the bedroom."

Kaely silently removed the afghan and waited for her mother to sit up before helping her back to bed. She noticed pictures of herself and Jason on her mother's dresser and realized there wasn't a single picture of her family in her condo. In fact, there weren't any pictures at all. It was a place to work and to sleep. Except for Mr. Hoover and what she called her "war room"— a special room full of files, pictures, and newspaper clippings about open or cold cases—there wasn't anything there she cared about. When she was home, she worked. She'd finally canceled her cable because she never watched TV. Her whole life revolved around chasing monsters. She'd pushed her family out of her mind completely.

Until Jason came back into her life, that is. At least she'd reconnected with her brother. But she wondered if she would ever have a good relationship with her mother again. Frankly, it was beginning to look like Marcie might die before that happened.

Kaely helped Marcie get into bed and made sure she was comfortable. Then she went back to her own room. After closing the door, she slid down to the floor, put her head in her hands, and began to cry.

TEN

Kaely was surprised when Jason came over the next morning to fix breakfast. She wasn't expecting to see him until that evening. He looked refreshed. Obviously even a single night away had helped him. Kaely felt badly. Dealing with Marcie wasn't easy. He'd been shouldering the load alone for too long.

Jason made Denver omelets for the three of them. When they sat down to eat, Jason said, "There was another fire last night. I thought you should know."

"Is that why you came over?"

Jason nodded. "I wasn't sure you'd heard about it."

Kaely glanced over at her mother, who had her head down and was picking at her omelet.

"Actually, I drove over there last night," Kaely told him.

"You left Mom alone?" he said, frowning.

"She wasn't gone very long," Marcie said. "I was just fine."

Kaely was surprised to hear her mother cover for her. She thought about telling Jason the truth, but if Marcie wanted to keep it between them, maybe it was best to leave it alone.

Jason stared at Kaely for a moment, but then went back to eating his breakfast.

"It looked really bad," Kaely said. "Do you know if anyone was hurt?"

Jason nodded. "Two of the family members are in the hospital. Not sure which ones. I guess a teenage son was staying the night at a friend's." He took a long sip of coffee before saying, "The house next door was a total loss too, along with a car in the garage. Thankfully, the family got out in plenty of time. Got their two dogs out safely as well."

"Thank God for that," Kaely said. "Where did you learn about this? In the paper?"

Jason snorted. "No, this isn't St. Louis. The newspaper here only comes out once a week. I saw it on the news last night." He took another sip of his coffee. "And I saw Sam outside his house on the way over here. He was just getting into his car."

"Sam?"

"Yeah. Sam Lucas. The firefighter I told you about."

"Was he there last night?"

Jason nodded as he chewed. "This is a volunteer fire department, sis. Most towns this size have them. But don't make the mistake of thinking they're not professional. They go through as much training as career firefighters."

"Yeah, I know that. They put their lives on the line because they want to help, not because they're drawing a paycheck."

"Yep. Makes them heroes in my book."

"Mine too," Kaely said. "What's Sam's regular job?"

"He's a veterinarian."

Kaely laughed. "Okay. So this hero firefighter also takes care of puppies and kittens? Is he for real?"

"You'll find out. He had to run an errand, but he said he'd stop by on the way to his clinic. He should be here any minute."

As if on cue, the doorbell rang. Kaely noticed her mother adjust her robe. Then she reached up and patted her wig. Kaely knew how much it upset her when someone stopped by unexpectedly. But strangely enough, she didn't look bothered.

"He's a nice man, Jessica," Marcie said. She looked pale

this morning, but her voice was steady and her eyes were clear. Kaely took that as a good sign. "Please don't embarrass us by acting like you know everything. Sam is a professional. He doesn't need your . . . help."

Kaely looked at her brother, who shook his head slightly. The pleading look on his face made Kaely bite her tongue. Starting an argument right before someone walked into the house wasn't wise. She was truly surprised by Marcie's reaction to Sam. What made this guy so different?

And then he stepped into the room.

Kaely gulped. Sam Lucas wasn't just a hero. He was a hunky hero. The kind of firefighter who posed on those cheesy calendars, and Kaely could certainly see this guy on the cover. He was tall with thick blond hair. Bright blue eyes framed a strong face with full lips that turned up in a smile that made her heart skip a beat.

"Sam, this is my sister, Kaely," Jason said.

Sam stuck out his hand. Strong fingers, manicured fingernails. But they didn't look like they were done in a salon. This guy took care of his own nails.

"FBI, right?" he said. "Impressive."

Kaely took his hand. "Volunteer firefighter," she said back. "*Very* impressive."

Sam laughed. "I appreciate that, but my penchant for excitement shouldn't be confused with a desire to save the world."

"Hey, Sam," Kaely said. "I'd appreciate it if you'd keep the FBI thing to yourself. I'm here for personal reasons and would rather not let anyone else know what I do." She glanced at Jason. "I guess my little brother has a big mouth."

Sam nodded. "Not a problem. I'll keep quiet." He switched his attention to Kaely's mother. "How are you doing, Marcie?"

"Hanging in there, Sam," she said. "Thanks for picking up our groceries the other day."

"You're more than welcome," he replied. "Just holler if I can do anything else."

"I really appreciate it too," Jason said. "I just didn't feel right about leaving her alone. She was pretty shaky after her treatment."

"Happy to do it. Call me anytime, Jason."

"Thanks," Jason said. "Feel free to sit down. How about a Denver omelet?"

"Sounds great, but I already ate." Sam glanced at the coffeepot. "I could sure use a cup of coffee though."

For just a moment, Kaely thought about jumping up and getting this dude's java. She didn't usually react this way to good-looking men, but she was human. Of course, she wasn't looking for a man. So why did her eyes shift to his ring finger? No ring. It took a few seconds for her to wrangle her thoughts under control. She wasn't responsible for visceral reactions, but she was liable for her thoughts and feelings once an uncontrolled physical response passed.

As Jason poured a cup of coffee, Sam sat down in the vacant chair next to Kaely. "I think my sister has some questions for you," Jason said, placing the cup where Sam could reach it.

Sam's eyes shifted toward her and a slow, lazy smile stretched across his face. Kaely was dismayed to find it hard to speak for a second. Shaking off the ridiculous school-girl feelings and once again trying to wrestle her analytical mind into submission, she nodded at him. It was then she caught a whiff of his aftershave. Understated. Musky.

Shoot.

She cleared her throat and took a deep, calming breath.

70

"You've had a lot of fires this winter," she said, stating the obvious.

He took a sip of coffee and nodded. "Too many. All caused by mishandled space heaters."

"Mishandled or faulty?"

"Hard to say. So far, most of them have been in the wrong place—next to curtains or clothes, or tipped over on the carpet." He shook his head. "You'd think people would know better, especially after we issued a warning."

Although his argument sounded convincing, Kaely saw something in his body language that said something else.

"What is it that bothers you about these fires?" Kaely asked.

Sam's eyes widened. "What makes you think I'm bothered by something in particular?"

"FBI. Behavioral analyst."

"I thought you were a profiler."

Kaely smiled. "Same thing. You're showing signs of uncertainty. Why?"

Sam hesitated a moment. "Look, it's nothing . . . solid. It's just . . ." He put his cup down and focused his blue eyes on her. "It feels wrong. I checked out each fire. Couldn't find anything that pointed to arson, but I've never seen this many fires caused by space heaters being misused." He stared down at his coffee cup. Kaely could see the conflict in his expression. Finally, he said, "The third house had signs of a break-in. But the cause seemed so obvious, that I dismissed it as something that happened earlier. Or something we did."

"But now you're not sure?"

"The first two fires . . . no problem. We had survivors. They admitted to buying space heaters, although they swore they set them up safely. Couldn't figure out how they ended up near flammable material. Again, I decided to ignore it. In these situations, almost everyone claims it wasn't their fault. Can't admit they were to blame. They're afraid they'll be found liable or lose out on an insurance payoff. Then I discovered that all the space heaters came from the same store. That's when I started to wonder if they might be faulty. I checked it out, but they were different brands."

"The same store?"

"Well, to be fair, this is Darkwater. We only have two stores that sell them."

"Still, that's a coincidence. I don't believe in coincidences."

"I don't either. That's why it continued to gnaw at me. And then last night—"

"The house over on Mayfield?"

Sam leaned closer to her. "The father and a daughter are barely hanging on. This has got to stop."

"I have a problem with these fires too, Sam."

"Tell me what you're thinking."

"Hold on a minute." Kaely jumped up from the table and got the newspaper from her room. As she carried it to the kitchen, she noticed the omelet Jason had made Marcie looked almost untouched. She'd taken a few bites, but not many.

Kaely sat down and opened the newspaper to the map. "Look at this." She pulled a pen from her pocket and drew a circle around the points on the map.

"A comfort zone?" Sam said.

Kaely thought he'd be surprised, but it was obvious he'd been thinking the same thing. "You almost expected this, didn't you?"

Sam took a deep breath and blew it out quickly. "As I told you, I've had some problems with this for a while. But then last night . . ."

"What happened last night, Sam?" Jason asked.

Kaely realized her mother and brother were listening with interest.

He leaned forward and cupped his large hands around his coffee cup. "The teenage son from the family in that fire? He swears they didn't have a space heater. Says his father hated them, especially after all the recent fires. Said he'd never buy one." Sam's eyes locked on hers. "But we found the charred remains of one in the house."

ELEVEN

Kaely's mother gasped at Sam's revelation. She frowned at her daughter but didn't say anything.

"Look, I'm not going to say anything for certain, Sam. That would be irresponsible. But my gut tells me you have a serial arsonist."

"Maybe you should talk to Chief Reynolds, Kaely," Jason said.

"Easier said than done," Sam said. "I approached him last night after the teenager told us about the heater. Tuck didn't want to hear it. Didn't believe it."

"If the arsonist actually brought a space heater into that house and started a fire, it means that family was targeted."

"I agree," Sam said. "I said the same thing to Tuck, but he wasn't having any of it. I had to back off."

"Most people think Chief Reynolds is a good man," Marcie said.

"He *is* a good man," Sam replied. "We've been friends since we were kids. But he's very pragmatic. I have no proof, and Tuck knows how often victims of trauma are wrong—or their memories are inconsistent. It would take more than my suspicions to make him willing to see this in a different light." He stared at Kaely. "I think Jason is right. Maybe if you could talk to him, he'd listen."

Kaely shook her head. "I can't do that. I have no authority here. You should contact the FBI field office in Omaha."

"Tuck would never allow that. A couple of years ago we worked an arson case with Omaha. A businessman opened fake businesses across the country, then burned down his stores to collect insurance profits. Let's just say that our collaboration didn't go well."

Kaely frowned. "Our people are usually very professional. We respect local police and fire departments."

"I believe that, but the agent in charge of the operation treated Tuck like a dumb country hick."

"I'm really sorry about that," Kaely said.

"The chief complained to a higher-up and that agent was . . . reassigned. John Howard, the special agent in charge for the field office in Omaha, couldn't have been more apologetic. Still, it left a bad taste in Tuck's mouth. He's had a chip on his shoulder ever since."

"What about your sheriff?"

Sam shook his head. "Same attitude. The fire chief and the sheriff are cousins and back each other up." He chuckled. "Of course, you'd never know it by looking at them."

"What do you mean?"

"Tuck was adopted by Josh's aunt and uncle, a white couple, when he was a baby. That's how Tuck and Josh became cousins. The family is very close. Our families all grew up together."

"So the fire and police departments get along? Sometimes they can butt heads. A kind of rivalry thing."

"Not here," Sam said. "Trust me, they'll band together and refuse to call in the FBI."

"Look, how about this? You bring me what information you can. I'll look through it and try to help. But unofficially. Off the record. You've got to keep this between us, Sam. If you don't, we could both get in big trouble."

He winked at her. "I've been in trouble before. I'm not afraid of it."

"I've been in more than my share too . . . and I'm a little nervous about it. Let's tread carefully."

Sam put his head back and laughed. "I like you, Kaely Quinn. I think we're gonna get along great." His phone suddenly rang, and he took it out of his pocket. When he looked at it, his smile faded. "I have to take this. Excuse me." He got up and left the table, going into the living room.

Kaely really liked this guy. She was certain they could work together. And after talking to him, Kaely was even more convinced that someone was setting these fires deliberately.

"Someone needs to get through to Chief Reynolds," Jason said.

"Look, I'll do what I can," Kaely said. "When I have some evidence, I'll give it to Sam. Let him take it to the chief."

Jason frowned. "Be careful, sis. Don't do something you'll regret."

"I'll be fine," Kaely said, "as long as we keep this to ourselves. I'm looking into this as a private citizen, not as an FBI agent. I won't be flashing my creds or using any FBI resources, although they sure would be helpful right now. Hopefully, I can find something that will cause Chief Reynolds to request help from the Bureau."

"I don't understand why Chief Reynolds can't handle this himself," Marcie interjected. "He's very competent."

Before Kaely could respond, Sam walked back into the room, his face tight with emotion. "The father didn't make it." He locked his gaze on Kaely. "Please help us. We can't stand by and let anyone else die. If there really is an arsonist, we need to find him as quickly as possible."

Kaely nodded. "I'll let you know if I uncover something that might help."

"I've got to go. I'll get in touch with you soon." Sam left without another word. It was clear that he was hurt by the father's death. That brought the human loss caused through these fires to two. She understood Sam's pain. Whether someone worked in law enforcement or public safety, they all felt responsible for the victims they couldn't save. It was part of the job. Carrying the dead with them.

Kaely finished breakfast and went to her room. Marcie had a doctor's appointment, and Jason had offered to take her. Kaely had tried to talk him out of it, but he insisted it would give her some time to work the case. She made a mental note to make sure she didn't take advantage of him. She came to Darkwater to help with her mother, not to look for a serial arsonist.

She didn't have much to go on yet, but she decided to get started anyway. She took out notebooks, sticky notes, pens, and tape from her tote bag. Not having her usual dry-erase board, she opened the closet door and began to tape notes and newspaper articles on the smooth wooden surface.

She'd been working for a while when someone rang the doorbell. Since Mom and Jason were gone, she sighed heavily and went to answer it. She was surprised to see Sam standing there. He didn't say hello. Didn't smile. He just handed her a folder.

"I never gave this to you. I wasn't even here." With that he turned and walked away.

Kaely watched him get into his car and head down the road. She stepped back inside the house and opened the file. It was full of copies of the original pictures and reports related to the fires.

Kaely smiled to herself. Now she could really get to work.

She headed back to her bedroom and sat down at the desk. She was reading a report from the second fire when her cell phone rang. She picked it up and saw that it was Noah. She smiled and answered.

"Hey there. What's going on?"

"Title III" was all he said.

"Oh no. I'm sorry." Wiretaps were usually the most boring assignment an agent could have. "Anything interesting happening?"

"Well, only if you're overly concerned about whether you should wear blue socks with a black suit to your aunt Muriel's funeral. Or if Antonio's Italian Restaurant uses too much garlic in their marinara sauce." He sighed. "It's that import/export business we've been working on for so long. I'm listening to their orders, but nothing stands out."

"They mostly import from China and South America, right?"

"Yeah. Clothing, electronics, and toys from China. Smartphone and computers from South America."

"Nothing unusual?"

"Let's see. . . . Before my mind went completely numb yesterday, a guy named Charles placed a huge order of figurines from China. That's the most interesting thing that's happened all week."

"Figurines?" Kaely said. "What kind of figurines?"

"China horses."

There was a long pause on the other end of the line as Kaely ran her hand over her face. She started to say something, but Noah's loud expletive cut her off.

"How could I have missed this? China horses. Heroin. I've messed up big-time, Kaely."

"You're just tired, Noah. It happens."

"No, I'm better than this. Thankfully, the shipment hasn't come in yet. I'll report it as soon as we get off the phone. Thanks." He sighed before asking, "How's small-town life? Are you bored out of your mind yet?"

"Actually, no. Darkwater has had a series of fires—"

"Did you say Darkwater?"

"Yeah. Darkwater, Nebraska."

"Wow. Sounds mysterious," he said. "Whereas Nebraska sounds—"

"Rather dreary?"

"A little. You mentioned some fires?"

Kaely told him about her suspicions that Darkwater had a serial arsonist.

"Let me get this straight," Noah said. "I've been going stir-crazy and you're tracking an arsonist. Life just isn't fair."

"Yeah, but now you're getting ready to bring down a drug cartel. Big stuff."

"Sure," Noah said. "But I missed the signs completely. I needed you to tell me what should have been crystal clear." He sighed again. "Tell you what, if we're right, and we expose these guys, I'll ask for some time off and come to Nebraska to help you. I really think I need to get away for a while, Kaely. I'm just . . . I'm just not myself."

Kaely's heart leaped with excitement at Noah's offer. She was a little surprised by her reaction, but if she was honest with herself, she'd have to admit she'd missed him over the past few days. A lot.

"Deal. Write down my mom's address." She started rattling off the address, but Noah stopped her.

"You're not going to make me share a bedroom with your brother or anything, are you? I don't do well around—"

"People?"

He laughed. "No. Families. I mean, I like mine and everything, but other people's relatives annoy me."

"Don't worry. There's a nice bed-and-breakfast not far from my mom's house. And Darkwater actually has motels. We'll find someplace where you can hide out from my family."

"Good. I have a feeling I might need to."

It was Kaely's turn to laugh. "Now make a note of this address." She waited while he wrote it down. "Keep me updated," she said. "I'd love to get another point of view on this thing. Just don't tell Solomon."

"Can't they bring in Omaha to work the case?"

"Apparently not. An agent there ticked off the fire chief, who passed his anger along to his cousin, the sheriff."

"You're kidding."

"Small-town politics," Kaely said. "And of course whatever we do has to be on the down-low."

"I can deal with that." Noah hesitated before saying, "Hey, I should have asked about your mother before anything else. How's she doing?"

"She's weak, Noah. Looks awful. Too early to tell anything though. She's just started some kind of experimental treatment."

"Okay. Well, you pray for her. You believe in that stuff."

Kaely chuckled. "Yeah, I believe in *that stuff*."

"I'll call you soon."

"Okay, Noah. Thanks. Bye." Kaely ended the call and stared at her phone. She really did miss him—more than she wanted to. She had to be careful. She'd already lost people she'd allowed herself to get close to. She didn't know what she'd do if she lost Noah.

TWELVE

Kaely spent the next couple of days taking care of her mother while Jason took some much-needed time off. When Marcie slept, which was a lot of the time, Kaely went through the information Sam had given her. She finally felt she had a handle on the case. She was certain her theory was right. But how could she convince the fire chief that he had a major problem?

She made lunch and then got Marcie settled on the couch so she could watch TV and take a nap. She'd just cleaned up the kitchen and was headed back to her bedroom when someone rang the doorbell. She hurried to answer it so it wouldn't disturb her mother. It was Sam. By his expression, it was obvious something was wrong.

"Can I talk to you?" he asked when she opened the storm door.

"Of course," she said. "Come on in."

After saying hello to Marcie, Sam followed Kaely into the kitchen. She gestured toward the table and then asked him if he wanted a cup of coffee.

"Yeah, coffee sounds great," he said. "It's freezing out there." He took off his coat and tossed it onto the chair next to him.

She noticed for the first time how tired he looked. "Rough night?"

He nodded. "Another fire. An elderly woman left a pot on the stove and went to bed. It's not connected to our other fires though. She's in rough shape. Not sure she'll make it."

"Oh, Sam," Kaely said. "I'm so sorry."

"According to the family, she had dementia. What were they thinking letting her live by herself? Someone should have been with her."

He cleared his throat as she handed him a cup of coffee. She was glad she'd kept the coffeemaker on.

"It's hard for children to see their parents as weak or in need of help, Sam," Kaely said. "I imagine her family truly thought she was okay. And she probably did everything she could to assure them of that. It happens a lot."

He ran his hand through his hair and sighed. "I'm sure you're right. Guess I'm just looking for someone to blame." He took a sip of coffee. "But that's not why I'm here. The chief called me this morning and asked me to bring you to his office."

Kaely frowned. "Why would he do that? Did you tell him who I am?"

"I'm sorry, but I did mention it, yes. He knows you can't help us officially, and he'll keep your identity to himself. He's trustworthy, Kaely. I hope you'll forgive me, but I can't stand by while people die." Sam shook his head. "Tuck is pretty upset. I think he's finally realizing that we may have a problem."

Kaely wanted to be angry at Sam for betraying his promise to keep her out of the investigation, yet she understood his reasons for approaching Tuck. Now that the cat was out of the bag, she didn't want to spend her time being angry. She needed to find a way to help the people of Darkwater.

"You'd think the sheer number of fires would alarm him," she said.

Sam nodded. "Sometimes he thinks . . . Well, he thinks I overreact."

Kaely's mouth dropped open. "Overreact? How many fires have there been in the last couple of months?"

"With last night? Five. Four of them suspicious."

"How many do you usually have?"

Sam shook his head. "We had two last winter. Both were electrical."

"But he's only now realizing there's a problem?"

Sam dredged up a small smile. "Not everyone sees patterns like you do, Kaely."

She could only nod. That was true. She'd realized years ago that she noticed things other people didn't, even before she joined the FBI.

"You were really upset about that family the other day," Kaely said gently, sitting down next to him at the table. "Did you know them?"

Sam looked away and for a moment Kaely thought he might not answer her question. Finally, he said, "It was a little too close to home. I think that's what pushed me over the edge. The reason I told Tuck about you."

"What do you mean?"

Sam clasped his coffee cup as if it were full of something more powerful than coffee. After a couple of deep breaths, he said, "When I was seventeen I got into an argument with my parents. You know, the kind of stupid stuff kids say that doesn't really mean anything. I told them they were terrible parents. Can't remember now what I was angry about. Might have been a party that I shouldn't have gone to anyway." His lips trembled as he fought to keep talking. "I stormed out of the house and went to stay with a friend. Refused to come home. That night our house caught fire. My parents and . . . my brother died. I was left behind to deal with what I'd said. And with not dying with them." He slowly looked up, and Kaely could see the pain in his eyes. "After that night, I decided to become a firefighter, just like my dad. Try to help others since I wasn't there to save my own family. I've never really forgiven myself for that night."

Without thinking, Kaely reached out and took Sam's hand. "It wasn't your fault. If you'd known what was going to happen, you'd have done anything to protect your family." She shook her head slowly. "If anyone understands guilt, it's me. Feeling guilty has never made me better. Never made me stronger. Sam, having an argument with your folks doesn't mean you wanted them dead. Surely you can see that."

"No. You don't understand." He looked into her eyes. "I know you're trying to help, but I carry the weight of that night with me every day. I always will."

Kaely's heart raced as she held his hand in hers. "Trust me, I really do understand. I've faced the same demons. But you've got to fight them. A lot of people depend on you. You've saved lives, Sam."

"I know you're right, but so far the lives I've saved haven't been enough to compensate for my poor decisions."

"What was it that made you compare that fire the other night to your situation?"

He smiled weakly. "Two teenage brothers and a space heater. That's how the fire in my house started."

"Wow. That's awful. I'm sorry."

Sam squeezed her hand and was quiet for a few moments. "What do you have to feel guilty about?"

Kaely gently pulled her hand away. "In my line of work, there are successes but also a fair share of failures. Every one of them stings." She hesitated before finally asking, "How well do you know Jason?"

"We haven't talked that much. Most of it in passing. I like him though. It's great that he's here taking care of your mom. He's a good man."

"Yes, he is." So Jason hadn't told Sam about their dad. Good. Kaely glanced at the clock on the wall. "When are we supposed to meet with the chief?"

"He'd like to see us around three this afternoon at the station."

"Hopefully he's come to the same conclusion we have."

Sam nodded. "I believe he has. Anyway, I hope so. We may be a volunteer fire department, but Tuck has the power to dismiss me. I love working for the department."

"I guess then you'd have to concentrate on saving all those sweet puppies and kittens."

Sam laughed. "Yeah, and I love that. I really do. But fighting fires is my way of bringing some kind of balance to what happened to my family. It means . . . Well, it means more than I can say."

Kaely was stunned by the similarities between her and Sam. She wasn't sure why she felt such a tug toward this tender-hearted hero, but she recognized that she was still damaged too. She wished she could just wake up one day and be whole, but God seemed to want her to face her fears before He delivered her from them.

She'd once heard a Bible teacher say that feelings buried alive never die. Kaely was beginning to understand that hiding from her pain would never bring healing. Facing it and applying the truth of God's love and promises was the only balm that brought permanent deliverance. Kaely wondered sometimes how long it would take for her to find true freedom.

Sam finished his coffee and gave Kaely the address to the

fire station. She promised to meet him there at three. After he left, she prayed their meeting with the chief would open a door to finding the person causing such destruction in Darkwater. Sam's story about his family bothered her since the arsonist might have planted a space heater in the last house. It was an odd coincidence, but she shook it off.

Kaely also hoped their appointment with the chief wouldn't affect Sam's work with the fire department. She remembered the pain of being asked to leave Quantico when the Bureau found out her father was a serial killer. She wouldn't wish that kind of grief on anyone. Especially Sam Lucas.

THIRTEEN

Noah was irritated with himself for not catching the code used by the traffickers earlier. It was a rookie mistake. He'd been trained to watch for just that kind of scenario. How could he have missed it? Of course, he knew the answer to his own question. He was distracted because Kaely was gone, and it was hurting his work for the Bureau. He had to get himself together. If Solomon ever guessed he wasn't operating at his best, Noah would probably never work with Kaely again. He couldn't allow that to happen.

He'd informed the case agent about the unusual order placed by the company. He didn't mention Kaely, and Noah knew she'd never bring it up. He felt guilty about it, but he wasn't willing to let anyone know he'd missed such clear signs. Now the Bureau would set up surveillance, request search warrants, and try to bring down the operation. By Thursday afternoon, Noah's part in the case was done. This morning he'd put in for vacation, fairly confident it would be approved.

He was trying to catch up on a few things that had gotten pushed aside by the surveillance assignment when Grace, Solomon's administrative assistant, called him to let him know the boss wanted to see him. Noah left his desk and hurried down the hall. Had Solomon discovered the truth about the surveillance? He felt sweat break out on his forehead. He wiped it with the back of his hand before he pushed open the door to Solomon's outer office. Grace smiled at him as he entered.

"Good to see you, Special Agent Hunter. He's expecting you. Go on in."

Noah nodded in acknowledgment and entered Solomon's office. He was hunched over his desk with a file open in front of him. He closed it when he saw Noah.

"Have a seat," he said amicably.

"Thank you." Noah slid into the chair in front of Solomon's desk, trying to look relaxed even though his insides were tied up in knots.

"Good job on the trafficking case."

Noah swallowed hard and bobbed his head up and down, guilt making him jumpy. He wiped his hands on his pant legs even though they weren't sweaty. He hoped Solomon couldn't read people the way Kaely did. If so, Noah had just sent a message that might cause his boss some concern.

Solomon leaned back in his chair. It squeaked loudly. Noah wondered why someone didn't oil the stupid thing. It was as if Solomon couldn't hear the irritating noise.

"You put in for vacation, I see," Solomon said suddenly.

Noah's eyebrows shot up in surprise. He had several weeks of vacation saved up, but HR usually handled vacation requests. "Yes," he said hesitantly. "Is there a problem?"

Solomon's mouth twitched as if he wanted to smile but couldn't quite push it through. "No, there's no problem," he said finally. "I'm glad you want to take some time off. Your whole life shouldn't be your job. I just find it odd that at the same time you request vacation, Agent Quinn is in Nebraska taking care of her mother. I assume you know that?"

Noah felt his cheeks grow hot. "Yes, I do."

"I looked up Darkwater, Nebraska. It appears there's an unusual string of fires occurring there."

Noah stared at Solomon, who met his gaze and didn't look away.

"Kaely thinks they have a serial arsonist," Noah said finally. "It seems that neither the fire chief nor the sheriff are willing to look into it."

"Are you going there to help her?"

Realizing it wouldn't do any good to deny the truth, Noah just nodded.

"You have no authority there. Neither does Kaely."

"We understand that. We were planning to work behind the scenes—"

Solomon held his hand up like a cop stopping traffic. "Too risky. You could get yourself in trouble and cause problems for me." He picked up a pen on his desk and pointed it at Noah. "Omaha is working a drug case involving MS-13. They're bringing in heroin laced with fentanyl from Mexico. The Bureau knows the gang has it, but the Omaha office is going after the person or persons behind the operation. They haven't been able to find strong evidence against the leader yet. There are several suspects they think might be working with him. They're under surveillance in North Platte, which is a little over one hundred miles from Darkwater."

Solomon fell quiet. Noah was pretty sure he knew what was coming.

"You and Kaely are on temporary assignment to Omaha," Solomon said. "They've asked that you take part in one of their details in North Platte. You'll be on surveillance from eleven at night until four in the morning. You'll be busy with paperwork before you head out." Solomon began absentmindedly tapping his pen on his desktop. "Just remember you're there under Omaha's jurisdiction, so watch your step. Omaha's not working these arsons, but they know you'll be poking around. You're covered by them as long as you don't step over the line. Understand?"

"Yes, I understand. When do I start?"

"You and Kaely will check in with Omaha on Monday at one in the afternoon. Once you're briefed, you'll go to North Platte. You should be able to start on Tuesday night."

"Okay," Noah said slowly. "How long do you think—"

"No way to know," Solomon said. "This is just a temporary assignment. Like I said, I'm setting it for thirty days, but if things wrap up quicker, I'll do my best to bring you both back. Omaha will have the final say." He leaned forward in his chair and stared at Noah, his expression serious. "The SAC in Omaha is John Howard. He's a friend. I've been candid with him. If you find anything of importance related to the fires, you have to turn it over to the local sheriff. He'll decide the extent of your involvement, so don't cowboy this thing. It could blow up in your face."

Noah nodded again, concerned he was beginning to look like a bobblehead doll. He stood up and extended his hand to Solomon. The older man got to his feet and shook it.

"You both need to be careful out there," Solomon said. "Your assignment in North Platte will pit you against a very violent gang. You and Kaely may also be putting yourselves in the cross hairs of a serial arsonist. You two watch your backs and stay safe. Okay?"

"You have my word, Solomon," Noah said.

His boss handed him a packet that included his plane ticket and other important case information.

Noah thanked him and left the office. He hurried back to his desk. Although he appreciated Solomon's efforts to help him and Kaely sniff out a possible arsonist, he worried that doing it this way would affect Kaely's time with her mother. Conducting surveillance for Omaha and working a case in Darkwater would take a lot of effort. Was this what Kaely wanted . . . or needed?

As he cleaned up his desk, he reminded himself that once Kaely was on the track of evil, she was like a dog with a bone. She'd be obsessed with catching and stopping this UNSUB. Noah could try to reason with her, but in the end, it wouldn't do any good. Kaely didn't see what she did as a job. That title was too mundane. Too normal. Kaely lived to track down monsters, and nothing would ever stand in her way—not even friends and family.

He clocked out and drove home, trying to stay somewhat close to the speed limit. He had a lot to do in order to get ready for this assignment.

Solomon's words kept ringing in his mind. *"Your assignment in North Platte will pit you against a very violent gang. You and Kaely may also be putting yourselves in the cross hairs of a serial arsonist. You two watch your backs and stay safe."*

He had every intention of protecting Kaely Quinn, although she didn't think she needed it. Even as he packed his suitcase, he wondered why he was willing to drop everything and follow this woman. She was incredible. And she was selfish. She had great insight into everyone except herself. But with all her flaws, for the first time since she'd left, Noah felt a twinge of anticipation. Was it because of the case?

Or was it because he couldn't find happiness without Kaely Quinn in his life?

FOURTEEN

When Kaely and Sam arrived at the station, several men stood in the engine bay. They nodded at Sam, but Kaely could see the tension in their faces and in the way they held their bodies. The fires were obviously taking a mental and physical toll on them.

Sam led Kaely to a door in the back of the bay. He pushed it open and stepped aside so Kaely could enter first. Sam cocked his head to the right. "The chief is this way," he said.

They walked down the hall to a door with a sign that read *Chief Tuck Reynolds.* Sam knocked, and a deep voice said, "Come in."

Sam swung the door open, and Kaely found herself being scrutinized by Chief Reynolds. He looked just like his picture in the local paper. His dreadlocks were tied behind his head, and his tight shirtsleeves revealed a man who worked out. Once again, Kaely was surprised by him. In a small town like Darkwater, she'd expected someone older, even if the office of fire chief was voluntary. However, she was struck immediately by his presence. He radiated confidence. His eyes locked on hers, his gaze intense. This man was serious about his job. Kaely suspected he didn't suffer fools gladly.

He nodded a dismissal at Sam, who shut the door behind him as he left. The fire chief gestured toward an old leather chair in front of his desk. High-end furniture that had seen better days was stationed throughout his office. Kaely gazed quickly around the room. There were two pictures on the bookshelf behind him. His family—and one that looked like it had been taken in another country. That explained it.

"You're the profiler?" he asked. His voice was well modulated.

"You're a dentist," she said matter-of-factly.

"Are you profiling me?"

"Not really. And actually, I was trained as a behavioral analyst. Some people call us profilers, but we don't refer to ourselves that way."

The chief's right eyebrow shot up. "Okay. So how do you know I'm a dentist?"

Kaely nodded toward the photos on his bookshelf. "First of all, your family photo. Your wife and sons all have perfect teeth. So do you. Then there's the picture of you with three children. It was obviously taken in another country. I would guess somewhere in Africa? If you were with some kind of charity, you would look concerned. But you're smiling. Has to be because you know you can help these kids."

"That's pretty good. I'm impressed."

Kaely flashed him a grin. "If that wasn't enough, your lab coat is hanging on the coatrack behind you with your name on it, followed by the initials DDS."

For the first time since she'd entered the chief's office, he seemed to relax. He even laughed, although it was quick and automatic. His serious expression slipped right back into place.

"You've been telling Sam that you think Darkwater has an arsonist." He stated it directly, not as a question. "Tell me why you believe that."

He was focused on her. She didn't see any signs of defensiveness. He wasn't challenging her. He was really interested in her responses. She took a deep breath. "The first thing I noticed was a pattern."

"What kind of pattern?"

"Do you have anything showing the locations of the fires?"

He nodded and reached into his desk. He pulled out a map of Darkwater and pushed it toward her. The location of each fire was marked with a red X. Interesting. Was this standard procedure, or was he curious about the fires as well?

"Here," she said, leaning over the chief's desk and pointing to the trail of X marks. "It's almost circular. As if someone was trying to stay away from his own home and reach out as far as he felt comfortable. But you've already noticed the pattern."

"I noticed it, but I wasn't sure," he said. "Anything else that led you to your conclusion?"

"Too many fires. The number and frequency of home fires for a town this size is way out of bounds, statistically speaking. And then with the early Tuesday morning fire, the boy who wasn't home when his house caught on fire was convinced his father wouldn't buy a space heater. Of course, all of this is circumstantial—but together it begins to add up."

The chief didn't say anything for a moment. Then he swore quietly. "I should have caught this sooner. I'm a very practical person. I don't get carried away by conspiracy theories or circumstances that sound . . . fanciful. Can you understand that?"

"Yes. But in my line of work, what's hard to believe usually turns out to be reality. Evil isn't something we're trained to accept. Facing the truth, realizing that someone actually wants to hurt innocent people, is extremely difficult to understand. Especially by someone like you who lives to protect life, not destroy it."

The chief didn't respond. He just reached into his desk and took out what looked like a letter. He unfolded it and then placed it in front of Kaely. "This came in the mail. It's the reason I asked you to meet with me."

She was surprised he was handling it without gloves. Careful not to pick it up and add her prints to the chief's, she leaned over and read.

Jack is nimble, Jack is slick.
Jack is knocking over the candlesticks.
Who am I watching? Who will I pick?
If you hope to catch me, you'd better be quick!

"It's . . . silly," the chief said slowly. "Ridiculous. A twisted child's nursery rhyme. I have to wonder if it isn't someone's idea of a joke. I have a hard time taking it seriously."

As Kaely stared at the note, a familiar feeling washed over her. This reminded her of another killer who'd sent letters, yet she sensed this was different. "I don't think it's a joke," she said. She looked up at the chief. "This is your arsonist. And he's not done. Please send this to the police. They need to check it for fingerprints." She frowned as she stared at the note.

"Something else bothering you?" the chief asked.

"This last call you went on, the one with the elderly woman," she said slowly, being careful not to let him know Sam had told her anything the chief wanted to keep private. "Did it fit the pattern of the others?"

The chief shook his head. "A clear accident."

"It's possible the arsonist sent this letter because of that fire."

"What do you mean?"

"It's difficult to be sure, but he could be upset that someone else rained on his parade. He may be protective of his . . . work. Doesn't want to share the glory."

"That's nuts."

"It might be nuts," Kaely said, "but he's been very shrewd. Don't underestimate him."

"All right. So what's going to happen now?" the chief said. "Is this guy going to send us more notes? Taunt us while he burns down this town?"

Kaely shook her head. "I'm not sure you'll get another message."

Chief Reynolds frowned at her. "Why do you say that?"

"It's just my sense of who he is. He communicates through his fires. Not with paper. Other serials have mailed letters to authorities because it made them feel powerful. Famous. They loved sowing fear. But this guy? He just wants to make sure you know he's behind them. The accidental fire spooked him. But now that he's made it clear he's out there, I think he's going to concentrate on what he really likes—setting fires. Killing people." She paused and locked eyes with the chief. "I don't believe he'll use space heaters anymore. Too much trouble. From here on out I suspect he'll revert to the usual gasoline or some other accelerant. Which makes him more dangerous."

"Why didn't he start his fires that way from the beginning? What's the deal with space heaters?"

Kaely had been wondering the same thing for a while. Why make it so complicated? She shrugged. "For now, anything I say would be a wild guess. I just can't be sure of his reasoning at this point." Sam's story about the fire that killed his family jumped into her mind. But that happened a long time ago. She couldn't see a connection.

Chief Reynolds was quiet, staring at the note. "Can you help us?" he asked finally.

"There's nothing wrong with asking my opinions, but unless I get permission from Omaha, I can't officially get involved. Have you thought about calling in the FBI?"

The chief shook his head. "No. I don't want to work with them again. I want you."

Kaely sighed. She'd hoped he would change his mind once he realized what they were up against. "Let me make a phone call. I'll let you know what I can do. A friend of mine is coming here. Together maybe we can—" At that moment Kaely's cell phone rang. "Sorry," she said. "I should have turned it off. I'm not expecting any calls." She pulled her phone out of her pocket, intending to silence it, when she noticed who was calling. What an odd coincidence. "Chief, I need to take this. Do you mind if I step out for a moment?"

"No," he said. "Do what you need to do."

Kaely got up and went out into the hall, closing the chief's door behind her. She quickly answered her phone. "Hey, Boss. Funny you'd call now."

She listened as Solomon told her about her temporary assignment. "Noah's on his way. On Monday afternoon at one o'clock you'll both check in with Omaha. From there you'll be sent to North Platte to do surveillance. In your off time, you can work the Darkwater case. Omaha will back you up, but they don't have a good relationship with the powers-that-be in Darkwater. Rather than trying to mend fences, we all agreed the best thing was to let you and Noah poke around under their jurisdiction. See what you can do to help. Even if Darkwater asks for help, Omaha can't do much right now. They have their hands full trying to shut down MS-13 and the drugs they're distributing in the area."

"Thanks, Solomon," Kaely said.

"What about your mother?" he asked gently. "I'd hate for this case to distract you from what's important."

"My brother is still here. I'm sure he'll cover for me." Even as she said it, she wondered how Jason was going to take this news. He'd seemed a little perturbed when she asked him to come over and watch their mother this afternoon.

"Please be cautious, Kaely. There are some mistakes we can't fix. Don't make a decision you'll regret later."

"I'll be careful. Thanks."

Kaely hung up and went back into the chief's office. As she told him about the assignment in North Platte and what she'd now be able to do in Darkwater, she couldn't shake Solomon's warning. Tracking this arsonist could easily consume her. Her mother was seriously ill. Could Kaely give her the attention she needed and still stop this murderer who called himself Jack?

She wasn't so sure.

FIFTEEN

When Jason came over to fix supper that night, Kaely told him about the assignment with Omaha. "I have to be in North Platte by eight o'clock on the nights we're called in. I'll be back in the mornings."

"What are you saying?" Jason asked. He was taking a casserole out of the oven. Kaely jumped as he slapped the metal pan down on top of the stove. "Sounds to me like I'm going to have to be here most of the time. Again."

"I'm sorry, Jason. People have died. If I can help . . ."

Jason came over and sat down next to her at the table. "Your job isn't everything, Kaely," he said, keeping his voice low. "What about Mom? Me? Does your family warrant any of your precious time?" He clasped his hands together. "Look, I respect what you do. I really do. I realize you're concerned about these fires, but Mom may be dying. Does she count?"

"Of course she does," Kaely snapped. "I drove all the way here just to help her. To help you."

"And now you've decided to chase an arsonist. And a violent gang. That's just great."

"I'm going to do the best I can to spend time with Marcie," Kaely said. "And to give you time to get away. I'm not abandoning you. Or Mom. But I have to do this, Jason."

"This isn't going to work, Kaely."

"It *will* work. I'll make it work."

Kaely couldn't understand Jason's attitude. Wasn't he concerned about Darkwater? About innocent people whose lives might be in danger? She wasn't going to abandon their mother. She would be here when she could. Didn't that count for something?

His attitude angered her. Why couldn't he understand that this was who she was? That she had no choice but to try to help the authorities find this guy before someone else died? He'd encouraged her to pursue this.

Jason took a deep breath before saying, "You know, when you left home, I felt abandoned. I resented you for that. It's the reason I didn't contact you when I finally left home. Didn't let you know where I was."

"I wasn't trying to be selfish," Kaely said. "I just needed to get out of there. You seemed to be doing okay."

Jason laughed bitterly. "Okay? I was just a kid. Left behind with a woman who couldn't connect with anyone and didn't even try. It was awful."

Was this the reason he was so upset with her now? Lingering resentment over something that happened so long ago? As she thought about it, she could understand how her leaving had felt like rejection. "I'm sorry, Jason. I really am. I didn't think. I wish I could take it back."

"I didn't tell you to make you feel bad," Jason said. "I just needed you to know. You thought I was trying to get away from our messed-up past. But the truth is, I was angry with you." He blinked away tears that filled his eyes. "I guess I feel kind of that way now."

"But this isn't the same thing."

Jason was quiet for a moment. Then he said, "I know. Sorry for getting upset. I can't pretend I'm happy about this situation, but I guess I understand. Anyway, I'll try to."

Kaely reached over and took his hand. "Forgive me?"

He gave her a tremulous smile. "I'm trying."

Kaely squeezed her brother's hand and then let it go. Her emotions were jumbled. She felt awful for hurting Jason, yet she was glad he'd been honest with her. It made more sense why he would be upset with her about not being able to stay with Mom as much as she'd planned.

Kaely and Jason could hear Marcie's bedroom door open. Jason got up and took plates out of the cabinet. Marcie shuffled in as he scooped helpings of the casserole onto their plates and put them on the table.

"What's this?" Marcie asked as she sat down.

"Chicken and broccoli with rice, Mom," Jason said. "Try it. It's good."

Marcie rolled her eyes. "You know I don't like broccoli."

Jason's face turned pink but he stayed silent.

"Then pick it out, Mom," Kaely said. "It smells heavenly."

They ate dinner in relative silence, Marcie making a big show of putting her broccoli on a small plate she got from the cabinet. After supper, Jason cleaned up the kitchen and left, not saying much to either Kaely or his mother. It was obvious he was still disappointed over Kaely's change of plans.

She spent the rest of the weekend with her mother, working the case in her bedroom at night or when Marcie took a nap.

On Sunday night, when Jason came over to fix supper, he took her aside. "Look, Kaely, I told you I'd do my best to deal with this, but you need to know that it can't go on forever. I need to get back to my business and to Audrey. She's very understanding, but I've postponed our wedding twice now."

"Well, then let's find someone to come in and help if we need it. No matter how Marcie feels about it."

"We may not have a choice, but first let's see how this week goes. You know Mom will pitch a fit if we try to bring a stranger into the house. Since you're convinced this will work out, that you can handle your job and care for Mom at the same time, let's give it a shot. I'm willing to see if you're right."

Kaely started to respond, but he waved her comment away. "I'll start looking around, see what kind of services are in the area. That way we'll know what our options are, okay?"

"I think that's a good idea." Kaely reached out and took her brother's hand. "I'm sorry, Jason. I don't want you to be angry with me, but I have to—"

"No, Kaely," Jason said, shaking his head. "You don't have to. You want to. You live for your job. It defines you. You need to learn that your job is just something you do. Not who you are." He gently pulled his hand from hers and walked away.

Kaely tried to dismiss his comments, but it wasn't easy. Who was she without her job with the FBI? It was a question she couldn't answer. She pushed away the confusion his comments caused. She had to concentrate on the case. The sooner the arsonist was caught, the happier everyone would be, including Jason. She prayed that God would help her locate the UNSUB and stop the destruction in Darkwater. After her prayer, she felt better.

Although she had a special way of profiling criminals, she didn't feel she had enough information to use it yet. She'd done some research on Rick Cramer, the high school history teacher, and ruled him out. He didn't come close to fitting the profile. Sam knew him and assured her he couldn't be involved. Besides, he was at a local restaurant celebrating his birthday the night of one of the other fires. She'd looked up his Facebook page, and there were pictures from the party. Devin, the odd young man living with his mother, wasn't a suspect either. He'd been in jail during the other fires and had been released the day before Kaely met him.

Kaely also checked with a couple of Aaron Pollard's neighbors. Sure enough, they confirmed that his mother had suffered a stroke while visiting her daughter. Aaron's daughter had phoned one of the neighbors who was friendly with his mother, Sally, and let her know Aaron was coming to watch the house. Sally had lived in Darkwater only for six months, and this was Aaron's first visit. He had no reason to set fires in the small town since he didn't know anyone and had no history with the people who lived here.

Kaely was back to square one.

She'd gone through background information on all the fire victims, wondering if someone might be attempting to cover up a crime by setting additional fires. It had happened before. But she couldn't find anything that pointed to that.

Thankfully, Georgie stayed away over the weekend while Kaely worked. She didn't want to be distracted. She needed to focus on the problem in Darkwater before more people died.

Kaely said good-bye to her mother on Monday morning after Jason arrived. Kaely had tried to explain the situation to Marcie the night before, but Kaely could tell by her body language that she was angry. Was she concerned about Kaely's safety? Or was she feeling slighted? It was impossible to know. Even though Kaely was well versed in reading physical clues, they only offered possibilities. There wasn't any way to actually see into a person's personal thoughts.

The drive to Omaha took a little over five hours. She arrived in town around twelve and decided to grab a bite to eat before checking in. She found the Chinese takeout chain she loved and went inside. As she approached the counter, she heard a familiar voice call her name. She turned to see Noah sitting at a table in the corner. Her mouth dropped open. She quickly ordered her food and then joined him.

"So ESP is now one of your specialties?" she asked with a grin as she sat down.

"It didn't take extrasensory perception to know you'd come here for lunch. It's close to the field office, and you're addicted to this food."

She reached over and squeezed his shoulder. "Yes, I am. And I must be addicted to you. I'm so glad to see you." As soon as she said the words, she realized he might take them the wrong way. When he didn't seem to react to her statement, she inwardly breathed a sigh of relief.

"When did your plane get in?" she asked.

"A couple hours ago. I rented a car and drove around for a bit. Then I came here to eat and wait for you. If you hadn't shown up when you did, I would have called."

"What do you think of Omaha so far?" she asked.

"It's nice. I've never been here before."

"I like it already since it has my very favorite restaurant."

Noah laughed. "So we're going to be on surveillance together. I'd say it's one of the most boring duties we've been assigned to, but now I'm not so sure. Listening in on inane conversations for hours and hours at a time still ranks as the most mind-numbing thing I've ever done as an agent."

"But you stopped a drug-trafficking scheme. That should compensate for the initial lack of excitement."

Noah grunted. "You're the one who deserves credit for that

bust. I don't know why I missed it at first. I know better. I've been . . . distracted."

"Probably because I wasn't there," Kaely joked.

An odd look flashed across Noah's face, but he shook his head. "As important as your presence is in my life is, I do have a life outside work, you know."

Kaely laughed lightly. "No, you don't." She glanced at her watch. "I better eat now or I'll be out of luck. Be right back."

She hurried up to the counter and found her order ready to pick up. The woman behind the counter handed her the bowl and the drink she'd ordered. Her favorite meal. Green beans and chicken. Kaely went back to the table where Noah waited.

"We're supposed to check into the field office at one," Kaely said. "We better finish and get going." She quickly ate most of her food, drained her glass of iced tea, and then reached for her purse. "Are you ready?" she asked Noah.

"I didn't know you could eat that fast," he said, grinning. "It usually takes you a while."

Kaely laughed. "I like to take my time, but when it's necessary, I can put it away faster than most men."

"I learn something new about you all the time." Noah stood up, picked up his empty bowl, and reached for hers.

Kaely smiled and handed him the remnants of her meal. Then she got to her feet and put her coat on. "Thanks. Since we're both driving, I'll meet you at the field office. Why don't we meet up in the parking lot and go in together?"

Noah nodded. "Sounds good. See you there." He paused for a moment, then smiled at her. "I'm really happy to be here."

"Let's see how pleased you'll be after five hours of sitting in a van, waiting for someone who may never show up."

"This may be the test of real friendship." He winked at her.

"We'll be okay. But be prepared to bring your best FBI stories. I'll need to be entertained."

"I think I can fill the bill," Noah said. "Meet you in the parking lot."

Kaely hurried out to her car. She really was delighted to see him. And frankly, it worried her.

SIXTEEN

John Howard, the special agent in charge of the Omaha field office, waited in his office for the agents sent to him from St. Louis. He knew one of them by reputation. Kaely Quinn was a name that had floated around the FBI for quite a while. Some agents thought she was the real deal. Others, like him, were a little skeptical. Could any behavioral analyst be that good? It didn't seem possible.

When someone knocked on his door, he sat up in his chair and found himself straightening his tie. He quickly put his hand down.

"Come in," he barked.

The door opened and a woman walked in, a man following closely behind her. John was surprised by Kaely Quinn. She was a small woman. He'd expected someone bigger. Her red curly hair was pulled up in a loose bun. But her eyes were her most startling feature. They were almost black, with something in them that drew you in.

The man with her was tall with dark wavy hair, a little longer than John liked for a special agent with the FBI. If this guy was one of his, he'd be getting a haircut ASAP. But there was an intense quality about Noah Hunter. Solomon had told him that these two were his best agents.

John was really grateful for the help. He knew the pair was working behind the scenes on a series of fires in Darkwater, but he didn't care. The Omaha office was dealing with a huge influx of heroin brought into the country through Mexico and distributed by members of MS-13. They'd flooded cities across the country. Now they had infiltrated Omaha, and his agents were working the case 24-7. Recently, a new branch of the gang had popped up in North Platte. Having agents like Hunter and Quinn help them out was a godsend. He had no plans to look a gift horse in the mouth.

He stood up and put his hand out. After shaking hands with both agents, he gestured toward the chairs in front of his desk. They sat down and looked at him expectantly.

"Glad you're here, Special Agents Hunter and Quinn," he said. "We appreciate the assistance."

"We're happy to be here, sir," Noah said.

"We need to get you up to speed quickly. You're scheduled from eight at night until four in the morning. Surveillance will be from eleven until four. You can go over case articles and pictures in the office from eight o'clock until it's time to leave. Make sure logs are up-to-date. If any suspicious vehicles show up during your surveillance, you'll need to request vehicle registrations so we know who's hanging around our target. I know most agents think this early morning shift is the quietest, but MS-13 doesn't keep regular office hours. They're normally very active after midnight." He stared at them for a moment. "I'm sure you're familiar with these procedures. Any questions?"

Kaely and Noah both said "no, sir" at the same time.

John stood up. "We'll arrange vehicles while you're working for us."

"If you don't mind, sir, I'd like to use my own car," Kaely said. "And after tonight Noah will be riding with me from Dark-water to North Platte."

"All right. Turn in your mileage. And you, Special Agent Hunter?"

"I have a rental car, sir."

"All right. Be sure to turn in your receipts. Now I'm going to take you to my SSA. He'll brief you on your assignment. Once again, I want you to know we're glad for the help. You both have excellent reputations, and you're not known in North Platte. Makes it easier to send you out since you won't be recognized by the locals. We've got to shut these guys down. The gangs are being controlled by someone else. First we need to arrest the leaders and put them away. Then we'll go after the gangs."

"We'll do the best we can for you," Kaely said.

"Follow me and I'll introduce you to Supervisory Special Agent Leo Moreland. He'll bring you up to speed on the case."

John walked around the desk, then headed down the hall to Leo's office. After the introductions, he left Kaely and Noah with Leo. As he walked back to his own office, he felt a sense of relief that these two great agents were here. Of course he hoped they'd bring the arsonist in Darkwater to justice, but right now he had to focus on the cartel and the gangs. This arrangement seemed to be just the solution they all needed.

After being briefed by the SSA, Kaely and Noah decided to drive to Darkwater rather than stay overnight in Omaha. Although Kaely tried to get Noah to book a room at the B&B where she'd originally planned to stay, he balked, claiming he wasn't a B&B kind of guy. Instead, he decided to check in to the same motel where Jason had been staying.

Noah followed Kaely to Darkwater. She waited outside while he checked in to the motel. After carrying in his luggage, he went out to find something for them to eat. He brought back cheeseburgers and fries from a nearby place called Bucky's Burgers. The burgers were surprisingly good. Charbroiled on the outside and perfectly cooked on the inside. Grilled onions, mustard, and pickles topped them off. And the fries were crispy and delicious. With a cup of hot coffee, it was a perfect meal after a long day. Kaely hadn't realized how hungry she was.

"So what do you think?" she asked Noah after taking another bite of her cheeseburger.

He wiped his mouth with his napkin. "About what? This drug case? Or the cheeseburger?"

She grinned. "The drug case."

He popped a French fry into his mouth, chewed, and swallowed. Then he washed it down with a big gulp of his soda. He set the cup down on the table, where he'd spread out his food. He was lucky to get a room with a small table and two chairs. Kaely had traveled a lot. Many of her meals had been consumed while sitting on the edge of a bed.

"I think we need to give it our best effort, just like you told Howard we would. We have to make sure we don't get distracted by the arson case and mess this thing up."

"We won't. We're too good for that."

Noah raised an eyebrow as he gazed at her. "You're pretty confident."

She laughed. "It's not that. I'm a pragmatist. I evaluate things based on facts. What I know. And I know we make a great team."

He nodded and smiled. "We do, don't we?" He took another bite of his burger.

Kaely could tell he had something on his mind. She kept quiet and waited.

"We've been through a lot in a short time, haven't we?" he said suddenly.

As soon as his question ended, a blast of wind from outside rattled the windows. Darkwater was under a winter storm warning. It wasn't supposed to hit until tomorrow. Hopefully, they'd be in North Platte before the bad weather arrived. Darkwater and Valentine were in the bull's-eye, but North Platte was on the edge. For some reason, the gust of wind felt like a warning. Where was Noah going with this?

"Yeah, we have," Kaely said. She munched on her French fries, waiting for him to continue. He didn't. "What makes you mention it?" she asked finally.

Noah stared past her. She could see hesitation in his expression. "Noah, is something bothering you? If it is, spit it out. There's nothing you can't tell me."

He shook his head slowly. "That's kinda what I wanted to say. I mean, the same thing. You . . . you can tell me anything too, Kaely. I mean, if something is bothering *you* . . ."

She frowned at him. "You're talking about my mom, I assume?" Kaely took a deep breath and blew it out quickly. "We've stored up years of personal baggage. I think we're trying to ignore it, you know? Marcie keeps saying hurtful things, which is her way of trying to deal, I guess. Sometimes I wish she'd just unload on me. Get it out. It would be more honest. I want to confront her, but I can't. I don't want to do anything to make her life . . . unpleasant. Right now the most important thing is that she gets well."

"Why would she unload on you? What have you done to make her angry?"

"Ignored her. She thinks I should have tried harder to see her, to connect with her. Even though I tried time after time."

She pointed a French fry at Noah. "I found out my brother was upset with me too. Felt like I'd deserted him when I left home. I tried to explain, but I'm not sure he understood." She snorted. "I get the feeling our pictures are in the dictionary under *dysfunctional*."

Noah chuckled. "So how is your mom? Do you think she's getting better?"

"Hard to tell, but Jason seems to feel she's got a good chance. I'm praying for her recovery."

"Just remember that I'm here. Don't keep things to yourself, okay?"

Kaely was grateful for Noah's concern and willingness to be a sounding board, but there were some things she had no intention of sharing. Not because she didn't trust him. She did. To a point. She confided in him more than anyone else. But events over the past couple of months had changed her. Made her more careful. She couldn't make herself vulnerable again. Giving away too much to people had backfired badly. She wouldn't allow it to happen again.

"I'm fine, Noah. Thanks. Sure, it bothers me that my mom's sick, but there's nothing I can do except pray. Hopefully we can improve our relationship." She smiled at him. "You've been good to listen to me when I needed someone. I don't think you could do more than you have. It means a lot to know you're there for me."

"Good," Noah said. "I'm glad. Just remember that I have big shoulders, and I'm always willing to listen without offering advice."

"A man who doesn't want to tell you what you should do to solve your problems? Impossible. Aren't you guys hardwired for that?"

He laughed. "We are, but we do it because we care. I guess we want to fix things. After doing the wrong thing many, many times, I finally learned to just listen. Tracy taught me that."

"I really appreciate it, Noah," she said softly. "If I need to talk about what's going on, I'll come to you. You have my word."

"Good." He yawned. "I'm tired. Why don't you go home and let me get some shut-eye?"

Kaely popped the last bite of her cheeseburger into her mouth. Then she gathered up the paper that the cheeseburger was wrapped in and the cardboard sleeve that had held the French fries. She threw everything in the trash and grabbed her coat. Another blast of winter wind shrieked outside.

"What time do you want to head to North Platte tomorrow?" she asked Noah.

He was quiet for a moment. Finally, he said, "Why don't we take off around four? The storm is supposed to get here sometime around five tomorrow evening. I realize we'll get to North Platte early, but we can get supper before we check in. I want to make sure we beat the weather."

Even though she didn't want to spend two or three hours filling time before they started their assignment, she knew he was right. "Okay," she said. "Why don't I drive? I think my SUV will make it through any snow we might encounter on the way back."

"Are you saying my rental compact car isn't as tough as your SUV?"

"That's exactly what I'm saying."

"Okay," Noah said. "We'll take your car. Do you want me to drive to your house or do you want to pick me up here?"

"I'll pick you up. The motel is close to the highway. But when we get back, I want you to come over for lunch or something. I'd like to introduce you to my mom. I mean, if you want to meet her." She smiled. "The safe bet would be to say no. She can be a handful."

She saw surprise in his eyes, but he quickly recovered. "I'd like that very much, Kaely. Thank you."

She nodded, grabbed her purse, and opened the door. "Bye," she said before pulling the door shut. She hurried to her car. When she got inside, she worried that she'd made a mistake. She'd been trying valiantly to keep her friendship with Noah at a place where she felt comfortable. The invitation to meet Marcie had slipped out before she had a chance to rein it in. She sighed. Noah and Marcie. That should be interesting.

Kaely started her car and headed back to her mother's house.

SEVENTEEN

Kaely pulled into the motel parking lot a little before four. The promised winter storm was bearing down on Dark-water a little early. She and Noah would just barely miss it. Jason had left the motel and was staying at the house. He was still unhappy with her. He wasn't saying anything directly, but she could tell he felt Kaely had let him down.

In an effort to smooth things over, Kaely had taken her mother to her doctor's appointment that morning. She'd sat in the waiting room while Marcie saw the doctor, but when she was done he came out with her. He was an older man who exhibited a persona of self-confidence. Yet, when he spoke she could tell he had a gentle spirit.

Dr. Branford had put his hand on Marcie's shoulder. "Your mother is doing very well. I couldn't be happier with her prog-ress. I suspect that having her children near her has helped her outlook. That can make a big difference in the results of her treatment."

Kaely had nodded dumbly at his comment. So far her mother hadn't shown any sign that she was happy Kaely was here. She found it hard to believe her presence was having any positive impact on Marcie's attitude.

After her father went to prison, Kaely knew she'd been hard to deal with. Recurring nightmares caused her to scream out in the middle of the night. At first her mother had come to her room and tried to comfort her. But then one night, when Kaely was sixteen, she didn't come. She never came again.

When Kaely was eighteen and announced she was moving out, her mother's obvious relief had been like a gut punch. It was then that Kaely decided she'd never let anyone get too close again. She'd learned she had to protect herself, since even those closest to her couldn't be trusted to have her best interests at heart.

Many years later, she'd found God. Although He was leading her to trust more, recent events had made Kaely more cautious. She was trying to gain back the ground she'd lost, but she was self-aware enough to realize it wasn't going to happen overnight.

Kaely glanced at her watch. This wasn't the time to rehash her relationship with her mother. She and Noah had a job to do. She started to get out of the car so she could knock on his door, but before she could, Noah came out and jogged toward the car. They'd both dressed down for the operation, wearing jeans, T-shirts, and beat-up jackets to hide their weapons. The idea was to match the neighborhood.

Although they were both hopeful they could find their target quickly, it would probably be a long, boring night. They were watching for a man Omaha suspected was one of the leaders of the cartel that was distributing heroin laced with fentanyl. In the past few years, heroin had become a major problem in the United States. Getting it over the border was too easy, and several cartels had taken advantage of that. Agencies in Washington were working hard to cut the flow of the dangerous drug, but dealing with politicians made it tough to get something done. It was frustrating.

Noah opened the car door and got in. "Do you want me to drive?" he asked.

Kaely shook her head. "I'll do it. Maybe you can drive back."

"Oh, I see. I get to drive after we've been up all night. I suppose you'll be sleeping on the way back."

"You make me sound so . . . devious."

"You? Heavens no." Noah shook his head as he put the satchel he'd slung over his shoulder on the floor between his legs. He smiled as he opened it. He pulled out a thermos. "Lots of hot coffee for tonight. I also brought some snacks for the trip. Brownies. Fruit." He looked at her. "I went to the grocery store down the street when I got up this morning."

Kaely stared at him with raised eyebrows. "Wow, I'm impressed."

The snow began to get a little heavier, but she was confident they could get in front of it. Sure enough, about fifteen minutes later, the roads were clear.

"So what do you think our arsonist will do next?" Noah asked.

"He's made himself known. He's not going to stop. There will be another fire. Soon."

"You think the sheriff can handle it?"

Kaely looked out the window. She still hadn't met the man. "I wish we could bring CIRG in on this." The FBI's Critical Incident Response Group brought together some of the best investigative tools available in the world. Kaely was curious to see if there had been similar fires in other places. That information could be invaluable. She would love to have the envelope and letter from Jack looked at by the FBI's lab. The police were dusting for prints, but the FBI could find much, much more. There was also a communication database that could look for comparisons to the letter. Kaely sighed loudly out of frustration.

"This is really bothering you, isn't it?" Noah asked.

"I want to use the best resources available to find this jerk."

Noah was quiet for a moment. "I have confidence in you. *You* are the best resource available. You'll find him."

Kaely glanced over at him. "You're not getting my share of the brownies if that's what this is about."

Noah shrugged. "Well, I tried."

Kaely laughed. A comfortable silence settled in the car as they drove toward North Platte. Even though she loved being with Noah, she felt a little unsettled around him. He had a way of keeping her off-center. Out of control.

They arrived in North Platte around five thirty and found a restaurant not far from the local FBI resident agency. After checking in with Omaha to let them know they were in town, they sat down to dinner and quietly went over their assignment. They were looking for a Miguel Guzman. He'd crossed the border illegally four years ago and disappeared. Omaha considered him a kingpin in the cartel—not the man in charge, but high enough in the ranks to be dangerous. The FBI suspected that Guzman was arranging transportation for the drugs. He was also known as an enforcer who was ready and willing to kill for his leaders.

Tonight the FBI was going to be watching an apartment complex where a woman named Rosa Martinez lived. It was believed that she and Guzman had split up a few months back, but the FBI had just learned that Guzman was seen with Rosa at a club a week ago. Agents assigned to the case wondered if Guzman might be trying to hide their relationship, which could mean Rosa knew more about his operations than they'd realized. Guzman undoubtedly wouldn't want the Feds to talk to her.

Even though Kaely and Noah's main target was Guzman, they'd also be monitoring all other traffic in and out of the apartment complex. There were at least six known MS-13 gang members living there. The local office had provided Kaely and Noah with photos of all the players as well as a list of vehicles registered to Guzman and Rosa. In addition, they'd given them additional information about other known gang members and their associates who might be involved directly with Guzman.

While they ate, Kaely checked her phone. Sure enough, Darkwater was being hit with a storm that could dump up to six inches of snow.

"We may need to stay here tonight," Noah said, as if reading her mind.

"Let's wait for morning. See what the roads are like," she said. "If there's a possibility we can get back, I'd like to give it a try. Jason's pretty unhappy with me."

"Sorry you're going through this," Noah said. "I can see how tough it is on you."

"What my mother's going through is worse."

"Yeah, I get that. Doesn't make this easier though, does it?"

Kaely sighed. "No, it doesn't."

After finishing dinner, they ordered dessert and talked awhile. Around seven, they left the restaurant and drove over to the North Platte office. They checked in and spent a couple of hours poring through files and being briefed about the assignment. Then SSA Paul Turner, the agent in charge of the operation, introduced Noah and Kaely to the other agents who would be hiding around the corner from the complex, waiting for a signal should they spot Rosa or Guzman. It was important that everyone meet so no one would accidentally get shot by friendly fire. Not recognizing fellow agents could have serious consequences. Kaely noticed that one member of their team seemed especially uptight. She found it odd since there was no way to predict if their suspects would show up. This would probably be a long, boring night.

At ten thirty, Kaely and Noah were taken to a locker room, where they put on their bulletproof vests. After that they were led out to the parking lot where Special Agent Mark Fisher waited for them with a beat-up old van. He would drive them to their surveillance spot, then get out and walk away, leaving Noah and Kaely locked inside, hidden in the back. The van had specially tinted windows so they could see out but no one could see in.

Noah and Kaely climbed into the van and took their positions. They each had a place to sit, along with binoculars, cameras with long-distance lenses, notebooks for handwritten notes, and cell phones to communicate with other surveillance team members. Thankfully, there was a battery-operated heater that would keep them warm since the van wouldn't be running.

Fisher drove them to the neighborhood where they'd spend the next four hours. It had been described as sketchy, but that was probably a notch above the truth. Kaely wondered why the girlfriend of a guy rolling in drug money would live in a complex like this. It didn't make much sense and made her wonder if they were wasting their time. If Rosa Martinez was still seeing Guzman, he'd probably have her stashed somewhere nice or wherever he was currently holed up. Since the FBI had no idea where that was, they could only go back to the last place they knew she'd lived. And that was at this apartment complex.

Once they were parked, Fisher pointed out the location of the other surveillance vehicles parked down the street. Then he got out and walked away. After he left, Noah said, "Well, at least we don't have to worry about this piece of junk being stolen. No one's that desperate."

"That's the point," Kaely said. "Being carjacked could definitely cause us some problems."

Kaely and Noah settled in, but Kaely's thoughts weren't on Guzman or Rosa. She was thinking about the arsonist in Darkwater.

Was he planning a fire right now? While they were sitting in this van, waiting for someone who might never come? Was someone else in Darkwater getting ready to die?

EIGHTEEN

Tonight he doesn't need a space heater to hide his genius. The heaters have served their purpose. Besides, now the authorities know him. They are watching for him. But they will never find him. He's too smart. Under the cover of snow, he makes his way to the back of the small frame house. It only takes a few moments to pour the gasoline around the foundation. He takes out his lighter and laughs softly. Seconds from now, the beast will rise again, no match for the snow. No match for those who think they can stop him.

He hesitates, not wanting to move too quickly. After all, this is a sacred moment. A memorial to what went before and what is to come.

In the dark, the snow whirling around him, he whispers, "'Jack be nimble, Jack be quick, Jack jump over the candlestick. Jack jump high, Jack jump low, Jack jumped over and burned his toe.'" Under his breath, he speaks one more thing. His mantra. His reason for existing. He takes a deep breath and says, "319 Harbor Lane."

Then he clicks the lighter.

———

When the call came, Tuck swore under his breath. Not another one. What would it take to stop this scumbag trying to destroy his town?

Tuck called the station and found out that an engine and a

ladder company were on the way. He gave the order that other volunteers be called in as well. He realized he wasn't that far from the fire, so he turned on the siren in his squad car and headed to the scene, praying that no one would die this time.

As their surveillance entered its third hour, Kaely was feeling stiff. The only people going in and out of the apartment complex were two teenagers who appeared to be sneaking in after curfew and an obviously inebriated couple probably walking home from a nearby bar.

Kaely moved the small sliding door that was built into the partition that separated the front seats from the back of the van. It was there so they could get clear pictures. She studied the couple through the camera Omaha had provided. The long-distance lens clearly showed the faces of the couple. Not Rosa. Not Guzman. She snapped a few pictures just in case. She closed the door and shook her head at Noah, who called the agent supervising the assignment to let him know the couple wasn't their targets.

Kaely stretched, trying to get comfortable. She took a bottle of water from the cooler next to her. They'd been provided everything they needed to do the job. All in all, she couldn't complain, but sitting for this long wasn't her style.

Noah seemed to be doing okay. He hung up the cell phone and looked over at her. "Are you staring at me?"

"Kind of. Just thinking."

He frowned. "About?"

"About the arson case. Not sure we should talk about it now though. We need to concentrate on this assignment." She turned her head to watch the building through the darkened window on the side of the van. They had a clear view of the apartments.

"As long as we're doing our job, I don't see why we can't talk a little. I'm not going to get distracted."

"Okay." Kaely set the camera on her lap and picked up the water bottle she'd left next to her on the floor. "Most serial arsonists use unsophisticated methods to set fires. The usual motive is some kind of revenge or a desire to feel powerful, in control."

"I thought some of these guys just set fires because it excites them," Noah said.

Kaely nodded. "That's true in a few cases." She turned to look at him. "But their main motivation is anger caused by something that happened to them." She shook her head, then went back to watching the apartment complex. "But this guy . . . he's sophisticated. When he started, he broke into homes. He seemed to know if the owners had space heaters. How? And what about the house without a space heater? Was there something important about that house? Why would he add a heater?" She shrugged. "Or are we on the wrong track? Could our arsonist have a beef with the fire department?"

She sighed. "So many avenues of investigation." She chewed her lip for a moment, thinking. "And then when it becomes public that the last fire wasn't caused by an arsonist, he comes out and writes a letter to the fire chief." Kaely closed her eyes for a moment and wrapped her arms around the camera. Finally she said, "If he followed normal patterns, he would have stopped setting fires by now. He should be afraid of getting caught. But instead he decides to make himself known. Why?"

"You're asking a lot of questions I can't answer."

Kaely was quiet for a moment, trying to get into the arsonist's head. "This guy's different, Noah. He's on some kind of mission. He's not going to stop until he accomplishes what he's set out to do."

"Then we need to stop him."

"We have to talk to the sheriff, Josh Brotton. We can't work this case the way we need to without his assistance."

"Whatever happens, I don't want them pulling this away from us," Noah said. "I know that sounds selfish, but I really want to find this guy."

"We're on the same wavelength."

Noah started to say something but stopped when a car pulled up across the street. They turned to watch the driver get out and walk toward the apartment complex. Kaely opened the sliding door and raised the camera.

"It's Rosa," she said. "She's alone."

Kaely took several pictures as they watched Rosa heading toward her apartment. Suddenly, three men walked out of the complex. It was only at the last second Kaely realized one of them had a gun in his hand. She called for backup at the same time she headed toward the back door of the van, weapon drawn.

From behind her she heard Noah call out her name. Then he grabbed her and pulled her down to the floor as bullets began to fly, hitting the glass window and piercing the side of the van.

Noah covered Kaely with his body, making it hard for her to breathe. It seemed like forever before the shots stopped.

NINETEEN

K aely and Noah gathered with the rest of the team at the North Platte office. SSA Turner was furious.

"Anyone want to explain what just happened?" Turner thundered. They were all sitting in chairs in a room that appeared to be used for training. "Rosa Martinez is dead. Two of our agents are in the hospital, and we've got three dead gangbangers."

He was met with silence, which seemed to make his already red face darken more. Noah was afraid the guy was going to stroke out.

No one said anything, but they all knew the truth. There was a rat somewhere. Someone had told Guzman about the operation. It might not be someone in this group. There were other people who knew about the operation. Without some kind of evidence, there wasn't any way to know who'd been working with Guzman.

"Months and months of preliminary work just got flushed down the toilet." Turner glared at the men and women who sat silently, watching him. "I'm gonna find out what happened, believe me. If any of you know something, you'd better find me before I come looking for you. This operation is shut down for now. Get out of here. You'll be contacted for reassignment." He pointed toward Noah and Kaely. "Special Agents Quinn and Hunter. You stay. I want to talk to you."

Noah glanced over at Kaely, who seemed to be interested in

something on the other side of the room. He nudged her. "Did you hear Turner? He wants to talk to us."

She turned to meet his gaze. "Yeah, I heard."

They waited in their chairs until the room cleared. Turner stared at them as they got up and approached him. Noah couldn't read the expression on his face, but it made his stomach tighten with apprehension.

Turner waited until the door closed as the last agent left. "I'm glad you're okay," he said. "But you're on suspension pending an investigation."

Noah's mouth dropped open. "I . . . I'm sorry, sir. I don't understand."

"I know every agent that was in this room, but I don't know you."

"You think we're working with Guzman?" Noah choked out. "That doesn't make sense. We don't even know him. We're not from here."

"Guzman has long tentacles," Turner said darkly. "He could have easily gotten to you. Money talks. Maybe he bribed you." He scowled at Noah. "Where were you after the shooting started? Why didn't you get out of the van and confront those gangbangers?"

"We couldn't. We were in the line of fire. Besides, by the time we could have exited, backup had arrived and was already confronting the shooters." Noah glanced at Kaely. "It was my call, sir. If we made a mistake, I take full responsibility."

"I think Agent Quinn was capable of making her own decisions, Agent Hunter." He pointed his finger in Noah's face. "I'll find out the truth, trust me. And if you had anything to do with this, I'll make sure you spend the rest of your life in prison. Do you hear me, Special Agent?" He spat out the last two words as if they were pieces of rancid food he wanted out of his mouth as quickly as possible.

Noah realized that Kaely hadn't said a word. He looked down at her, wondering why she was so quiet.

But when she finally spoke, he wished she hadn't.

"I might know who your corrupt agent is, sir," she said.

Noah had to bite his lip to keep from telling her to shut up.

"I believe you're aware I was trained as a behavioral analyst?" she continued.

Turner didn't respond. He just stared at her icily.

"It's not a perfect science," Kaely said, "but sometimes we can analyze people's reactions. It helps to see into their minds."

"And?"

"I observed several behaviors by one of your people that caused me some concern. I'm not saying he's Guzman's person on the inside, but I believe you need to look at him closely."

Noah wanted to grab Kaely's arm and drag her out of that room. At this point he was hoping Turner wouldn't remove his weapon and dispose of them right there.

"So who do you think betrayed the Bureau?" Turner asked Kaely in a low, tight voice.

She hesitated a moment. "I don't know his name, but he sat on the third row, near the end. He wore a dark parka and a black shirt. He has brown hair with some gray at his temples."

Turner's expression hardened. "You're talking about Special Agent Frank Navarro, one of the best agents I've ever worked with. You're trying to tell me he's working for the Mexican cartels? Are you crazy?"

Kaely seemed a little taken aback, but she held her own. "I'm just suggesting you check him out, sir. That's all. Whether you do or not is up to you. I may be wrong. He could have something else on his mind. But in the group gathered here tonight he was the only one expressing behaviors that showed he was upset about something. Perhaps even expressing feelings of guilt." She held her hands out in front of her, palms up. "What you do with this information is up to you. I have no intention of following up on it." She put her hands down and nodded at him. "Good night, sir." With that, she turned and headed for the door, leaving Noah standing there with a furious SSA.

"Good night, sir," Noah echoed, then he quickly followed Kaely out of the building. When he stepped outside, the cold smacked him in the face like a fist. It took a second for him to catch his breath. "What did Navarro do that made you suspicious?" he asked Kaely, who stood by the door, waiting for him.

"He was upset before the operation even began. Why? We had no indication that Rosa or Guzman would show. Maybe it was some personal problem. But just now, I noticed that he kept rubbing his legs. It's called leg cleansing. It means he's under stress. He was trying to pacify himself."

Noah was dumbstruck. "You told Turner someone on his team is a rat because he was nervous before a dangerous operation and after we were fired upon, he rubbed his legs? Are you serious? Everyone in that room was under stress. Turner was mad enough to open fire on all of us."

"There were other signs, Noah. If I wasn't convinced there was something wrong with Agent Navarro, I wouldn't have said anything. Do you think I should have stayed quiet?"

Noah met her gaze. Looking into her dark eyes, he realized there was only one answer he could give. "No," he said. "You did the right thing." He sighed, and his breath turned to steam in the cold. "Did I mess up? Keeping us in the van while shots were being fired?"

"Of course not," Kaely said. "We had no way of getting out of there safely. If we'd gotten up, at least one of us would have been hit, if not both." She hesitated a moment before saying, "Look, I really appreciate what you did. It's possible you saved my life. To be honest, it wasn't until you pulled me down that I was aware we were in danger. Thanks."

Noah nodded but didn't respond. Agents were expected to protect their partners, but his reaction hadn't been based on his training. When he'd realized Kaely was at risk, Noah had been seized with the kind of fear no agent could afford to entertain. He had been more than willing to give his life for Kaely Quinn. And the reason scared him more than he could admit.

TWENTY

W e need to let Solomon know we've been suspended," Noah said, changing the subject. "I guess that means we have some time off." He stomped his feet, trying to chase away the cold. "How many inches of snow and ice do they have in Darkwater? Do you have any idea?"

Kaely took her phone out of her back pocket and pulled up a weather app. A few moments later, she said, "Four inches. That's not much. But I have a feeling . . ."

"Oh no. Not one of your feelings." Noah clapped his hands together. They felt numb.

"Yeah. I think something's happened." She took a deep breath. "We need to get back to Darkwater."

"All right, all right." Noah shook his head. "Let's go. I knew I'd lost this argument before we started. Besides, I'm freezing. If I don't give in, you'll just make me stand outside until you get your way."

"Why don't you drive?"

"So you think it's okay to head back to Darkwater, but you don't actually want to tackle the roads yourself?"

Kaely smiled. "See? You can profile too."

He chuckled and shook his head. When he'd first met Kaely Quinn, she rarely smiled. Things had changed. He assumed it was because she was learning to trust him. Sometimes he felt as if he'd be willing to give up a body part just to see that smile.

The drive back wasn't as bad as Noah had anticipated. Road

crews had treated the major highways, and even though some of the roads were down to one lane, they were passable. Still, he wondered what they'd face when they got to Darkwater.

They'd both checked their phones but couldn't find any stories about a fire in the small town. Had Kaely missed it this time? He doubted it. Her *feelings* were almost always on track.

"Have you tried out your special . . . procedure on our arsonist?" Noah asked. Even though he was aware the process had spiraled out of control, he still believed it was a valuable tool.

"No," she said quietly, "but I think I'm finally ready."

He could hear the hesitation in her voice. Was she afraid to try it?

"Kaely, you don't need to do this, you know. You're the best behavioral analyst I've ever met. Just profile him the way everyone else does. Seriously. If others can do it, you can too."

She turned her face from him and stared out the window. Although most of the snow had already fallen, light flakes fluttered around the car. The car's headlights seemed to set them ablaze. It was hard to keep his attention on the road and off the glittering dance that engulfed them.

"It's just . . . well, I know my method works." She turned her head toward him. "I don't do the dinner part anymore. That was leftover from meals with my father. It was the only time we talked. I always felt as if I'd missed something. I thought if I could just re-create those dinners, I could pick up on something that would have revealed who he really was." She clasped her hands together as if she was cold, but the interior of the car was warm and toasty.

Drawing on his courage, he decided to attack the situation another way. "Can I ask you what happens when you do this . . . thing?"

"This *thing*?" she replied. "You mean my profiling technique?"

He heard a trace of irritation in her voice. "Sorry," he said with a smile. "I was just curious. I've never seen you actually do it."

"And you won't. It would hurt my concentration." She was silent for a moment before saying, "All I do is put a file in front of me . . . maybe add my own notes to it . . . and begin to look it over. Then I start the profile. Sometimes I ask the UNSUB questions. As they answer, sometimes I begin to see them."

"You actually hear them speak?"

"Yeah." She frowned at him. "I've explained how the process works. Why are you asking me about it again?"

"No reason. Just trying to understand it a little better." Had he overplayed his hand? He focused on keeping his expression steady and not making any physical moves that would let her know he was nervous or being deceitful. He suddenly realized he was blinking too much. A sign of deception. He quickly put one hand up and rubbed his eyes. "The snow is bothering me," he said. He put his hand down and forced himself to keep from blinking. It wasn't easy.

She was quiet as she stared at him. Finally she said, "Sorry. You can ask whatever you want."

He looked over at her. "Not if it bothers you. We don't have to share everything in our lives just because we work together."

"It doesn't bother me. What else do you want to know?"

Trying to sound as nonchalant as he could, Noah said, "When they answer you . . . how does that work? I mean, you're just channeling your profile through their mouths, right?"

"Yes, basically that's true."

"Basically?"

A voice whispered loudly in his head, telling him to back off.

"What is it you really want to know, Noah?" Kaely asked quietly.

"You know what? Forget it. It's your process. We all have them." He looked at her and grinned. "I tried doing it your way once. Wasn't gonna tell you. Promise not to laugh?"

The corners of her mouth twitched. "And?"

"A dismal failure. No one showed up. I felt ridiculous." He shook his head. "I don't know how you do it. It's a real talent."

"Maybe."

"No, it truly is, Kaely. You've done some great work using that procedure. Anyone who makes fun of you is jealous. I know our parents used that line a lot when we were kids, and of course we never believed them. But this time it's the truth."

Kaely laughed. "My mother did say that. More than once."

Noah looked at the clock on the dashboard, feeling relieved that he'd gotten past the uncomfortable moment, but also a little sad she wasn't ready to tell him herself that she'd been having trouble with her technique. Would she ever trust him enough to be completely honest with him?

He realized they'd be in Darkwater in thirty minutes. "Should we stop somewhere for breakfast? It's early, but I noticed an all-night diner right outside of town."

He didn't hear her response and looked over at her. She was staring at him with an odd expression.

"Sounds good," she said. "And I'd like to talk to you about something. If it's okay."

"You can talk to me about anything," he said gently. "I'm your friend."

"I know that."

Noah only nodded his response, but inside, his heart suddenly felt full. He realized that more than anything, he wanted a chance to show Kaely Quinn that she would always be able to count on him. That he would never let her down. Was she ready to give him that chance?

TWENTY-ONE

Tuck Reynolds sped to the hospital. One of his men had been injured and he needed to be by his side. Sam Lucas disobeyed orders and ran into a house engulfed in flames. At first they'd been told the family was away. But then a neighbor who'd thrown a coat over her nightgown and pushed her way through the throng of people had yelled at the firefighters, begging them to listen to her. When Tuck and Sam finally walked over to where she waited, she informed them that the family had arrived home the night before. The father worked nights, but his wife and child might still be in the house.

Tuck had seen Sam's eyes widen. As Tuck yelled at him to stop, Sam ran toward the house and disappeared into the fire. Tuck was getting ready to order his men to redirect their hoses to cover Sam when suddenly he came running through the flames. He had one arm wrapped around a small woman whose body was totally limp. His other arm held an infant.

Tuck swore with relief. His wife's voice echoed in his head. *"Swear words are used by people who don't have anything important to say."* He shook his head and swore again. Right now he wasn't afraid of swearing. He was afraid that Sam's heroic effort had come too late.

He ran toward them and took the woman from Sam's arms. He carried her to the EMTs, with Sam running behind him, the baby next to his chest. The EMTs immediately began checking the mother's vitals and took the baby from Sam's arms. After they put a pediatric oxygen mask on him, he began to cry. A great sign. It was then that Tuck noticed Sam. His face was as white as the snow around them. Then he began to sway.

"He needs help," he told the EMTs. "Smoke inhalation." One of them jumped out of the ambulance and grabbed Sam.

"I'm okay," he mumbled.

"No, you're not," Tuck said. "You let them take care of you. That's an order." Most fire-related deaths were caused by inhaling too much smoke. Tuck knew how serious it could be. Fear clutched at him. Sam had risked his life to save two people. Would his heroism cost him everything?

At that moment, another ambulance pulled up and two more EMTs jumped out. They ran over and checked in with the first crew, then helped Sam walk over to the ambulance. Within minutes they had him safely strapped in, an oxygen mask on his face, and on his way to the hospital.

As both ambulances raced away, sirens wailing through the cold night air, Tuck Reynolds did something he hadn't done in years.

He prayed.

Noah and Kaely had just taken their seats in the diner when an old TV mounted on the wall broke in with news of another fire in Darkwater.

"We're told the fire is under control," the sleepy-looking reporter said. "Two people were pulled from the blaze. We don't have any information on their condition, but it seems a firefighter was injured trying to rescue them. We'll be back with more as soon as we have it."

The waitress was on her way toward them, but they waved

her away. Without a word, they ran out of the diner and got into their car. Neither one of them said anything as they raced back to Darkwater.

As they entered the town, Kaely called Tuck Reynolds. Unfortunately, her call went immediately to voicemail. Next she called the fire station. The phone was answered by a man who sounded exhausted. Kaely told him she was a friend of Tuck's and wondered what was going on.

He told her Tuck was okay and the fire was out. When she asked about the injured firefighter, he declined to give her any details. Thinking she could get more information from Sam, she asked to speak to him. The silence that followed her question told her what she wanted to know. She thanked the tired firefighter and hung up.

"Sam's been hurt," she told Noah.

"Are you sure?" he asked.

"About as sure as I can be."

"Should we go to the hospital?"

Kaely nodded. "We need to find out how he is, and we need to talk to Tuck."

The streets weren't as clear in Darkwater as they'd been on the highway. Noah's grip tightened on the steering wheel. He drove as carefully as he could while trying to get to the hospital as quickly as possible. He pulled into the parking lot about fifteen minutes later and parked the car. Noah and Kaely got out and ran through the emergency entrance, where they found Tuck and several other firefighters either seated in the waiting room or pacing the hallway.

When Tuck saw them, he came over. He gestured toward a

spot near the entrance, away from the firefighters waiting for information on their injured comrade.

After introducing himself to Noah, he said, "Don't know anything yet. Sam disobeyed orders and went into an almost fully engulfed house. Brought out a mother and an infant. Stupid fool may have saved two people but put his own life at risk."

"Anything on the mother and baby?" Noah asked.

Tuck rubbed his bleary eyes. "Looks like they're both going to make it. The mother was touch-and-go when they brought her in." He put his hand down and sighed. "Hopefully, we'll get the same good news about Sam." He nodded to them. "I want this guy. I want him badly. Can we talk?"

Kaely nodded. "Of course."

Tuck looked at his watch. "Let's go to the hospital cafeteria. It's just past six. They're open now."

Before they had the chance to head toward the cafeteria, a tall blond-haired man came through the entrance doors and walked over to where they stood.

"What's going on, Tuck?" he asked.

While Tuck filled him in on the fire and Sam's condition, Kaely watched the man closely. She recognized him from the newspaper. This was Sheriff Brotton.

When there was a pause in the conversation, Tuck turned toward them. "Josh, these are the two FBI agents I told you about. This is Special Agent Kaely Quinn and Special Agent Noah Hunter."

Kaely extended her hand to the sheriff. At first, she wasn't sure he was going to take it, but he finally did. Then he shook hands with Noah.

"It's nice to finally meet you, Sheriff," Kaely said. "I've been hoping for a chance to talk to you."

"I know you're here because you think we're incompetent, Agent Quinn, but we're not. I really don't think we have anything to discuss." He turned toward Tuck. "Please keep me updated. I want to know how Sam is doing." With that, he walked back out the way he'd come in.

Kaely looked over at Noah and rolled her eyes. It was clear they wouldn't be able to rely on help from the sheriff. And that was going to make things much more difficult.

TWENTY-TWO

S orry about that," Tuck said. "I'm working on him. His nose is still out of joint because of what happened the last time we dealt with the FBI."

"You don't need to apologize," Noah said. "But at some point we'll need his cooperation. We've got to work together."

Tuck nodded. "I know. Josh thinks his department can find this guy on their own. I'll convince him that they need your help. It just might take a little time."

"I'm not sure time is something we have a lot of."

"I agree. Let's go to the cafeteria. I need coffee. Badly."

Noah and Kaely followed Tuck down the hall to the cafeteria. Noah was pleasantly surprised. They had a buffet with delicious-looking scrambled eggs, hickory smoked bacon, maple sausages, and light and fluffy biscuits with gravy, for those who liked that kind of thing. Noah was happy with a little butter and strawberry jam on his biscuits. They had that too.

After filling his plate and getting a cup of coffee, he and Kaely sat down with Tuck, who had a plate of biscuits and gravy. The aroma of the gravy made Noah second-guess his opposition to the combination. He glanced over at Kaely's plate. It figured. A bowl of fresh fruit and a bagel with blueberry cream cheese. He didn't care. He was starving. He picked up his fork and dug in while he waited for Tuck to open up the conversation. The food was wonderful. Even the coffee was great.

After a few bites of food and a gulp of coffee, Tuck put his cup down. "Who is this guy and how do we catch him?"

Kaely didn't answer him at first. She just stared at her plate. Then she lifted her eyes and met his. "I have to be honest with you," she said slowly. "He confuses me."

Noah almost choked on the piece of sausage he'd stuffed into his mouth. Kaely was confused?

"Most arsonists don't have clear patterns. This guy does."

"I don't understand," Tuck said. "You told me there was a pattern. Now you say there isn't one?"

"Do you know anything about these victims?" Kaely asked, seeming to ignore his question. "Are they connected in any way?"

Tuck shook his head. "I wondered the same thing, so I did some digging. The families didn't know each other. None of them worked at the same place, went to the same church. No connection to each other at all. My department has never had any interaction with them." He frowned. "Josh checked them out too. No problems with law enforcement. Maybe we missed something, but I don't think so. They seem like normal families."

"You just pointed out what they have in common. Families." She looked back and forth between them. "Every targeted house belonged to families. No elderly couples. No singles. All families."

Kaely's revelation surprised Noah. That hadn't occurred to him. He could see Tuck was as taken aback as he was.

"You're right," he said slowly. "He's after families?"

She nodded. "Most arsonists are unsophisticated. This guy isn't. Most common motives for setting fires are revenge, excitement, vandalism, profit, or crime concealment."

"What's this guy's deal?" Tuck asked.

"I think he's out for revenge," she said. "But it's just a guess at this point."

"Maybe someone set his house on fire?" Tuck asked.

"Maybe," Kaely said. "But why not just burn down the house of the person he blames for that fire?"

Noah was silent as he considered her question. Tuck's expression made it clear he was puzzled too.

"If this guy hates families," Kaely said quietly to herself, "he's burning down their houses because they have something he doesn't."

"But these people had nothing to do with whatever this guy's problem is," Noah said.

"I know. But remember the first case we worked together?"

"The dead body in the park?"

Kaely nodded. "Yeah. That killer copied George Anderson, a serial killer who murdered guys who had the lifestyle he couldn't have."

"You think that's it?" Tuck asked. "This nut is killing innocent people because Mommy and Daddy didn't treat him right?"

Tuck's anger was palpable, but it was also understandable. He had an injured firefighter. Two people were dead. This was personal to him.

Kaely started to answer when one of Tuck's firefighters walked up to the table. He was young, maybe twenty-five. He held a phone in his hands and was visibly upset.

"No news on Sam yet," Tuck said. "We should hear something soon."

"That's not why I'm here," the man said. "A friend sent me something from the fire. You need to see it."

Tuck frowned at him. "Show me."

"Privately?"

"Nothing you can't say to me in front of them," Tuck said. "What is it, Greg?"

The young firefighter sat down next to Tuck, across from Noah and Kaely. "A friend of mine lives near the scene of the fire. He was sitting on his front porch, having a cigarette early this morning. He noticed a guy walking down the street, going toward the house that burned down. A little later, the same guy comes back, moving pretty quickly, looking around. My friend thought he was acting oddly, so he recorded him. Then a few minutes later my friend smells smoke. And not long after that he could see flames."

"Your friend may have recorded our UNSUB?" Noah said. He couldn't keep the excitement out of his voice.

Greg held the phone up so the chief could see it. "Sir, this guy . . . well, he looks a lot like Sam Lucas."

TWENTY-THREE

For several seconds no one said a word. Then Tuck let loose a string of profanity that filled the cafeteria. Kaely knew it was born out of shock. People turned to look at him. Parents with children glared his way.

"I don't believe it for a minute," Tuck said. "That's not possible."

Greg sat down. "Look, I don't believe it either, but I had to bring this to you. I think this guy could be our firebug."

Tuck grabbed the phone and stared at it for a moment. "You can't tell for certain it's Sam," he said with disgust. "It's too dark."

"I realize that," Greg said. "But you have to admit it could be him."

Tuck shook his head. "This could be anyone. It could be Sheriff Brotton, for crying out loud."

Greg's cheeks turned red. "I just wanted you to see it. I'm sure it's not Sam. To be honest, I was so shocked when I saw it. . . . Maybe I overreacted." He leaned back in his chair and sighed.

Kaely could see the young man was exhausted.

Tuck ran the video again. "You're right. It's not Sam, but it could be our arsonist."

"Can I see it, Chief?" Kaely asked.

He handed the phone to her. Despite the chief's insistence that it wasn't Sam Lucas, it certainly looked like him. The guy was tall with light-colored hair peeking out beneath a dark hoodie. The features were similar to Sam's, but the video was grainy, and it was hard to make out details. Not clear enough to use as evidence.

She showed it to Noah and then gave the phone back to the chief, who handed it to Greg. "Take this to Sheriff Brotton. I'll call him and ask him to look at it. His tech guy can turn it into a photo. Make it larger so we can see everything. I want this photo so clear I can see the hairs in this guy's nose." He pointed at his young firefighter. "You tell your friend to keep this quiet. I don't want some stupid rumor going around that Sam is our arsonist. Do you understand me?"

Greg nodded. "He won't say anything."

"Good." Tuck stared at Kaely. "That's not Sam."

"You're certain?" Noah asked.

"Positive. Unless his twin brother has come back from the dead . . ." His eyes suddenly widened. "Forget I just said that. I misspoke. I'm so bushed I'm punchy."

"Sam told me about what happened to his family," Kaely said to the chief.

"He did?" Tuck asked. He looked surprised. "Sam doesn't share that with many people. Of course, most of us who've lived in Darkwater awhile know about it. But new people? I can't remember the last time he told an outsider the truth about that terrible night."

"I didn't know Sam's brother was a twin."

The chief nodded. "So alike you couldn't tell them apart. Except for the scar."

"What scar?"

"Sam's brother had a scar on his right cheek from a bike accident when he was a kid." He shook his head. "Look, let's focus on finding this arsonist. I'm tired of this guy trying to burn

down our town. Sam almost died trying to save that family."
He looked back and forth between Noah and Kaely. "Help us."

"You won't like this," Noah said, "but the first thing we need to do is prove Sam didn't set that fire. I agree the video is difficult to make out, but it's the first lead we've had."

"I had a few other suspects," Kaely said. "People who were hanging around the fire on Mayfield, but I ruled them out." She hesitated. "We really need to talk to Sam. Give him a chance to view the video and see if he has an alibi for an hour before the fire call came in."

Tuck's face turned red, and he started to say something, but Kaely held up her hand. "You know as well as I do that this has to be our next step. People surprise us, Chief. It's happened to me more times than I can count. You're not naïve. You know it too."

"Yeah, I know it. But not this time. I'd bet my life on it."

Kaely glanced over at Noah. She saw the same doubt on his face that she felt. She hadn't seen anything in Sam to suggest he was capable of something like this. No deception. No attempt to hide some kind of inner anger. She would almost stake her career on his innocence. Still, she couldn't deny that the man on the video looked surprisingly similar to Sam Lucas. Tuck was obviously seeing what he wanted to and not being objective. That attitude wasn't going to help. Of course, they needed rock-solid evidence. Innocence and guilt hinged on it. Without it, all that was left was opinion.

"Maybe I should have kept this to myself," Greg said. "Asked my friend to just delete it."

"No, you did the right thing." Tuck gave Greg a weary smile. "Don't worry about it, okay? Just get the video to Josh. And text it to me too."

"And me," Kaely said. She gave Greg her cell phone number.

Greg nodded, tapped some buttons on his phone, then quickly stood up and left the room. Kaely wanted to look Sam in the face as he denied that the man in the video was him. She needed to see his reaction. See if she could detect guilt or an attempt at self-protection that didn't ring true. Still, her heart told her Sam wasn't an arsonist. The pain of losing his own family would have kept him from destroying the lives of others in the same way. Besides, an arsonist wouldn't rush in to save people the way Sam had unless he had a hero complex. Something else Kaely didn't detect in him.

Even as she built a case for Sam's innocence, she couldn't deny that many times people we trusted in the daylight could betray us in the dark.

Tuck was just getting ready to say something when a doctor came into the cafeteria, his eyes sweeping the room. When he saw Tuck, he headed their way. Tuck was silent, his dark face looking as if it were carved from stone. Kaely could feel tension flowing from him in waves.

It felt as if the doctor was walking in slow motion, even though Kaely knew that was impossible. When he finally reached them, Kaely read his body language before he spoke, and relief flooded her body. However, now that she knew Sam was okay, she would be forced to see him only as a suspect. Not a person she admired. Anything else could throw her off. Cause her to miss something.

"He's doing great," the doctor said right off the bat. "His lungs took in a good amount of smoke, but I don't see any permanent damage. He'll be as good as new in a day or two."

"Are you releasing him today?" Tuck asked.

"Yes. I want to watch him for a few more hours, but I don't

see any reason to keep him here. He'll probably be more comfortable at home." The doctor looked around. "Smoke inhalation is a lot more dangerous than people realize. It can affect the lungs and the heart. I've had patients seem fine and then suddenly suffer a major heart attack. Thankfully, I don't find any signs of that in Sam. Unless I see something that concerns me, he'll be out of here this afternoon."

"Doc, I need to talk to him," Tuck said. "Is that okay?"

Kaely read the doctor's badge. *Dr. Rodger Price.*

The doctor nodded. "Sure. He's awake. Just don't stay too long, okay? He needs as much rest as he can get."

"We'll be careful."

The doctor frowned. "We? I thought you were the one who wanted to see him, Chief."

"I'd like them in the room with me, if possible." Tuck gestured toward Kaely and Noah.

"Let's keep it to no more than two, okay?"

"I'll sit it out," Noah said. "Not a problem."

The doctor nodded at Noah. "I appreciate that. Thanks."

Tuck stood up and extended his hand to Dr. Price. "I can't thank you enough, Doc. We're lucky to have someone like you in Darkwater."

"Thank you." With that, the doctor turned and walked quickly out of the room.

Tuck turned to Kaely "You can come in with me. But I don't want you to mention the video. I mean it."

"You'll have to tell him eventually," Kaely said. "If he's released this afternoon he might go to the station. What if Greg brings it up? Sam should be prepared."

"I know that. And I'll talk to him about it. But it's got to come from me. Not from anyone else."

Kaely paused for a moment. Tuck was being led by his emotions. By his concern for a longtime friend. Kaely really needed to hear Sam's explanation for the video, and time was of the essence.

"The sooner we hear his side of the story, the faster we can find the truth and stop the arsonist," Kaely said. "You understand that."

"Of course I do," he snapped. "I'm not an idiot." He exhaled slowly. "I'm sorry. First Sam is injured and now . . ."

"If it makes any difference," Kaely said, "I believe your first instinct is right. I don't see Sam as our arsonist. Why risk his life to save a woman and her child if he's trying to burn down homes with women and children inside?" She shook her head slowly. "I feel like something else is going on here." Although she sounded confident about her assertions, she wasn't. Why couldn't she get a handle on this case?

Tuck stood to his feet. "Sorry to make you wait for us," he said to Noah.

Noah shook his head. "It's fine." He eyed Kaely. "I'll be here, eating for both of us, I guess."

She smiled. He was right. Whenever a case presented her with something interesting, she lost interest in everything else. Even food. Her mind became burdened with questions and scenarios. Her thoughts kept her so busy, eating seemed like something foreign. Something unnecessary.

"I'll be back as soon as I can," she told Noah.

She followed Tuck toward the area of the hospital where Sam was being cared for. Tuck seemed to know his way around. He'd probably been here before, maybe with other injured firefighters. Although she wasn't expecting any calls, Kaely reached into her pocket, took out her cell phone, and turned it off. The last thing she wanted was for it to go off in this part of the hospital. It seemed disrespectful.

Up ahead, Dr. Price stood outside a door. When they reached him, he said, "We're giving him breakfast in a bit. If you could keep your visit short . . ."

Tuck nodded. "Sure. I understand." He turned to Kaely. "Are you ready?"

She nodded, but to be honest, she wasn't certain she was. Who was Sam Lucas? The kind hero she'd immediately liked the first time she met him? Or a twisted killer?

TWENTY-FOUR

As Kaely followed Tuck into Sam's room, she tried to empty herself of her previous opinions. She wanted to evaluate him through fresh eyes. He could be a serial arsonist. Yet when she saw him lying in his hospital bed, her instinct told her this man would never purposely hurt another human being.

Tuck walked straight up to Sam's bed and put his hand on the firefighter's shoulder. "How you feeling?"

"I'm fine," he said, his blue eyes drifting over to Kaely. The weariness on his face was the only clue that pointed to the ordeal he'd recently endured.

"I'm glad you're okay," Kaely said. "We heard that the woman and baby you saved are doing well."

"Yeah, the doctor told me," Sam said. "I'm really grateful."

"You saved their lives," Kaely said. "What you did was heroic."

He shrugged. "Just doing my job. People shouldn't make such a big deal out of it."

"Actually, you weren't doing your job," Tuck said. The gruffness in his voice sounded forced. "You were told not to go inside that house. Didn't you hear that command?"

Sam's eyes widened. "I didn't hear anything like that, Boss. Of course, the sound of the fire was so loud . . ."

"Yeah, yeah." Tuck sighed loudly. "I guess you're gonna stick with that?"

Sam frowned at the fire chief. "I'm sure I don't know what you're talking about."

Tuck didn't respond, just turned toward Kaely. "You want a chair?" he asked.

As she shook her head, Sam gave her a quick wink. She tried not to smile, but she couldn't keep the corners of her mouth from edging up.

Tuck rolled his eyes at her and turned toward Sam. "You're not coming back until you get medically cleared. If you give me a hard time, I might have to research your claim of temporary deafness. Do you hear me this time, Sam?"

"Look, Chief . . ."

"I mean it, Sam. I really do."

Kaely almost found it hard to believe the two men were the same age and that they'd grown up together. Sam treated Tuck as his superior, showing nothing but respect for his position. Somehow it made Tuck seem older, more mature.

She leaned against the wall as they debriefed the fire. She perked up when Sam said, "Any news on our arsonist? Are we any closer to finding him?"

Tuck went suddenly silent. His reaction wasn't lost on Sam. He stared at Tuck and then at Kaely. "What's going on?" he asked. "Is something wrong? Did you find him?" He hesitated a moment. "Is it someone we know? I mean, whoever's doing this seems to know how to set a fire and get out in time."

Tuck held his hand up, bringing Sam's flow of words to an end. He took a step closer to the bed. "Something's come up, Sam, but I want to wait until you're out of here before we talk about it."

Sam frowned. "Why would we need to wait until I'm home? Anything that brings us closer to catching this scumbag will only make me feel better."

Tuck's silence only increased the look of confusion on Sam's face. Finally, his eyes narrowed as he stared at the chief.

"Surely no one's saying I had something to do with this. I mean, that would be insane." He frowned at his childhood friend. "Tell me, Tuck. Tell me the truth right now."

Tuck took a deep breath. "Greg Washington was contacted by someone who lives near the house that caught fire last night. This guy was smoking a cigarette on his front porch, looking at his phone, when he noticed a man walking down the street. A little later, the same guy came back, heading the other way. Greg's friend decided to record him just because he felt the man looked suspicious. A few minutes later, the fire became visible."

"Well, that's good, isn't it?" Sam asked, his eyebrows arched in excitement. Kaely felt strongly that his reaction was real. Sam Lucas had no idea who was on that video. Her every instinct as a behavioral analyst told her he was innocent.

Sam waited for Tuck to answer him. The silence was so full of tension Kaely had to bite her lip not to say anything. But finally Tuck said, "The man on the video looks a lot like you, Sam."

Sam's face went white. "Tuck, you know better than that."

Kaely couldn't stay quiet another moment. "Where were you last night?" she asked Sam. "About an hour before the fire started?"

He stared at her like he'd never seen her before. His shock was genuine, Kaely was certain of it.

"I . . . I was at the station. I was on shift and I was tired. Went upstairs and took a nap. The guys at the station will tell you the same thing."

Tuck nodded. "We'll check that out. Thanks." Then he reached into his pocket and took out his cell phone. After a few clicks, he handed it to Sam. Sam reached out and took the phone. He pressed his fingers on the screen and then stared at the video.

A few seconds later, his face went slack, and the machine attached to him began to beep loudly. The phone slid from Sam's hand onto the bed as he slumped back on his pillows. Tuck grabbed the phone before it fell off the edge of the bed and then leaned over the distressed firefighter.

"Sam? Sam, are you okay?"

A nurse came running into the room. She quickly glanced at the machine next to Sam's bed. "I'm sorry," she said, "but you need to leave. Now."

"Is he going to be all right?" Tuck asked.

"I mean it," the nurse said again. Her gaze swung to Kaely. "Will you help your friend out of here?"

Kaely went over to Tuck. "Come on. We'll wait outside. I'm sure Sam will be fine." She tugged on his arm. "Let's go."

Although the chief didn't move at first, he finally looked at Kaely and nodded. She led him out the door and into the hall. They saw Dr. Price hurrying toward them. He didn't say anything before rushing into the hospital room and closing the door behind him.

"He was just shocked, Tuck," Kaely said. "He'll be okay."

Tuck went over to a line of chairs next to the wall and seemed to almost collapse, as if he had no strength in his legs. "He was beyond shocked," he said, his voice shaking. "He was wounded by even the suggestion that he could do something like this. I just hurt one of my best friends." He took several quick breaths. Kaely was about to ask a nurse to check him out when his dark eyes locked on hers. "I need to tell you something. It's going to sound unbelievable and it probably is, but it's been bothering me ever since we got that letter."

Kaely sat down next to him.

"Sam Lucas couldn't walk away from a fire even if he wanted to. He's a firefighter through and through. His father used to be the fire chief in Darkwater. It's in his genes."

"Okay," Kaely said slowly.

Tuck took another deep breath and let it out slowly. Finally, he said, "I'm beginning to wonder if the man in that video is Sam's brother."

Kaely was prepared for almost anything but this. "Surely you're not serious."

"I know it sounds impossible, but I can't quit thinking about it. I need you to help me prove it—or disprove it."

"Let me get this straight," Kaely said. "You actually believe that Sam's dead brother is setting these fires?"

Tuck shook his head. "I know how it sounds. But you know that house on Mayfield? The one that didn't have a space heater? You wondered why the arsonist cared so much about that house?"

Kaely nodded.

"The teenager who wasn't home was a twin."

Kaely couldn't believe what she was hearing. How could someone as smart as Tuck allow himself to be convinced that Sam's brother was running around setting fires?

"Did you know that the cause of the fire that killed Sam's family was a space heater?"

Kaely nodded. "Sam mentioned that. I agree that these are disturbing coincidences, but I don't think . . ."

He held his hand up. "I didn't say anything earlier because

. . . well, because it sounds so ludicrous." He rubbed the back of his neck, a pacifying gesture. "Some kids in school used to taunt Sam's brother with the same nursery rhyme that was in that letter."

"Why?"

"Sam's brother's name was Jack."

TWENTY-FIVE

After finding out that Sam had stabilized, Kaely made arrangements for her and Noah to have dinner with Tuck. Then she dropped Noah off at the motel and headed back to her mother's house. She didn't tell Noah that Tuck thought Sam's long-deceased brother was their arsonist.

When Kaely walked into the house, she found Marcie in the living room, watching a soap opera. Jason was in the kitchen, cleaning up from breakfast.

"How'd it go last night?" he asked when she came in.

"Not well." Kaely had decided to keep most of the information about the failed FBI operation to herself. No reason to upset Jason and her mother with something they couldn't do anything about. "We're on hiatus." She caught Jason's eye. "I'll be around more. At least for a while."

Jason nodded. "Good. We've missed you."

She walked up next to him. "What can I do to help?"

"You must be exhausted. Sit down, and I'll get you a cup of coffee."

Kaely plopped down at the kitchen table. She was tired. Inside and out. And grateful that Jason didn't seem angry with her. "How's Mom?"

"She did okay last night."

"Great." Kaely breathed a sigh of relief.

"So you'll be here tonight?"

Kaely shook her head. "I've got to meet Chief Reynolds around seven. I'm not sure how long we'll be."

Jason didn't say anything, but Kaely saw his body tense.

"I'm sorry, Jason. I really am. I didn't come here planning to work a case."

"Two cases, if you count Omaha."

Kaely clasped her coffee cup as if it were a life preserver. "I know you think I care more about catching this arsonist than I do about you and Mom." She looked up at him. "It's not true, Jason. You're . . . you're everything to me. My brother. And I love Mom too, no matter how she acts toward me. It's just . . ." She blinked back tears that sprang from weariness. "This is who I am. I can't help it."

Jason hung his head for a moment before saying, "You *can* help it, Kaely. You just don't want to."

She started to protest, but he shook his head. "Get some rest. I'll be here tonight to take care of Mom."

"Thanks. You can leave after I get home. I really am sorry."

"I know you are, Kaely. I just wish . . ." He shook his head. "Never mind. I'm going to check on Mom." He'd started toward the kitchen door when he stopped and turned back. "I'm trying to be understanding, Kaely. I really am. Just be sure you make the right choices—that you won't have any regrets if something should happen to Mom. I'm not sure you can handle any more emotional baggage." His eyes locked on hers. "I'm worried about you, you know. We all have our breaking points." He stared at her for a moment more before leaving the kitchen.

Kaely wasn't sure what Jason was trying to say, but she was too tired to do anything about it. She trudged to her room. After changing into her sweats and an old T-shirt, she collapsed on the bed. She was certain she'd fall asleep as soon as her head hit her pillow, but instead she could only stare at the ceiling.

Tuck's assertion that Jack Lucas could be their arsonist was tickling her mind. It was absurd. But the fire on Mayfield bothered her. Why had the arsonist gone to all of the trouble to actually bring a space heater into the house? Was he trying to re-create a fire that happened almost twenty years ago?

She finally pushed herself up into a sitting position. Then she got up, grabbed the desk chair, and pulled it close to the bed. Kaely grabbed the file from the desk, sat down on the bed, and opened the file on her lap. She took a deep breath and began to talk.

"It's clear you're angry about something," she said, staring at the empty chair a few feet away from her. "This is more than thrill seeking." She looked down at the file and ran her finger down the page. "For some reason you have a thing about families. Why?"

She looked up at the chair again. Unfortunately, no one was there. "Maybe you like to start fires so you can save people. Be a champion. Feel like a big man. Is that right, Sam?" Still nothing. Kaely rested her chin in her hand. Exhaustion was beginning to overcome her.

She stared at the empty chair. "Okay, let's try this. Years ago your house burned down. You lost your entire family. Somehow you survived." Something vile slithered through Kaely's thoughts. She gulped involuntarily. "You hated your family," she whispered. "You started that fire. You wanted to kill everyone, but your brother wasn't there. He ruined your plan. Now you're back to finish the job, but first you want to destroy Sam's reputation. Make it seem as if he's the one setting these fires."

As she watched, a body tried to form in the chair, but it faded away. Kaely sighed. Had to be because she wasn't convinced their UNSUB could be Jack. There was something missing, she could feel it. What was it?

She got up and put the file away. It was too early. She wasn't ready.

As Noah got dressed for dinner with Tuck, he wondered what was up. It was obvious something had happened between Tuck, Sam, and Kaely. Kaely's only explanation was that they'd talk about it tonight. Tuck had mentioned a Mexican place in downtown Darkwater that was popular. Kaely told Noah she'd pick him up and fill him in on the way to the restaurant. Was she going to tell him Sam had admitted to setting the fires?

He tucked in his shirt and stared at himself in the mirror for a moment. He had to admit that Sam didn't seem like the kind of person who could do something so violent. So destructive. Of course, Noah wasn't the profiler.

He gazed at himself as if the man in the glass might suddenly have answers to whatever it was that was really bothering him. Seeing Kaely here, trying to deal with her family, made her seem more . . . real. More human. The feelings that flooded him had to be quenched. And he was determined to do it.

Filling his mind with images of Tracy helped. He would never love like that again. Any other relationship would be second rate, and he wasn't planning to settle. Loving wildly, without limits, could destroy a person. He couldn't survive losing that kind of love again.

He walked away from the mirror, got his coat, and sat next to the window, watching for Kaely. It had begun to snow again, but it wasn't supposed to add much to the previous amount.

A few minutes later, Kaely's SUV pulled into the parking lot and stopped in front of his room. Noah got up, walked out the door, and then made sure it was locked. He got into Kaely's car, grateful it was already warm.

"What is it you have to tell me about Sam?" he asked, his curiosity aroused. What could she possibly say that she couldn't have told him earlier?

Kaely was quiet for a moment. "Don't react until I finish talking. Sometimes you're . . . very negative."

Noah looked at her in surprise. "Negative? What do you mean?"

She glanced over at him. "I'm extremely pragmatic, but I'm also open to . . . unusual circumstances. If you don't entertain the possibility that sometimes things aren't what they appear to be, you may miss the truth."

Noah shook his head. "Why don't you just tell me whatever it is you and Tuck talked about? I'll keep an open mind."

Kaely breathed deeply. "Okay. When I first heard this, I dismissed it as a fairy tale. But after thinking about it . . . I don't know. But here goes. Sam Lucas had a twin brother who died in a fire when they were seventeen—or so everyone thought. Tuck seems to think it's possible that he's alive and that he's setting these fires."

Noah had to run Kaely's words over in his mind a couple of times before he could grasp what she was saying. He gaped at her in disbelief. "Are you seriously trying to tell me that Sam's brother is our arsonist? Really?"

"I know it sounds fanciful, but I can't ignore the possibility. The fire where the arsonist brought a space heater into the house? Twin teenage boys lived there. The fire that killed Sam's family was also caused by a space heater. And Sam's brother? His name was Jack."

Noah couldn't believe what he was hearing. He had no idea what to say to Kaely. This was insane.

Kaely glanced over at him, but then swung her eyes back to the road. "I guess some kids in school used to tease him, using the words of that old nursery rhyme, 'Jack be nimble. Jack be quick . . .'" She looked back at him again. "You have to admit it's fascinating."

Noah didn't respond. He was dumbstruck not only by the ridiculousness of her suggestion, but also because it was obvious Kaely was intrigued by the idea.

Had this incredibly brilliant woman finally gone off the deep end?

TWENTY-SIX

When they arrived at the restaurant they found Tuck waiting for them. As Noah and Kaely sat down, Kaely noticed Tuck searching Noah's face for a reaction to his theory. To Noah's credit, he didn't show his disdain for the possibility Tuck had presented, even though she knew he didn't buy it.

After greeting each other, the group was quiet as the waitress took their drink order. When the waitress came back, Kaely and Noah took Tuck's recommendation and asked for cheese enchiladas with tamales on the side. Kaely ordered guacamole for the table.

"I know you both think I'm crazy," Tuck said as the waitress walked away. "But every firefighter at our station swears Sam was with them when that last fire was set. That he was upstairs. I stick by my opinion that the video isn't clear enough for us to be sure."

"You might be seeing what you want to see," Kaely said, feeling the need to play devil's advocate. Her practical side was at war with the part of her brain that wanted to accept the possibility.

"I don't believe that," Tuck said.

"Did anyone actually see him upstairs?" Noah asked.

Tuck grunted. "Well, no. We don't usually stare at each other when we're sleeping."

Kaely and Noah glanced at each other.

"That doesn't mean he wasn't there," Tuck insisted, noticing their skepticism.

"But no one can prove it, Tuck," Noah said. "Is it impossible he could have snuck out, set the fire, and been back in time for the call to come in?"

Tuck glared at them. "It is possible? No. Because Sam isn't your guy."

They weren't getting anywhere. Kaely looked out the window next to their booth. The snow was getting heavier. One of the staff had started a fire in the fireplace across from them. The ambience was so relaxing that it eventually helped to calm the atmosphere. Kaely noticed Noah's shoulders loosen up. Of course, the margarita he'd ordered might have helped as well. Kaely stuck with iced tea. She didn't drink. Didn't like anything that made her feel like she was giving up a measure of control.

"I know you think I'm crazy," Tuck said, "but I talked to Josh about Jack. He and I went to the medical examiner's office this afternoon. He's new to Darkwater and didn't know about the fire. He went through the files and found the information about the Lucas family." Tuck shrugged. "According to the ME, everything checked out. Although Jack's corpse was burned beyond recognition, he was officially identified through dental records. And there was a bracelet on his wrist. Jack loved that bracelet. Never took it off."

"So that's it," Kaely said. She felt a sense of disappointment—and something else. A personal alarm going off inside her. That alarm had served her well. Why was it alerting her now? Something was wrong somewhere. What was it?

Tuck took a sip of his drink. "Look, I may not be trained in all the latest FBI procedures, but I know people. Sam didn't start those fires. You can choose to dismiss my opinion, but I'm right about this. I'm convinced with every bone in my body that something was wrong with Jack Lucas's autopsy. No matter what some new ME says."

"So you believe the remains identified as Jack Lucas belonged to someone else?" Noah asked. "I can't imagine a medical examiner allowing a mistake like that. Besides, if it wasn't Jack, who was it?"

"I don't know, but we need to keep following this lead until it's proven beyond a shadow of a doubt that Jack Lucas is dead."

"Have you gone back over all the fires?" Kaely asked. "Can you prove where Sam was when they were set?"

Tuck shook his head. "This is a volunteer fire department. We all have other lives. Jobs. None of us hangs around the fire station all the time. Since Sam lives alone, proving where he was is almost impossible. I'm sure there are times he can't account for. Just like the rest of us."

"You should at least talk to his staff at the clinic. Check out his alibis."

"His alibis?" Tuck's face flushed red with anger. "As far as I'm concerned, Sam doesn't need an alibi."

Kaely caught Noah's eye. Tuck's unbridled loyalty to Sam made him useless to them. Noah and Kaely needed him to be objective, but it seemed that wasn't possible.

"Okay," Kaely said. "If we pursue the theory that Jack Lucas is alive, then Sheriff Brotton needs to check missing persons during the time the fire happened. See if anyone disappeared. They found a body in that fire. If it wasn't Jack, who was it?"

Noah made a sound and Kaely glanced over at him. He was staring at her like she'd lost her mind.

"Just covering all the bases," she told him. "Seems to me it's the logical thing to do."

"Logical," Noah said under his breath. "None of this is logical."

Tuck looked back and forth between Kaely and Noah. "Look, I know you think I'm crazy. Maybe I am. I don't know anymore. But unless I personally see Sam Lucas set a fire, I won't change my mind. I'm sorry if that upsets you. I appreciate everything you're trying to do for us. I truly do."

Kaely sighed in frustration. She needed more resources than she had now. If only someone in ViCAP could check for similar cases. She could also request that they run a timeline from NCIC for every time law enforcement ran a check on any suspect they had and any vehicles he had access to.

That could identify places Sam might regularly travel, vehicles used, anything that might help them to find out where he'd been. The National Crime Information Center could also put out a general query to all law enforcement for similar MOs that matched their arsonist. Kaely remembered an agent she'd met at Quantico who was with NCIC. They weren't friends, but they'd gotten along well. Might as well give her a call. Ask for a favor. What could it hurt?

Just then, the waitress showed up with their food.

When she walked away, Tuck reached down and picked up an expanding file he'd brought with him. He handed it to Kaely. "This is everything I could find on the fire that killed Sam's family. And Josh coughed up his information too."

"Do I need to return this after I've looked it over?" Kaely asked.

Tuck shook his head. "Just keep it. Those are copies."

"Thanks."

"I just hope you can find something that will help Sam."

Kaely hesitated for a moment before meeting Tuck's gaze. "And if it goes the other way?"

"Then we'll deal with it," Tuck said quietly. "People have died. They deserve justice."

Kaely took a bite of her cheese enchilada. It was made with cheddar cheese, the way she liked. She ate some tortilla chips with guacamole and offered some to Tuck and Noah.

Tuck dug in immediately, but Noah shook his head. "It's green," he said. "I don't like green food."

Kaely couldn't hold back a laugh. "Wait a minute. I've watched you eat green beans. You like green peppers on your pizza. And what about salad? Lettuce is green."

"Yeah, but none of that stuff is mashed up into some kind of . . . I don't know. It looks like something someone regurgitated."

Tuck's stare was piercing. "Not really something to bring up while we're eating, is it?"

Noah blushed and Kaely giggled. She smiled as she took another bite of her enchilada. The food was good. The atmosphere in the restaurant was perfect. Even though their conversation had been a little tense, Kaely was enjoying herself.

Still, she couldn't stop that warning bell going off in her mind. What did it mean?

TWENTY-SEVEN

Kaely and Noah spent the rest of the evening listening to Tuck's stories about being the fire chief in a small town. A lot of them were hilarious, and Kaely really enjoyed them.

When it was time to leave, Noah and Kaely walked out to the parking lot with Tuck, where they all said good-bye.

"Nice guy," Noah said as he pulled away. "But this theory about Jack is absurd." They stood under a large streetlight near the road that ran past the parking lot. "Look, we can't ignore this much longer. Sam should be questioned by the police. Investigated."

"Let's wait until I have time to go through this new file," Kaely said. "Tuck is completely convinced of Sam's innocence. There's no doubt in his mind. And you have to admit that the video we saw isn't conclusive evidence."

Noah sighed. "I think there's a hint of frostbite on my nose. Can we get in the car now?"

Kaely chuckled. "Good idea. Does it ever get this cold in St. Louis?"

"No. This is the coldest it's ever been in the history of the United States. Has to be."

"You're a goof."

Noah grinned. "So you've told me more than once."

They walked over to the car and got in. Kaely started the car but sat there a few minutes to give the heater a chance to overcome the frigid temperatures. She used the time to run Tuck's

179

scenario through her head. Finally, she turned toward Noah. "Look, I need to spend some time with my mom. Jason needs a break. I've pushed him past his limit, I'm afraid. Can you go to Sam's office tomorrow? See what you can find out?"

Noah sighed. "Yeah, I'll do it. I don't know what you think I can discover. The fires were at night. The clinic would have been closed."

"Just covering our bases."

Noah shrugged. "Okay. I'll see what I can come up with."

"How about coming in for some hot chocolate when we get to the house?"

"What if your mom's up?"

Kaely studied him. "Are you afraid of my mother?"

"No, of course not." He was quiet and stared out the window, not saying anything.

"Oh, Noah," Kaely said, her heart sinking. "Tracy died of cancer. What's wrong with me? I've been so focused on this case I didn't think."

He nodded slowly. "My father had cancer too. He recovered. But Tracy didn't. It's a terrible disease. I hate it."

She sighed. "Let me go inside first. She's probably in bed. I doubt you'll run into her."

"No, I'm just being stupid. I can't hide from everyone who's sick just because I lost my wife. Let's go to your house."

"Are you sure?" Kaely asked softly. "I could get my notes and we could go somewhere else."

He turned toward her. The look in his eyes made it hard for her to breathe. She could see the love he had for his wife and the grief he still carried from losing her. She couldn't help but wonder if she'd ever be loved like that.

"I'm sure. Let's go."

Kaely put the car in gear and pulled out of the parking lot, praying her mother really would be asleep by the time they got to the house. She wasn't sure how Marcie would react to Noah. Kaely was a little nervous about it. She glanced at the clock on the dashboard. Eight thirty. Marcie was usually in bed by nine, but sometimes she liked to retire earlier so she could watch TV in her bedroom. There was no way to know if she would be up when they got there.

"Do you need anything from the store before you go back to your motel room?" Kaely asked suddenly.

Noah shook his head. "There's a store not far from the motel. I picked up supplies earlier."

"Do you mind if I stop to pick up a few things? I won't take long."

"Just long enough to make sure your mother is asleep when we get there?"

"I'm starting to rub off on you. Quit reading me."

Noah laughed. "Look, if you'd like to get a cup of coffee and wait a bit, it's fine with me."

Although she wanted to accept his offer, she realized he was willing to face his fear and she wasn't. She felt ashamed. "No, let's go to the house. It's all right."

"Are you afraid she won't like me?" he asked.

"No. I'm afraid . . . I don't know. It sounds ridiculous. I guess I'm afraid you'll see me differently." She glanced over at him. "Does that make any sense at all?"

"Yeah, it does," he said quietly. "It's why I didn't like it when you and Solomon decided I might be a good partner for you because of Tracy. Because you knew I wasn't looking for romance. It felt too personal. Like a violation of my privacy."

He understood. Somehow it made her feel better. "We're

more than partners now. We're friends. I may not have a lot of experience with having adult friends, but I'm pretty sure sooner or later you have to allow your real life to seep in." She took a deep breath. "I'm willing if you are."

"I'm willing too. Thanks, Kaely. It means . . . well, it means a lot to me."

There was something about the warmth of the car and the beautiful ballet performed by the snowflakes that surrounded them. Kaely felt something stir inside her. She wasn't sure what it was, but it felt powerful and wonderful. She caught Noah's eye and smiled at him. As her reservations melted away, a voice inside whispered that she was opening a door she might not be able to close again.

TWENTY-EIGHT

They were quiet as she drove to the house. Kaely parked and got out. Noah followed her to the front door. When Kaely unlocked it and stepped inside, she expected her mother to be sitting on the couch, but instead Jason was there alone, watching TV. He stood up when he saw Noah.

"Good to see you again," he said with a smile. They shook hands. They'd met in St. Louis and seemed to like each other.

"Is Mom in bed?" Kaely asked. "I wanted to introduce her to Noah."

"She wasn't having a good night. She's been in bed for over an hour."

Jason looked tired, and Kaely felt guilty. "Sorry about not being here."

Jason shoved his hands in his pockets and nodded toward the door. "If it's okay, I'm going to get my coat and get out of here."

"Sure." Kaely could feel the tension in the air and wondered if Noah picked up on it.

Jason went over to the coat closet and pulled out his jacket. After putting it on, he looked at Noah. "Why don't you come to supper tomorrow night?" he asked. "I'm a pretty good cook."

"I'd like that," Noah replied. "I'll be here."

"I hear I might be running into you. I've got a room at the Darkwater Inn. I like it. Nice rooms. Economical."

"Yeah, I'm comfortable there. I'm in room 205. Stop by sometime when I'm not following your sister around town."

"That appears to be a very small window of time," Jason said, his eyes drifting toward Kaely. "What are you two planning for tonight?"

"Hot chocolate," Kaely said. "Then I thought I'd take Noah to my room and show him my notes about the arsons."

"Well, it's more creative than wanting to show him your etchings," Jason said, grinning.

Kaely sighed. "Not funny. Time for you to leave, brother dear?"

"I think it is." He turned off the TV, but before he buttoned his coat, he stopped, a look of concern on his face. "Are you planning to take Noah back to the motel when you're done?"

Kaely nodded. "It won't take me more than twenty minutes. Surely Mom can be on her own for that long."

Jason shook his head. "I'm not comfortable with that. What if she needs something? Or gets up and finds herself alone?" He sat back down on the couch. "You two go ahead with what you're doing. I'll wait. I can take Noah back to the motel when you're finished."

Kaely felt a quick flash of irritation, but she had to admit that maybe Jason was right. She'd left Marcie alone once already, and that had turned out badly.

"Thanks, Jason. We won't be long." She gestured to Noah. "My room is this way."

She took off down the hall, trying to calm her jumbled emotions. She knew she was being unreasonable. The truth was, she felt guilty. Like Jason was the good kid and she was the bad seed. Was it true or was she overreacting again?

When she reached her room, she opened the door. Noah walked inside and looked around. "Wow," he said, going over to the bookshelves. "What a great collection." He picked up one of the Sherlock Holmes anthologies. "I love these stories." He turned and smiled at her. "We have the same tastes in literature."

Maybe it was seeing him here, in her mother's home, casually looking through the books that gave her comfort as a child . . . but all of the sudden, Noah's presence felt intrusive. Too close to her past. Kaely suddenly wanted to grab the book out of his hands and tell him not to touch her things. What in the world was wrong with her? She knew she could trust him. Why was she waffling between feeling she wanted to be closer to Noah and resisting the idea with a vengeance?

"You know, you could move to another motel," she said, trying to change the subject and slow her racing thoughts. "The Darkwater Inn is pretty basic."

"I like basic," he said. "It's clean and has everything I need." He frowned at her. "You don't want me around your brother?"

Kaely sighed and sat down on the bed. "I don't know. I'm sure you can tell he's displeased with me."

Noah put the book he'd taken from the shelf back in its place. "Why?"

"He thinks this investigation is more important to me than he is. Than my mom is."

"Is he right?"

Kaely stared at Noah, her body tight with annoyance. "We came here to talk about the case. Not my mother."

Noah nodded slowly. "Okay, then. Let's get to work."

Kaely pulled another chair up to her desk. "Sit here," she said. As he took a seat, she walked over to the closet and opened the door.

"Wow," Noah said when he saw all the notes and pictures taped to the inside. "You've made your own incident board."

"I had to improvise, but it's working well enough," Kaely said. "Give me a few minutes. I'll get our cocoa."

Noah nodded absentmindedly and got up, walking toward the closet. "Can I look this over?"

"Of course. I'll be right back." Kaely went to the kitchen and quickly fixed two cups of hot chocolate. It was made from a prepackaged powder mix, but it was pretty good. She finished each cup off with a mound of whipped cream. When she got back to her room, Noah was still studying her notes. He took a cup from her hand when she held it out to him and then sat down again.

"I'm still not sure what you think I can find out from the people at Sam's clinic," he said.

"You can't tell them you're with the Bureau."

Noah rolled his eyes. "What would you like me to say? I'm doing a census report?"

"No, smarty-pants. How about telling them you're thinking about bringing your pet in for an appointment? Then you can ask all kinds of questions."

"Sure," Noah said, sipping his hot chocolate. "Uh, 'I'd like to bring Fido in for a checkup. And by the way, does Dr. Lucas seem to have an unusual interest in fire?'"

Kaely sighed. "I trust you'll figure it out somehow."

"I'm worried about Omaha." He shook his head. "I can't believe Turner thinks we're corrupt."

"He's just angry that his operation went south. They lost months and months of work."

"You really think the guy you pointed out to him was involved?" Noah asked.

"I only know he was worried about something," she responded. "It's not possible for me to narrow it down like that.

But it would be odd for him to be upset about something else after two agents were shot. My guess is that he had no idea Guzman was taking Rosa out."

"He must not have told those gang members that we were there. They seemed surprised."

Kaely nodded absentmindedly.

"What are you thinking?" Noah asked.

She looked into Noah's gray-blue eyes. "I'm concerned about Navarro. I pray Turner took my concerns seriously. If he tells Navarro what I said . . ."

"No SSA is going to do that, Kaely. Even if he disagrees with you."

"I hope you're right. But if Navarro really is working for Guzman, we could be in trouble. We need to keep an eye out, okay?"

Noah smiled. "I always do."

"You know, if you're really worried about visiting the clinic tomorrow, you could tell them Tuck sent you."

"Yeah, until Tuck finds out. Not sure I want to tick him off."

Kaely thought for a moment. "Let's ask Tuck to back you up. You know, to help you prove Sam couldn't have done it."

"But I'm not sure that's what we're going to find."

"I know. But Tuck is so certain, he'll probably tell you it's okay to drop his name." Kaely sighed softly. "I wonder if we should ask Chief Brotton to bring us in under Domestic Police Cooperation? If we get officially kicked to the curb by Omaha, it'll be hard to stay current on the case."

Noah raised one eyebrow. "I guess it wouldn't hurt to try, but we need to actually talk to him first. He sure doesn't seem willing to do that."

Noah turned to stare once more at the mock incident board

Kaely had set up on her closet door. "I'd love to spend some more time looking over what you've come up with, but I think I need to let your brother get back to the motel before the roads get worse. I don't want him to be more irritated with you than he already is." Noah finished his hot chocolate and stood up.

They were walking down the hall when Jason came out of Marcie's bedroom, his face white. "Help me, Jessie. Mom's stopped breathing."

TWENTY-NINE

Noah, Kaely, and Jason followed the ambulance as it raced to the hospital through the dark streets, lights flashing in tandem with Kaely's pounding heartbeat. The EMTs told them Marcie was still breathing, but her respiratory rate was very low. When they arrived at the hospital, Marcie was rushed to the back somewhere, and they were told to stay in the waiting room until someone could talk to them.

About an hour later, a doctor came out to tell them that Marcie was stable. He looked at them over his glasses. "Your mother is very weak. Her current treatment has simply overwhelmed her body. I've contacted her oncologist to let him know how she's reacting. Not sure what they can do since she needs this medication, but he'll have to decide that."

"When can she go home?" Jason asked.

"I'd like to keep her for a few days," the doctor said. "Her condition needs to improve, or she'll just end up back here. Let's give her some time to rest and get stronger."

"Thank you, Doctor," Kaely said. "Can we see her?"

The doctor shook his head. "She's sleeping. Right now she needs rest."

Jason nodded and stood up, extending his hand to the doctor. "Thank you."

The doctor shook his hand and walked away.

Jason turned to Kaely. "I'm staying here. I don't want her

to wake up alone. You can go on home. I'll call you when she can have visitors."

"Are you sure?" Kaely asked. "I can stay."

"I napped this afternoon while Mom did," Jason said. He stepped closer to Kaely and gave her a quick hug. "It's okay, sis. It really is."

Kaely's eyes grew moist. She was amazed at how mature her little brother was. She felt a rush of pride in him and in the way he'd turned out—especially considering everything they'd been through. Being raised by a serial killer could mess anyone up, but here they were. Brother and sister. They might have scars, but they were still standing.

"Let's go," Noah said to Kaely. "You look beat."

After saying good-bye to Jason, Kaely and Noah headed for the front entrance. Before they reached the car, Kaely grabbed Noah's coat sleeve. "I'm sorry," she said. "I didn't mean to drag you into all of this."

He stared down at her. "Friends share things like this," he said quietly. "Maybe sometime I'll tell you about Tracy. What I went through. What I still go through every day." He looked deeply into her eyes. "Trust goes both ways, doesn't it?"

His statement made Kaely's breath catch involuntarily. He was right. She suddenly felt incredibly selfish. Was she so self-involved she had to always be the person who needed healing but was never the healer?

Noah mistook her reaction as a response to the cold. "You must be freezing," he said. "Let's get you warmed up."

They got into the car. Kaely started it up while Noah turned on the heater. After a couple of minutes, welcome warm air began to flood the interior.

"Better?" Noah asked.

"Yeah. Thanks. I'm just worried about my mother. I've never seen her so helpless like this. It's scary."

"I know. I'm sorry. But if she's anything like her daughter, she's a fighter. Don't give up hope."

"I'm praying she'll recover." Kaely believed it was God's will for her mother to live, but Marcie seemed to want nothing to do with God. How could Kaely encourage her to pray for help from someone she didn't believe in?

"I'll drop you off at the motel," she told Noah.

"If you don't mind, I'd rather stay at your mother's house. With you."

Kaely glanced over at him. "I'm okay, Noah. Really."

He turned to meet her gaze. "Look, Kaely. We don't know what's going to happen to your mom. You've been through a lot lately. I want to be near you in case . . . in case something goes wrong."

"In case my mom dies?" Kaely hated even saying the words. They felt like dirt in her mouth. She wanted to argue with Noah, but she realized she really didn't want to be alone. "You'd have to sleep on the couch."

"I've slept on my share of couches," he said, laughing lightly. "It's not a problem."

"Okay. Thanks, Noah." Kaely tried to concentrate on her driving. The slushy streets had refrozen. They were slick and needed her full attention. Still, her mind kept drifting. She thought about the friends she lost after her father was arrested, the agents at Quantico rejecting her because she was related to The Raggedy Man, other important friends who were gone now. Would she be forced to say good-bye to her mother as well? And what about Noah? He was getting close. Closer than anyone else ever had. Would he cause her pain too?

Kaely was relieved when she finally pulled into her mother's driveway. "Thanks for being here, Noah," she said because she felt she needed to. "I can't tell you how much it means to me."

"I wouldn't want to be anywhere else," he said, his voice deep and husky.

They got out of the car and hurried to the front door. The wind had picked up. It felt like icy fingers were trying to grasp at her, scratching at her face. She quickly unlocked the door, and she and Noah stepped inside. As Kaely closed the door behind them, she heard a strange sound. Like someone taking a deep breath. In the next second, she realized exactly what was happening. Before she could speak, she saw fire at the back of the house, consuming the structure like a fierce, hungry animal devouring everything in its path.

THIRTY

Kaely cried out as the flames gained strength. She started to run toward the door when anger overtook her. She wasn't going to let him get away with this. She turned to Noah. "I have to get something."

"No!" Noah yelled. "We have to leave. Now."

Although he tried to grab her, Kaely pushed him away. She closed the door to the kitchen, trying to keep the fire contained. Then she ran toward her bedroom, quickly grabbing her Go Bag and stuffing her files and notes inside. She also tore the notes off the closet door and jammed them inside the bag. Tears ran down her face as she stared at her books. She didn't want to lose them. She wrestled some of them from the shelves and turned to leave. Smoke was starting to fill the room.

A second before she headed for the door, she thought she saw someone tall with blond hair walk past her window. Was she imagining things?

Suddenly, she was seized from behind by Noah. "You're getting out of here right now!" he yelled. "Don't argue with me."

He pulled her from the room, her bag in one hand, her books in another. Noah tried to take them from her. "Leave them," he shouted.

"I can't." Kaely tried to be heard over the roar of the flames that had burned through the kitchen door and were now filling the living room, but she could only croak as smoke seemed to fill her mouth and push its way through her body, trying to possess her.

They were almost to the door when Kaely lost her grip on her bag. "Noah!" She tried to scream but her voice was choked.

Noah pushed her violently toward the front door, and she fell to her knees. "Go!" he bellowed. "I'll get the bag." Even though she wanted to argue with him, she couldn't find the strength to talk—or even walk. She crawled toward the doorframe, still holding on to her books. She noticed the purse she'd dropped by the door when the fire started and grabbed it. She kept trying to edge herself away from the fire, but she wasn't moving. Her body had no strength left.

Suddenly hands grabbed her and pulled her out of the doorway and into the middle of the yard. Kaely turned over on her back, gasping for air. Sam stood over her. She pointed toward the house. "Noah," she whispered. "Noah."

Sam's eyes grew large, and he ran toward the out-of-control flames. But he didn't get there before the front of the house collapsed. With Noah still inside.

Jason woke up when someone shook him lightly. He hadn't meant to fall asleep. Had something happened? He opened his eyes to find a nurse standing next to him.

"Is it my mother?" he asked, fear chasing away any remnants of sleep.

"No, she's resting comfortably," the nurse said. She was older and had a kind face. "We got a call. Your mother's house is on fire."

Jason jumped to his feet. He couldn't believe what he was

hearing. Panic made his chest tighten. "Thank you. I need to go." He stumbled toward the door of the waiting room, pulling his coat on at the same time. He ran out to the parking lot before he realized he didn't have his car. Thankfully, a taxi sat near the hospital entrance, its engine running. He hurried over to the cab, got in, and gave the driver his mother's address.

Although it seemed as if it took forever to get there, Jason was at the scene a few minutes later. The house was still burning. It was clear to see it was fully engulfed. He started to run toward the house but was stopped by a police officer. "I'm sorry, but you can't go any farther."

"But that's my house," Jason said frantically. "Actually, it's my mother's house."

The police office's expression turned serious. "Was your mother inside?"

"No. She's in the hospital. But my sister might have been. Please let me through!"

"Sir, I can't let you into the fire ground." He pointed to an ambulance across the street. "I suggest you check with them. If your sister was injured, they'll know about it. They may even have her. One ambulance has already left for the hospital."

"Thank you," Jason croaked out. Was Kaely in that ambulance? Was she okay?

He stumbled toward the ambulance, slipping on the frozen sidewalks. Everything was covered with ice and snow. The streets, the ground. Even though he knew he should be careful, he kept running. Although the ambulance was across the street from his mother's house, the heat from the fire was almost overpowering. The side of the neighbor's house next to his mother's was black. Thankfully, it wasn't burning now.

He had to run around three large fire trucks until he could

clearly see the back of the ambulance. Jason's heart was beating so hard he was dizzy. He felt almost possessed by fear.

He called out his sister's name and expelled the breath he felt he'd been holding ever since the nurse woke him up at the hospital. Sitting on the edge of the ambulance was Kaely. Her face was streaked with soot, but she looked all right. Her eyes lit up when she saw him.

"Is she okay?" Jason asked the EMT who stood nearby. "I'm her brother."

"She should be fine," he said with a smile. "She inhaled some smoke but not enough to cause any damage. We gave her oxygen . . . until she ordered us to take it off. She's kinda pushy."

Jason found himself laughing with relief. He was so grateful to find Kaely unharmed, he couldn't stop the well of joy that sprang up inside him. His previous irritation with his sister vanished like the smoke drifting up into the air above them.

"Noah was hurt," Kaely said, her voice rough and low. "They've taken him to the hospital."

"What happened?"

Tears streaked Kaely's soot-smudged face. "I was trying to get my notes and files out of the house. And at least a few of my books." She tried wiping her face but only smeared the soot around. "I dropped my bag and he went back for it. The front beams of the house collapsed on him."

"Collapsed?" Jason repeated with apprehension.

"Your friend is on his way to the hospital, sir," one of the EMTs said. "He's got a broken arm. Some cracked ribs. A few burns. And we're a little concerned about his breathing. He may have a punctured lung. They'll check him out further. Hopefully, there aren't any internal injuries. That's something we can't tell."

Jason thanked the EMT. "Were you in the house when it caught on fire?" he asked Kaely.

She looked at him and coughed. "Yes," she said, nodding. "The fire was already in the kitchen when we stepped inside the front door."

"You risked your life for some notes . . . and your books?" Jason asked, suddenly angry. "Kaely, you could have died. And Noah was injured. . . ."

"I know, I know," she said. "It sounds stupid, but I couldn't let all the work I've done burn up. I want to catch this guy. Even more now." She shook her head. "I realize it's my fault Noah's in the hospital."

Jason wanted to chew her out. How could she do something so reckless? But when he looked at her face, he could see this wasn't the time to chastise her. She needed his support.

Jason sat down next to her on the back of the ambulance. "It's okay, sis. Don't worry. I'm grateful you made it out of the house in one piece."

"I almost didn't," she said. "Sam pulled me out."

"Sam Lucas?"

When he said Sam's name, someone came around the side of the ambulance. It was Sam. His face was also blackened by smoke.

"Sam!" Jason said. "I thought you were in the hospital."

"Got out late this afternoon," he said. His voice was deeper than usual. "Since I'd been resting all day, I was still up. Then when I smelled smoke, I came outside and saw the house on fire."

"I was lying by the front door right before the house collapsed," Kaely told Jason. "Sam pulled me out into the yard and then went in and got Noah."

"I didn't want to move him," Sam said, "but I didn't have a choice. Hopefully I didn't cause any damage."

"Sounds like you saved his life," Jason said. "And Kaely's. Thank you, Sam. I'm so glad you were around."

Sam took a ragged breath. "I couldn't believe she would put herself in danger for a few books, but it was clear she wasn't going without them." He smiled at Kaely. "This woman is incredibly stubborn."

"I know," Jason said. "I'm just praying that someday it doesn't get her killed."

He watches, congratulating himself that he'd timed everything just right. Waiting until the profiler was inside. She saw him through the window. Perfect.

As usual, neighbors spill out onto their lawns. He loves to observe them. It's like being in a band and enjoying the applause of the audience after you play your song. Although he hadn't thought about it quite this way before, he realizes that fire is his composition. His opus.

He feels excitement rise in him as the fire reaches up into the sky. When he hears the distant sounds of sirens, he moves. It's time to present his final oeuvre. Kaely Quinn has no idea how important she has become to him. To his creation. Although she believes she can bring his song to an end, instead she will raise the baton for his finale. Her presence has only added to his pleasure.

He laughs. Even though he appreciates her part in his masterpiece, when his song is finished, the last stanza will include the death of Kaely Quinn.

THIRTY-ONE

Kaely stood over Noah's bed. His arm was in a sling, and his chest was bound tightly with bandages. She'd tried to get to the hospital as quickly as she could, but Tuck had insisted she stay behind until he could interview her about the fire. She decided not to tell him that she thought she'd seen someone out of the window. She honestly wasn't certain her imagination hadn't been playing tricks on her.

Once he was done, Kaely raced to Noah's side, but when she arrived he was in surgery to repair his shattered arm. The doctors had also inserted a chest tube to help his punctured lung. Thankfully, the surgeon assured her Noah would recover completely. This was the second time Kaely had been forced to visit him in a hospital. He'd been shot by a deranged killer a few months earlier, but the bullet had hit his bulletproof vest, which had protected his life. He'd escaped death and serious injury twice since becoming her partner. Kaely didn't want to chance a third time.

Noah wouldn't be able to return to work for a while, and physical therapy was certainly in his future. His left arm was the one that was broken, but thankfully Noah was right-handed. She'd called Solomon to let him know what was going on. He'd made her promise to keep him updated.

Noah mumbled something nonsensical and went back to sleep. Kaely sat down in the same chair where she'd spent the last several hours. She'd tried to nap when she could. She glanced at her watch. Almost eleven in the morning.

She and Jason had been able to grab breakfast before their mother woke up around nine. They'd gone in together to tell her about the house. To Kaely's surprise, her mother seemed to take it pretty well, even telling Kaely she was grateful she'd made it out okay. Kaely figured at some point Marcie would figure out that the arsonist had been after her daughter and blame the loss of her house on Kaely's insistence on investigating the fires. But at least for today, there weren't any recriminations. Kaely was thankful for small favors.

After coming out of surgery, Noah had been given a morphine pump. He could give himself a dose when he felt he needed it. Every time Kaely thought they might get a moment to talk, he'd push the morphine button and drift away again. Kaely had to question the wisdom behind giving drugged-up patients the ability to medicate themselves. Didn't make much sense to her.

The door to Noah's room opened, and Kaely looked up to see SSA Turner standing there. The last person she expected to see.

"I heard about Agent Hunter. How is he doing?"

"He's going to be okay," Kaely said, wondering why he was here. Did he come to inform them he was filing a formal complaint? Was her career on the line? If he was there for some kind of confrontation, Kaely didn't have the strength to do battle.

Turner slowly walked over to a chair next to hers and sat down. After not saying anything for a long moment, he finally spoke. "I wanted to talk to you. I called your cell phone, but you didn't answer."

"Sorry. I turned it off. Don't like it going off in certain places. Like hospitals."

He nodded. "That's when I called Josh Brotton. He told me what happened."

Kaely frowned at him. "You know Sheriff Brotton?"

"I used to be on the police force here. I met Josh a little while before I went to the Bureau, back when he was a deputy."

"Why are you here, sir?"

"You were right about Frank Navarro. I'm sorry I didn't listen to you." He spat out the words as though he wanted to get rid of them as quickly as possible. "Frank and I met at Quantico. He was more than an agent who worked for me. He was a friend. In all the time we worked together, I never saw any reason to suspect he was dirty." Turner paused and cleared his throat. He was clearly emotional, and he looked tired and defeated. Kaely felt compassion well up inside of her.

"People wear masks, sir," she said. "I've learned that almost everyone has a price. They may not start out with the intention of being disloyal. Human beings are just that—human. That makes them fallible and, many times, untrustworthy."

"They still shouldn't be part of the Bureau."

Kaely studied him for a moment. "Do you have children?"

He frowned at her question. "Yeah. Two kids. Why?"

"If one of your children was dying from a terrible disease and the only treatment cost more money than you had, would you cut a deal with the devil to save him?" Although Turner didn't say anything, Kaely saw the answer in his eyes.

"But Frank doesn't have any kids. Seems he sold his soul just for the cash. Nothing noble about that."

"No, there's not. But whatever his reason, it made sense to him. And it wasn't anything against you personally."

Turner's eyebrows shot up. "Well, it feels personal. Why are you defending him?"

Kaely leaned back in her chair, trying to ignore how weary

she felt. "I'm not. I'm just trying to give you a way to understand your friend and maybe someday forgive him. If you don't, it could torture you. Make you weaker. Believe me, I know. You need to be your best. Not just for the Bureau, but also for your wife and those kids. Do you understand?"

Turner stared down at the floor for a moment. When he looked up, his eyes were shiny. "Thank you, Special Agent Quinn. I'll keep that advice close to my heart." He looked away for a moment. It was clear that he was struggling.

"What's going on with the investigation?" she asked.

"Nothing," he said. "It's shut down for now. We don't know how much information Frank gave Guzman, and we've lost Rosa. I can't risk losing anyone else. Besides, Guzman would see us coming if we tried again. Of course, Omaha is investigating the shooting." He squared his shoulders. "I'm going to tell them this was my fault. Maybe if I'd pulled Frank from this assignment, it would have not only saved lives, but it might have protected our operation." He rubbed his face with his hand. "Thank God our agents will recover, although Special Agent Burroughs may spend the rest of her career behind a desk. She won't like that."

"I'm sorry."

"I am too." He leaned forward in his chair, resting his arms on his legs. He nodded toward Noah. "Was this fire connected to your arsonist?"

"I think so. Need to see what the fire department says."

"But your gut tells you this was your UNSUB?"

"Yeah."

"Josh said this was your mother's house?"

Kaely nodded.

"That's disturbing. Isn't this a break in his pattern?"

Kaely's eyebrows arched. How did Turner know about the arsonist's pattern?

He smiled at her surprised look. "I've been following the case a little. I find it interesting. Glad you're poking around. The worst fire I ever remember happening here was around eighteen years ago. Family named Lucas."

"You were here when that happened?"

He nodded. "Whole family killed, with the exception of one of the twin boys who wasn't home. Boy, that kid was so filled with guilt when he found out what happened. Kept saying he could have saved them if he'd been there."

"He's a volunteer firefighter now. Saved my life and Noah's last night."

"Really?" For the first time since he'd entered the room, Turner smiled. "I haven't kept in touch with folks in Darkwater since I left."

"Could you tell me what you remember about that fire?" Kaely asked. "I know it sounds strange, but anything you could share might be helpful."

Turner hesitated, then said, "You know, there's something about the situation that's bothered me all these years."

"What's that?"

"There was a terrible grain elevator explosion at the same time as that fire. Several deaths. The local ME's office was overwhelmed. Some medical examiners and assistants came in from neighboring counties, but . . ."

"You had some concerns about the autopsies?" Even as Kaely asked the question, somehow she knew the answer.

"Yeah. Dr. Roberson was the medical examiner back then. Although I think he tried to make sure everything was done properly, it was too much for him. One of the MEs from another office told me that the bodies from the fire may have been re-leased without a sufficient autopsy." He shrugged. "The ME couldn't be sure and didn't want to raise a stink, but he thought the bodies were cremated too quickly. He said the dental records that belonged to the father and son arrived after the bodies were given to the mortuary—after they'd been cremated."

Jack's autopsy wasn't complete?

"Are you okay?" Turner asked. "You look a little pale."

"Yeah. Sorry. Just tired."

"Hope my story didn't upset you."

"No. You may have helped more than you know. Thank you, sir."

Turner stood up and walked over to Kaely. He stretched out his hand. Kaely shook it. "Thank *you*, Agent Quinn. It's been an honor."

"I'll pray everything works out for you."

"I appreciate that. I really do." He managed a strained smile. "I'll check back later to see how Agent Hunter is doing. If there's anything he needs . . ."

"I'll let him know that when he's lucid."

"Good."

Turner walked out, leaving Kaely in shock. She felt glued to her chair. Couldn't move. Was it possible? Could Jack Lucas have lived? If so, why was he in Darkwater? And why was he setting his town on fire?

THIRTY-TWO

Since Noah was still asleep, Kaely grabbed a notebook she always carried in her purse and started making notes about the case. As she wrote, she remembered Tuck had said last night that he'd ask Sheriff Brotton to check the missing persons reports around the time of the Lucas fire. She wondered if he'd done it yet. She decided to take a chance and call the police station. At first she didn't think the woman who answered the phone was going to put her through. Even though she didn't want to, she told the woman she was with the Bureau, hoping she'd take the call more seriously.

After being on hold for a few seconds, Kaely heard, "Sheriff Brotton."

"Sheriff, this is Kaely Quinn. I'm sorry to bother you, but Tuck said you might look into any missing persons around the time of the Lucas fire. I'm wondering if you found anything."

The silence on the other end of the phone went on so long Kaely began to wonder if they'd been disconnected.

"Can you meet with me?" Sheriff Brotton asked suddenly, actually making Kaely jump.

"I'm at the hospital with Agent Hunter."

"Why don't I come down there? We could talk in the cafeteria."

"That would be great," Kaely said. "I'd appreciate that."

"How about noon? I have some things to clear up here first."

"Noon sounds good." Kaely started to say good-bye but realized the sheriff had already hung up. His abruptness was a little unsettling. It was hard to get a read on him. He didn't show much emotion and appeared to have a razor-sharp focus on his job. She was surprised he'd been defeated in the election and wondered just how hard it would be for him to walk away from his interim position.

At ten minutes to twelve, she put her notebook back in her purse and checked on Noah once more. He was still out. Before she realized what she was doing, she bent down and lightly kissed him. Shocked by her automatic action, she quickly straightened, praying he wasn't conscious enough to remember what she'd done. Perturbed by her behavior, she hurried out of the hospital room.

When she reached the cafeteria, she scanned the room until she spotted Sheriff Brotton sitting toward the back. His cap was pulled down low and his head was down. Kaely wondered if his attempt to hide from the public was a waste of time. In a town this size everyone knew who he was.

She noticed he already had food, so she bought a large chef's salad and an iced tea. She carried them to the table and sat down. He looked up at her. "Thanks for agreeing to meet with me."

"Glad to. Thanks for checking on this for us, Sheriff."

"Just call me Josh. We're pretty relaxed about titles in Darkwater."

"Sure, Josh. And you can call me Kaely."

He offered her a small smile. A real breakthrough from their previous interaction. He really was a handsome man. His serious demeanor had made it hard to notice his looks. But Kaely was still a little skeptical of his sudden change in attitude.

He picked up one of the files sitting on the table. "We had

four missing persons right around the time of the Lucas fire. They were all eventually located, except for one. He was reported missing a few days after the fire and the grain mill explosion. His name was Raymond Berger." He pushed the file toward her. Attached to the papers was a school picture. Raymond was a gawky-looking kid with dirty blond hair and crooked black glasses that were way too big for his face. Kaely doubted he was very popular in high school.

She looked up at Josh and noticed he was interested in something over her shoulder. Before she had a chance to see what it was, she heard a voice. "Hope it's okay if I sit in on this. Josh called me."

Sam slid into the chair next to her. Kaely was surprised to see him, but glad to see he was up and about. "How are you feeling?" she asked him.

"Totally back to normal," he said.

"Not sure that's saying much," Josh said teasingly.

"You could be right." Sam pointed at the photo Kaely had in front of her. "Raymond Berger. Josh thought I might be a good person to tell you more about him."

"You knew him?"

"Jack was closer to him than I was." He glanced toward the food offered in the cafeteria. "Can you give me a minute to grab something to eat?"

Kaely nodded. "Sure. Not a problem."

Sam got up and headed for the food line.

"You can take that file with you," Josh said. "But I'm going to need it back eventually." He reached down and took another file, this one much larger, from a briefcase sitting next to his chair. "These are copies of the files of anyone caught setting fires in Darkwater over the last five years. We've combed through them and couldn't find anything. Maybe you'll have better luck."

He handed her the file folder.

"Thank you. I really appreciate that."

"Not a problem," Josh said. "I really want this guy."

Kaely stabbed at her salad. "I . . . I'm sorry you lost the last election. You seem like a very dedicated sheriff."

Josh shrugged. "To be honest, my heart wasn't in it. I campaigned, but not with a lot of enthusiasm. The other guy wanted it more than I did. I only lost by eighty-six votes."

"Boy, that was close. I don't mean to be nosy, but do you mind if I ask why you weren't that interested in winning?"

"No, it's okay." Josh put his fork down. "Believe it or not, even though Darkwater is a small town, this job requires lots of overtime. It was getting to where I only saw my wife at night after I climbed into bed. And my kids? I've missed too many important events—baseball games, school plays, meetings with teachers. The list goes on and on. I wanted to be with them more than I wanted to be sheriff."

Kaely could understand his reasoning. She realized how different she was from Josh. Of course, she had no idea what it was like to have her own family.

Sam returned to the table with his food and sat down.

Kaely was amused to see Sam's plate. It was loaded with fried chicken, mashed potatoes and gravy, buttered corn, and two rolls. He and Noah shared the same tastes.

Sam looked back and forth between her and Josh. "I don't want to interrupt your conversation. You two looked pretty serious."

"Nothing important," Josh said. "So what can you tell Kaely about Raymond?"

As they waited for Sam to chew and swallow, Kaely noticed

how much they looked alike. Josh was tall with blond hair and blue eyes, and had similar facial features to Sam. They could be related.

Sam took a drink of his pop and then said, "It's hard to say negative things about your brother, but to be honest, Jack wasn't the nicest person around. He wasn't really a bully or anything, but he was a manipulator. Had a way of getting people to do things he wanted them to do, you know?" He stared down at the table. This was obviously tough for him. "Raymond was a shy kid. He'd show up at school with dirty, wrinkled clothes. No lunch. Jack took an interest in him. At first I thought it was out of compassion. But Raymond was just an easy target, someone my brother could control. Raymond followed Jack around like a loyal little puppy."

He sighed, picked up his glass, and took another drink. When he put it down, he looked up and met Kaely's eyes. "My parents were nice to him. My mom had Raymond bring his dirty clothes over so she could wash them. And she gave me money to pay for Raymond's lunch at school."

"You say you didn't know him very well," Kaely said, "but your mom sent his lunch money with you?"

Sam picked up his fork and pointed it at her. "Very perceptive. Yes, because she couldn't trust Jack to use the money for Raymond."

"Your parents didn't trust Jack?"

"No. I'm afraid when we were in high school, Jack made life pretty tough on them. It wasn't fair. They were great people." Sam's voice cracked a little. He scooped up a big forkful of mashed potatoes. Kaely gave him a moment to collect himself. She couldn't imagine the trauma he'd endured, losing his entire family in one fell swoop.

"Sam, you were seventeen when the fire happened," Kaely said. "What happened to you? Where did you live?"

"He moved in with me," Josh said. "It was only a few months until he turned eighteen, so family services looked the other way."

"I'm sorry for what you went through," Kaely said. "And I'm glad you had friends to support you."

"Thanks," Sam said. "I don't know what I would have done without Josh and his folks."

He smiled at her and her heart lurched. *Get ahold of yourself, Kaely.* She hesitated to ask her next question, but she couldn't avoid it. "Sam, is it possible the remains found in the fire at your house didn't belong to your brother?"

He frowned at her. "Look, I know you heard Tuck's theory, but it's impossible. First of all, what about the medical examiner's report? He identified Jack's remains. He even returned Jack's silver bracelet to me, the one he wore all the time. Besides, even if Jack was alive—and I'm sure he isn't—why would he do something like this after all these years?" He shook his head. "I just don't buy it. I think you're barking up the wrong tree."

"I have to agree," Josh said. "I've been going over and over this video and the picture we blew up for you." He reached into the inside of the coat flung over the chair next to him and pulled out a picture. "This was taken from that cell-phone footage the night of the Mayfield Street fire. I don't think this is Jack Lucas. It could be anyone. Frankly, it could be me."

"Do you see a scar on his cheek, though?"

"It looks like a shadow to me. Or even a glitch in the video."

Kaely looked closely at the picture. Was he right? Was she seeing a scar because someone put the idea in her head?

"Maybe," she said slowly. "What about the letter? What about the rhyme?"

"What letter? What rhyme?" Sam asked.

Kaely knew Tuck hadn't wanted the letter shared until he was ready, but she'd assumed he'd told Sam. She caught his eye. "I'm sorry," she said. "I thought . . ."

"You thought what?" Sam's voice had taken on a more insistent tone. "What's she talking about, Josh?"

"There was a letter, Sam. It doesn't matter. It's not important."

"What did it say?" Sam's meal was forgotten.

Josh reached into his coat pocket again and pulled out a folded piece of paper. "I'd decided to show this to you when we were alone." He scowled at Kaely as he handed the paper to Sam. "Of course, this is just a copy. We checked the original for prints. There weren't any except for Tuck's."

Sam unfolded it. When he read it, the color drained from his face, and Kaely was afraid he was going to pass out.

Sam stared at Josh, his eyes wide. "Why didn't you tell me?"

"Because I knew you'd overreact, Sam. Just like you're doing now. Anyone could use this rhyme. It doesn't mean—"

"Of course it does. Kids used to taunt Jack with this same nursery rhyme. He hated it." Sam stared at the note again before looking up at Kaely. "But my brother is dead. How can you possibly think he could be setting these fires? This is impossible."

THIRTY-THREE

After lunch, Kaely found a spot in a hospital hallway and called Josh. She wanted to ask him something without Sam listening in. Thankfully, he was already back at the office.

"Sorry to call you so soon, but I have a favor to ask. I'd like to talk to the medical examiner who was in office at the time of the Lucas fire. Can you help me?"

"I'm not sure I'm your man. He was retired by the time I became sheriff. Tuck knows him a lot better than I do. They were friends."

"Thanks," Kaely said. "I'll call him."

"Let me know what you find out," Josh said. "I have a hard time believing Jack is alive, but I guess we need to follow every lead, no matter how ridiculous it sounds." He sighed. "I didn't want to say this in front of Sam, but Jack scared me. Like he said, Jack was a manipulator. He had a way of making people do things they didn't want to do. And he had a horrible temper. He would come unglued when he didn't get his way. He went after several people in school he didn't like. He even put one kid in the hospital. There was a girl in our class that Jack had a crush on. When she rejected him, her cocker spaniel went missing. They found him a couple of days later. Someone had dumped him near the highway out of town. It was a miracle he wasn't hit by a car. I always wondered if Jack was behind it."

Did Josh realize he was describing a psychopath? Even more reason to wonder if Jack was their arsonist.

"Please be careful, Kaely," Josh said. "And call me if you need help."

"I will. Thanks. I really don't think the arsonist intends to approach me directly. It's not his style. Setting fires and running away seems to be his modus operandi."

"I hope you're right, but I wouldn't be so sure. The Jack I knew was capable of almost anything."

After Kaely hung up, she thought about what Josh had said. Another contradiction. Arsonists didn't normally have direct contact with their victims, but the person Josh described hadn't seemed afraid to get up close and personal with those he wanted to punish.

She realized she needed to be on her guard. She'd always felt completely capable of taking care of herself. But now she felt alone and wished Noah was here by her side. She chided herself for feeling she needed a man to protect her and shook off her qualms. She was smart and able to defend herself, if necessary.

She dialed Tuck's number, hoping he would answer. Sure enough, she heard his deep voice on the other line.

"I'd like to meet the former medical examiner," she said immediately.

"Hello to you too. I assume this is Special Agent Quinn," he said.

"Sorry. Yes. Josh said you knew him pretty well."

"As well as anyone, I guess. Doc Roberson lives on the edge of town. I can visit with him if you want me to so you can stay with Agent Hunter. Just tell me what you want to know."

"No, I want to go with you," Kaely said.

"Because you think you'll know if he's telling the truth and I won't?"

Kaely didn't respond. She didn't want to offend Tuck, but he was right. Finally she said, "Because of my training it's possible I might pick up on something you wouldn't."

"My ego isn't that fragile," he said, chuckling. "I'd like to have you there. When do you want to go?"

"Tomorrow morning, if possible," Kaely said. "Can you set it up, Tuck?"

"Let me call him now. I'll get right back to you."

He hung up. Kaely stared at her phone, waiting for it to ring. Even if Dr. Roberson agreed to talk to them, would he tell Kaely what she needed to know? If his office had made mistakes, would he admit it?

As she waited, she saw Jason walking down the hall. He came over and sat down on the bench next to her. "I called the motel. They don't have any vacancies tonight, but I reserved a room next door to me for tomorrow. Of course, no one's staying in Noah's room, but it's on the other side of the complex. Why don't you stay in my room tonight? I think you should remain close to me, sis. If the arsonist you've been looking for set Mom's house on fire, I seriously doubt he selected it randomly. Didn't you say he was targeting families? Where there were mothers, fathers, and children? That's not us."

"You're jumping the gun, Jason. Give the fire department time to investigate. That will help us to figure out what's going on."

Jason took a ragged breath. Kaely could see how upset he was. She wanted to tell him about the figure she saw walking past the window during the fire, but she couldn't. It was clear to her that it might push him over the edge. He was worried about Mom and had watched her house burn down. Now he was afraid a madman was targeting his sister. She needed to keep him as relaxed as possible. She didn't have time to worry about him. She needed time to think. To figure out why the arsonist had targeted her.

"I need to contact Mom's insurance agent," Jason said. "Thankfully, I have his card. Not long after I got to town, a pipe in Mom's basement burst. The agent was really helpful."

"Where will Mom go when she gets out of the hospital?" Kaely asked.

"The insurance company will provide her with a place to stay. Probably an apartment. Something she can handle."

"We need to talk about home health care once she gets into her apartment," Kaely said. "I can't stay forever, Jason. And neither can you."

"I know that."

Kaely put her hand on her brother's arm. "I won't desert you. We're family. We'll make it through this together."

Jason blinked back tears. "I'm so glad you're okay. If I'd lost you . . ."

"You're not going to lose me, I promise. I know my job seems scary, but just remember, I'm packing heat, and I'm not afraid to use it."

Despite the situation, Jason laughed. "You know, I don't remember you being funny."

Kaely patted his hand. "We didn't have much to laugh about when we were kids, did we? Dad wasn't big on laughing. Found it annoying. Do you remember that? It got to where we felt it was . . . inappropriate."

"I remember," he said softly. He smiled. "Audrey taught me to laugh."

Although she didn't say anything, Noah was the person who'd brought humor into her life. And so much more.

"Look, just stay close, okay?" he said again. "Make sure I know where you are."

Kaely started to say something, but Jason held his hand up. "I know, I know. You can take care of yourself, blah blah blah. But to be honest, I'm not afraid for you—I'm more afraid *of* Noah. Once he's not so doped up, he's gonna jump all over me if I don't tell him I'm keeping an eye on you."

Although Kaely wanted to object to her brother's offer, she couldn't. He was exactly right. It was the first thing Noah would say.

"Okay. I accept. I'm about ready to drop, so I'll head over to the motel as soon as Noah wakes up. Please tell me your room has two beds."

He smiled. "Well, we used to climb into bed together when we were kids, remember? You'd read to me until I fell asleep. I'd wake up next to you, and there would still be a book clutched in your hand."

"I hope you're not counting on an encore."

Jason laughed. "No, I've learned how to read all on my own."

Before Kaely could respond, her phone rang. "Give me just a minute," she said. "I need to take this."

As soon as she answered, she heard Tuck's deep voice. "Marvin said we could come by tomorrow around ten. I told him it was about an old case, but I didn't mention which one. I didn't want to give him the chance to say no."

"That's great, Tuck. Can you text me his address? I'll meet you there in the morning."

"Sure thing. See you there."

Kaely hung up and put her phone back in her pocket.

"Where are you going in the morning?" Jason asked.

"Going to talk to a guy who used to be the medical examiner. I have some questions about an old case." She nudged her brother. "I'll be safe. I'll be there with Tuck."

"All right," Jason said slowly. "But keep in touch. And either come here or go to the motel when you're done, okay?"

"I will." She leaned up against her brother's shoulder. "Thanks for watching out for me."

He put his arm around her, and they sat there for a while. In the crook of her brother's arm, Kaely felt safe, as if nothing bad could possibly happen to her.

THIRTY-FOUR

Kaely spent the afternoon in Noah's room, looking through the files Josh had given her. Noah woke up several times but would drift off after a while. He kept asking Kaely if she was all right. She assured him more than once that she was fine.

"He knows who you are, Kaely," he mumbled one time when he seemed coherent. "Please be careful. I'll get out of here as soon as I can. I'll protect you."

"I'm fine," she told him. "Don't worry about me."

"Sorry I didn't get to check out the veterinarian clinic. I'll do it tomorrow. I'm a little tired right now."

After that, he fell asleep again. Had her obsession with this arson case almost cost Noah his life? Guilt overwhelmed her. Most of it came from her relief she had her bag with the case notes—and her books. That made her feel even worse. What was wrong with her?

She gazed at Noah. He deserved better. Someone who didn't put a case before her partner.

The doctor stopped by and told her he was doing well, but that he would be in the hospital for several days. "We want to make sure his lung heals adequately," the doctor said. "A punctured lung can be very serious. So far, we've kept him out of surgery. I hope we won't have to use that option. We need to make sure he stays still and doesn't fight the tube in his chest."

Kaely assured the doctor she'd do what she could. She didn't tell him that Noah was pretty stubborn. Keeping him in a hospital bed for several days might be tough.

Kaely wrote in her notebook some, but around three in the afternoon she finally fell asleep with her head on her hand. She was awakened by someone calling her name.

She looked up to see Noah staring at her. "Hi," she said. "How are you feeling?"

"Tired and sore," he said. "And drugged. What is this?" He cocked his head toward the morphine pump.

"Something you need to lay off of for a while. You've been pushing that stuff into your body since you got out of surgery."

"Surgery?" he said, looking surprised. He looked down at his bandages and then noticed the tube. What little color he had drained from his face. "What happened?"

"Don't panic. A broken arm that will heal just fine. You had surgery to repair it, so stay still. You have some cracked ribs, and your lung was punctured. That's the reason for the tube. You have some third-degree burns on your legs and arms. The doctor said you'll be fine as long as you follow orders."

"Thank God." He tried to take a deep breath, but he grimaced in pain. He nodded toward the side of the bed. "Could you adjust this thing so I'm sitting up?"

Kaely got up and found the automatic control for the bed. She raised the back slowly, not wanting to put pressure on Noah's chest.

"That's good," he said when he was in a more upright position. "Thanks." He looked around the room. "I remember being in the house. Pushing you out. Don't remember much after that."

"In a nutshell, after probably saving my life, the house fell on you when you went back for my bag." She took his hand.

"I'm so sorry, Noah. I wasn't thinking. I should have left the bag behind."

"Yeah, you should have, but then you wouldn't be Kaely Quinn." He squinted and shook his head slowly. "Wait a minute. How did I get out of the house? You couldn't have pulled me out."

"I didn't. Sam showed up. He pulled me out into the yard. Then he went back inside for you."

"Sam was there?"

Kaely nodded. "Saw the fire and showed up just in time."

She wanted to tell him about seeing someone out the window during the fire and about her conversation with Josh, including how she was going to see Dr. Roberson tomorrow. But she couldn't. Noah needed to rest and heal. Getting riled up would make it harder for him to stay calm.

"Guess who showed up this morning?" she asked, hoping to divert his attention from the arsonist case.

He shrugged and then winced. "I guess I can't do that for a while."

"Turner came to the hospital. He found out Frank Navarro was working with Guzman. He came to apologize. We're off the hook, I guess."

"So now what? Will we be called in for something else?"

Kaely chuckled. "You're done, my friend. You've got physical therapy in your future. Besides, Turner said they were suspending the operation for now. Actually, he told me to work on the arson case with his blessing."

"Are you talking about SSA Turner or someone else with the same last name?" Noah asked, a look of incredulity on his face.

"I'm pretty sure it was our Turner," Kaely said. "I felt bad for him. I guess he and Navarro were friends. He just couldn't believe he would sell out the Bureau."

"Everyone has a price," Noah said with a shrug. "Ouch. Why don't you stop me from doing that?"

"Not sure I can."

Noah locked his gaze on Kaely. "The fire at your mom's wasn't random, Kaely. You know that right?"

"Yeah, I know. Please don't overreact. I don't have another house to burn down. I'm pretty sure he won't torch the Darkwater Inn."

"What if he comes after you again, Kaely? Some other way?"

Kaely tried to answer him without actually lying. "Arsonists are cowards, Noah. They like to do their damage from a safe distance. I'll be fine."

"Still, I wish I was with you." He pointed his finger at her. "I want to talk to Jason. Send him by here."

"I will. Hey, I need to head out. I haven't really slept for quite a while. Just catnaps waiting for you to wake up. And I need to check on Mom before I leave."

"How's she doing?"

"About as well as can be expected when you have cancer and find out your house is gone," Kaely said. "The hospital is going to keep her until she's stronger, and Jason is checking with her insurance company. He thinks they'll arrange for her to move into an apartment until her house can be rebuilt."

"Tell her I'm thinking of her, will you?" Noah was starting to blink a lot. It was clear he was still sleepy.

"I will. You take care of yourself and do what the doctors and nurses tell you to do. I'll be back tomorrow."

"Okay. Hey, where's my cell phone?"

Kaely went over to the small closet near the bed and looked through the bag with Noah's clothes and belongings. She found his phone and brought it over.

"Humor me," he said. "Check in with me every few hours, okay?"

"Can we start that tomorrow? I'd rather not have to wake up several times during the night."

"Very funny. Call me only when you're actually awake. If you wait too long, I will call you. You know that right?"

She smiled at him. "Yeah, I know that. Anything I can do for you before I go?"

"Some water would be nice. My mouth is so dry."

Kaely poured some water from the pitcher on Noah's tray into a small glass and handed it to him. He drained the glass and put it back on the tray. "Thanks. That's better."

Kaely could hear a rattling sound outside the room. She stuck her head out and saw a large cart with trays. She went back over to Noah's bed. "Supper's on the way. Hope you get something good."

"Me too. I'm surprisingly hungry."

Kaely snorted. "Yeah, that's shocking since you're such a light eater."

Noah stuck his tongue out at her. "Get out of here. Get some shut-eye. Call me tomorrow."

"You got it." She stood there a moment, unsure of what to do. The urge to kiss him was strong. Instead, she patted his un-wrapped shoulder. "Be good," she said, her voice husky. Before she said or did anything embarrassing, she left the room, almost running into a woman carrying a tray into Noah's room. Kaely apologized and hurried down the hall. She was having feelings for Noah she couldn't handle. She wanted him in her life, but things couldn't go on like this. They just couldn't. Her job was everything to her, and she couldn't allow anything to get in the way. Even Noah.

THIRTY-FIVE

Kaely took the elevator up to her mother's room and found that she was also having supper. She stayed for a while but finally begged off by telling Marcie she'd been up all night and needed some sleep. After she left, she stopped by a local department store to get some clothes, makeup, and other personal items. Then she drove to an Italian fast-food place that had pretty good lasagna. She bought lasagna and a salad, along with a drink, and drove to the motel. She was just getting out of the car when her phone rang. It was Solomon.

"Just wanted you to know that I talked to SSA Turner. He told me what happened. He had nothing but good things to say about you, Kaely. Wishes he would have listened to you."

"He's a good man, Solomon."

"I know. That's why he's taking full responsibility for the failure of the operation. I'm not sure what will happen to him."

Kaely didn't say anything.

"So have you found out anything helpful about the fires?" he asked.

"Not sure. One of the possibilities is just . . . well, it's hard to accept."

"Want to tell me about it?"

Kaely would like Solomon's opinion, but she was afraid to tell him about Sam and Jack. He'd probably think she'd gone off the deep end. "Not yet," she said finally. "Not until I have more information. But thanks."

"How's your mother?" he asked, clearly not offended by her rejection of his offer.

"She's involved in some kind of clinical trial for treating the cancer, but she just recently had a setback. My brother still seems very encouraged by her prognosis. To be honest, he knows more about her condition than I do. I've been so busy with Omaha and the arsons in Darkwater that I haven't spent as much time with her as Jason has."

"Be careful, Kaely," he said. "Don't do anything you'll regret later. Your mother is more important than any case."

Although she knew he was trying to help, for some reason she felt a little defensive. "Okay," she said. "I'll keep you updated."

"Is it too soon for me to talk to Noah?"

"I'd give him a little time. Not unless you want to know how Noah Hunter sounds drugged up," she said.

Solomon laughed. "I think I'll pass. I'll call him tomorrow."

"Thanks. Talk to you soon." She hung up, still feeling a little irritated about his admonition to put her mother ahead of her investigation. However, as she got out of the car, she admitted to herself that the case had been a way to escape from her mother and what she was going through. As Kaely unlocked the door to Jason's motel room, she heard a small, still voice remind her that she'd spent the last few years pushing people away. Her mother was toward the top of that list.

Kaely shook her head. She needed to get her mind on the case. She'd have to think about Mom later.

She pulled the door shut behind her and put the bag of food on the table. Then she took off her coat and changed into a comfortable T-shirt and a pair of sweat pants she'd picked up at the store. She sat down and flipped on the television so she could watch it as she ate. The local news was just starting. She was surprised to see Josh being interviewed by one of their reporters. She quickly turned up the sound.

"Sheriff, some citizens say we're dealing with a serial arsonist, one that you don't seem capable of finding and arresting. What do you say to those people?"

Josh, who looked angry, replied, "I'm not sure who those people are, Andrea. Maybe they need to talk to me instead of spreading false rumors. The truth is, we don't have any proof there's a serial arsonist in Darkwater. Of course, we realize the recent rash of fires seems unusual, and we are looking into the reasons behind them. *If* we determine this actually is the work of an arsonist, we'll let our citizens know immediately. For now, I will repeat what I've been saying all along: Don't buy cheap space heaters. Make sure you're not overusing your electrical outlets, and keep covers in front of your fireplaces. That's all I have to say." With that, he stormed off, ignoring questions from the other reporters gathered around him.

Josh knew there was an arsonist, but he was trying not to scare the town. Kaely felt even more pressure to figure out what was going on. Unfortunately, Josh himself was one of her suspects. He'd recently lost his bid for sheriff. Even though he said he didn't care, what if he was lying? What if he'd decided to pay the town back for rejecting him? He could have been the man in the video. And he could be the person she saw walk past the window before the fire started at her mother's house.

And then there was Jack. If he was alive and angry at Darkwater for the fire that cost his parents' lives, then the body found in the remains of the house was probably that of Raymond Berger. Kaely sighed with frustration. It was true the boy had disappeared, but it was a stretch to believe something so implausible. Kaely got up, grabbed her notebook, and wrote

Find out if Raymond's family still lives in Darkwater. Talk to them. Although she wasn't certain what they could tell her, she needed to cover all the bases.

Then, of course, there was Sam, who had an alibi for the first fire that happened after she arrived—and who had saved people, including herself, from two different fires. She wanted to rule him out, but she wasn't ready to do that yet. She'd never picked up one hint of deception from him. It was almost impossible for someone not trained in body language to fool her.

She had to consider the note sent to the fire chief. Of course, Tuck, Josh, and Sam all knew the nursery rhyme had been used to tease Jack when he was a kid. Was it a joke most people would know? Would anyone else connect it to Jack?

Did that put the three men at the top of her list of suspects?

THIRTY-SIX

Kaely ran her hand through her hair, trying to sort out her thoughts. It was difficult because everything was so jumbled. Her mother's illness and Noah's injuries weren't helping her ability to concentrate.

"You're having trouble with this one, aren't you?"

Kaely looked up. Georgie was sitting on the edge of the bed, watching her.

"Yes. It's driving me nuts." Kaely could hear the impatience in her voice, but she couldn't help it. There were too many possibilities and not enough evidence. Her frustration was beginning to bubble over. "I've gone through all of Josh's files, but I haven't found anyone I'd call a good suspect. Well, a couple of them could fit, but one's dead and the other's in prison."

Georgie nodded. "Was the guy in prison an arsonist?"

Kaely sighed. "Yeah, but not the kind I'm looking for. He set his fires in fields and ditches, places void of people."

"He could have changed. Maybe he has an accomplice."

"I thought of that," Kaely said, "but I can't find a motive." Her conversation with Georgie had been so natural, so fluid, that Kaely hadn't realized she'd shown up on her own again. "What are you doing here?"

Georgie's brown eyes narrowed. "You need me."

Kaely took another bite of her lasagna and washed it down with a quick drink of soda. Georgie was right. Kaely was alone and needed someone to bounce ideas off. It helped her to think.

"Nothing makes any sense," she said with a sigh.

"Talk it out. What doesn't make sense?"

"I put Sam at the top of the list of suspects but . . ." Kaely turned to look at Georgie, who was listening intently.

"But you have a hard time believing he's behind these fires?"

"A very hard time. Everything I know about evaluating people tells me it's not him."

"Then why not rule him out?"

"Because logically it has to be him. I saw someone who looked just like him before the fire started at Mom's house."

"Wasn't it dark out? How could you see him?"

Kaely turned the question over in her mind. The answer came to her suddenly. "You're a genius, Georgie. You know that?"

Georgie laughed. "I think you're congratulating yourself, but thanks."

"I noticed my first night at Mom's that the next-door neighbor had an automatic light on their side porch. Whoever it was trigged the light."

"Well, that proves it wasn't your imagination. It came on because someone really was out there."

"Right," Kaely said slowly. "But that doesn't mean it was Sam. Or Sheriff Brotton."

"Did it look like him?"

Kaely started to say yes, but then she stopped. "You know what? I don't know. It was so fast. I got the impression it was a tall man with blond hair who was wearing a hoodie."

"How could you see his hair?"

Kaely chewed her lip as she thought about it. The truth was, she wasn't sure she saw the guy's hair. "I think I saw what I expected to see."

"You expected to see Sam?"

Kaely looked at Georgie and nodded. "I guess it could have been anyone. Even the next-door neighbor. I expected to see Sam because I can't rule him out. Even though I want to."

"But deep down inside you know it's not him, right?"

Kaely rubbed her temples. She could feel a stress headache coming on. "I can't prove it's Sam. I can't prove it's not Sam. I can't prove it's anyone. Maybe it's someone not even on my radar. Someone I don't know."

"Now, you know that can't be true. Whoever set the fire at your mother's house knew you—was targeting you."

Of course Kaely was aware of that, but exhaustion had caused her to forget. She was grateful that Georgie had reminded her.

Georgie leaned back, her arms behind her, her legs dangling off the edge of the bed. Georgie always wore a short, colorful patchwork dress with black Keds and a purple ribbon in her curly hair. It was the real Georgie's favorite outfit when they were kids. Even though Kaely's Georgie was grown up and Kaely's age, that's still how Kaely saw her, and she had no intention of changing the image she had—no, needed—of Georgie.

"What else is bothering you?"

Kaely took a sip of her soda as she thought. When she put the cup down she said, "I keep going back to the studies that say arsonists cause destruction from a distance. They like to watch what they've done, but that they usually don't like close contact with their victims."

"You're thinking about Jack?"

Kaely nodded. "Let's just say for a minute that our arsonist *is* Jack."

"Okay."

"Jack doesn't fit the profile. He wasn't afraid to confront

the people he didn't like." She gazed at Georgie. "That's what bothers me about this case. I can't find anyone who fits the profile perfectly." Kaely rubbed her eyes. She needed sleep. Being so tired wasn't helping her powers of deduction. "And you're right. The person who set Mom's house on fire knows me. But why go after me? No one here has a reason to want me dead."

"Say Jack is alive. Why would he come back after all these years and set fires?" Georgie asked suddenly.

Kaely pointed her finger at Georgie. "That's the big question, isn't it? What's his motivation? And why go after families? It doesn't seem like he was mistreated. There's no reason for him to hate his family enough to kill innocent people." She frowned. "Okay, let's say Jack set the fire at his house. Left Raymond inside to take his place. Made sure he was wearing his bracelet. What about that night connects him to today? Makes him want to burn down homes? A lot of kids hate their parents. They don't burn down their houses. And wanting your twin dead? Twins usually have a strong bond. Something's missing, and I can't seem to get a handle on it."

"But Jack's a psychopath," Georgie added. "He didn't react like everyone else. Let's say for a moment he is the one setting the fires. Forget everything you just said. What's his motive?"

Kaely took a deep breath. "Sam escaped. Jack's back to finish what he started. He wants to destroy Sam."

"First he wants to ruin his reputation," Georgie said softly. "And then . . ."

"The end game is to kill him."

Kaely sat up straight in her chair. The Jack angle finally made sense. Except . . .

"Why now?" Georgie asked, putting into words exactly what Kaely was wondering.

"Something stressed him. Pushed him over the edge. I won't know what that was unless I can talk to him. Interview him." Kaely slapped her hands on the table. "I'm talking like Jack is really here. Like he's alive. But that's ludicrous."

"Perhaps what you're missing is right in front of you. You've got to eliminate the impossible. Once you do that . . ."

"'Whatever remains, no matter how improbable, must be the truth.'" Kaely shrugged. "I'm well aware of that quote from Sherlock Holmes. But it doesn't apply here . . . does it?"

"Does it?"

"I'm going to talk to Dr. Roberson tomorrow. I'll see if there's any reason to think the body found in the fire isn't Jack's." Kaely rubbed her eyes again. "I've got to shower and get some sleep." She smiled at Georgie. "Thanks. I really appreciate your help."

"Just be careful," Georgie said. "Noah's not with you. I feel . . . something."

"Yeah, I know. 'By the pricking of my thumbs, something wicked this way comes.' That was a little overly dramatic, wasn't it?"

"Hey, blame yourself for that. You're the one who loves Shakespeare. But you feel it, Kaely. I know you do. Pay attention. Your instincts are always right."

"Not always, but thanks. Now let me get some sleep."

Georgie faded away.

Kaely picked up the remnants of her meal and put them in the trash. She kept the soda since she had a lot left and was really thirsty.

She was gathering some clothes together for her shower when she decided maybe it was time to *see* their unknown subject.

She got up and grabbed the file she'd put together, along

with what she'd gotten from Sam and Josh. Then she sat back down at the table and began to review her information. She stared at the chair across from her and said, "You're not the average arsonist. You're organized, skilled at what you do. You began with space heaters. Then, when the authorities started getting suspicious and a fire happened that wasn't your creation, you came out of hiding. You only wrote one letter. You felt it was enough. You're not getting all of your excitement through public attention. Your real thrill comes from feeling like you have control over this town." She scooted forward in her chair. "Some arsonists get their jollies from burning things, but I don't think that's you. No, this isn't just vandalism. You're too sophisticated."

Finally, a dark shape appeared. No features. Nothing to indicate his identity.

Kaely just stared at him. Was it Sam? Josh? Was the return of Jack the impossible thing Georgie mentioned? Or was it just improbable? She couldn't be sure. "Okay," she said. "Let's say you're Jack Lucas, and you've come back from the great beyond. Why? What's your motive? Why would you run away, change your name and your identity, and then years later come back here to kill people you don't even know? Try to kill me? I don't get it."

"You won't catch me," a raspy voice said. "You're going to fail. More people will die. You will die."

Kaely scowled at the shadowy figure. "Stick to the script. You can't just say anything you want. So, what are you trying to achieve? You're angry. At who? And why? Josh would have a reason if he really wants to stay in his position at the sheriff's department. Sam has no reason at all. And Jack?"

"'Jack be nimble, Jack be quick, Jack jump over the candlestick. Jack jump high, Jack jump low, Jack jumped over and burned his toe.'"

Kaely shook her head. "I know that old nursery rhyme. Why is it important to you? Are you Jack . . . or are you pretending to be him?"

A thought suddenly occurred to her. Something she should have seen. A jolt of something akin to electricity caused a quick intake of breath. "Raymond? Did Jack actually die that night? Are you back to exact some kind of revenge? Because he betrayed you? Tried to take your life?"

The shape in the chair grew denser and darker, making a growling sound. But there was no face. No features to tell her who it was.

"'By the pricking of my thumbs, something wicked this way comes. Open, locks, whoever knocks!'"

"Okay, you're good at quotes. Now stop it and answer my questions."

"You're going to die," the shape said. "It will not happen here, in Darkwater, but it will happen. And soon."

"Stop it!" Kaely said, her voice trembling. This wasn't how this was supposed to go. The images she conjured had no way to take control like this. "I'm commanding you to leave. Now!"

A deep laugh came from the darkness in the chair across from her. "You need to be careful, Kaely Quinn. Very careful."

The image suddenly disappeared. Kaely sat looking at the empty chair, her confidence shaken. What had just happened? She'd been having trouble with her procedure for a while, but it was her greatest weapon against the monsters. Against evil.

She shook this off as an aberration. Something that wouldn't happen again. She couldn't stop using the method she'd created. She just wouldn't. Yet she felt a heaviness in her spirit.

A warning she couldn't deny. She had to fight to push back the feelings that tried to invade her mind. She had work to do.

She went back to the files, searching for something, anything that could help her find this guy. She found a note about Raymond Berger, and something she hadn't considered before popped into her head. Kaely pushed her chair back. Had he left town because he'd lost the only family that cared about him? Because he lost Jack? But why wait almost twenty years to come back?

Kaely rocked back and forth as she thought. She needed to talk to Raymond's family. First thing in the morning she intended to call Josh and ask him to go with her to visit the Bergers. It was a long shot, but Raymond was the one person they'd ignored. If Jack Lucas died in that fire, where was Raymond Berger? Maybe she was grasping at straws at this point, but she just couldn't admit that their UNSUB was Jack Lucas.

She stared once again at the chair across from her. Had all of Georgie's warnings put something in her head that caused her process to deviate so wildly? Or was there something else going on? Something she really had no way to influence? The idea frightened her, but she had no intention to stop. She was a monster-fighter, and she wouldn't let the monsters win.

THIRTY-SEVEN

Kaely was rethinking her profile when Jason knocked on the door. He opened it slowly. "It's me," he said. "Don't shoot."

Kaely laughed. "Why do you think I'd shoot you?"

"I meant to call you and let you know I was coming, but I forgot. I didn't want to spook you."

"I expected you. But you probably should call next time. Just to be safe."

Jason came in and sat down in the chair across from his sister. "I will. I'm so tired right now, it might be better if you did shoot me. I could go to the hospital, sleep, and have food served to me. Sounds pretty good right now."

"I'll bet Mom would trade places with you in a heartbeat."

Jason nodded. "Good point." He sniffed the air. "You smell like smoke."

"I know. I've been smelling myself all day." She got up and found her bag, which she then realized also smelled strongly of smoke. She removed the books she'd saved from the fire. Sherlock Holmes. Father Brown. Two novels by Charles Dickens. Kaely stacked them on top of the nightstand between the beds. Although she was glad she'd saved them, she still felt guilty. They weren't worth Noah's life. He was lying in that hospital bed because of her.

"If you're planning to take a shower, I have a pair of clean sweat pants and a T-shirt you can sleep in," Jason said.

"Thanks. I stopped by a department store on the way here and picked up a few things. I'm good."

"I saw Noah before I left the hospital," Jason said. "He's really concerned about you."

"I know. I tried to tell him I'd be okay, but I don't think he believed me."

"So you admit this guy tried to kill you?"

"I think that might be what he hoped would happen, but he's a firebug, Jason. I honestly don't think he'll come after me again as long as I'm not somewhere he can burn down. Houses are one thing. Motels and hospitals are something else."

"I . . . I guess that makes sense." His eyebrows knit together. "Why does he want you dead?"

"Hard to say. Maybe I'm getting too close. Maybe he doesn't like anyone who challenges him."

"Do you have any idea who this guy might be?"

"A few suspects, but no evidence to prove anything."

"But how would he know who you are, sis? I don't get it."

"Maybe he's met me. Or seen me with someone he knows like Tuck or Josh. At this point all I can do is guess. But don't worry. We'll get him."

Kaely had included Noah in her promise to bring the UNSUB to justice. But he wasn't here. She didn't like feeling as if she was less without him. She wasn't. She was fully capable of finding this guy and turning him over to the police.

"Look, we can talk about this later," Kaely said. "I'm headed to the bathroom unless you need to get in there."

"I'm not as stinky as you are. You go first."

"Very funny."

She went into the bathroom. Thankfully, there was just a small window. Not large enough for someone to get through.

She covered it with a towel. Then she took off her clothes and got into the shower. Although finding the arsonist was her immediate concern, she couldn't get Noah out of her mind. He'd risked his life for her. And for what? It was more than her notes about the case. Kaely had been putting her work first for years—but she'd also gone back for her books. Surprisingly, she still cared about the little girl she'd once been. About the family she'd been a part of.

As the water from the shower washed over her body, it was mixed with Kaely's tears.

When she got out of the bathroom, she found Jason sitting in the chair, watching TV. She told him about the towel over the window.

"Whatever for?" Jason asked. "The glass is frosted. No one can see in."

"But a shooter can see a shape in front of a window. A good marksman could take a successful shot."

Jason looked at Kaely with his mouth open. "Is this how you live? Worrying about people burning you up? Shooting you?"

"When they're not drugging me or trying to get me to shoot myself."

Jason sighed. "Suddenly I feel a deep desire to get my own room."

Kaely walked over and hugged her brother. "Hey, it's just like the sleepovers we used to have when we were kids. It will be fun."

"Yeah, but you weren't armed back then," he said wryly.

"Look at it this way. You've never been as safe as you are right now. You're sharing a room with a trained and armed FBI agent. You can relax."

"Well, when you put it that way . . ."

Kaely pointed at the door. "Don't open the door for anyone. Period."

"I won't."

For all her bravado, she was secretly grateful that she wasn't alone, that Jason was with her. Someone wanted her dead, and she really had no idea who it was.

They talked for a few minutes, but Jason nodded off in the middle of a sentence. She thought about waking him up so he could get a shower and change clothes, but she decided to leave him alone. He was exhausted and could do all of that later. She got a blanket from the closet and covered him. Then she got into bed and rolled over onto her side. Within a few minutes, she was sound asleep.

Almost immediately she began to dream. She could see a dark figure hidden in the shadows, starting a fire. Kaely watched as he poured gasoline around the foundation of a house. It was as if Kaely was there but invisible. She looked in a window and saw Noah, Jason, and her mother. She tried knocking on the glass to get their attention, warning them to get out. But they couldn't seem to hear her. She began to pound louder. She screamed their names, but there was still no response. Then she realized that the person setting the fire had heard her. He walked around the side of the house. She looked at him, trying to see his face, but she couldn't. Then he turned around, and she realized he had another face on the back of his head. She still couldn't make out his features.

"Stop doing this," she yelled to the arsonist.

"I'm not doing anything," he said in a low growl. "You have the wrong man." Then he took a long-handled lighter out of his pocket and leaned down. When he clicked the lighter, the house went up in flames. Kaely ran to the front of the structure, thinking she could get inside and save Noah and her family, but the house didn't have a front door. As she raced around the building, she realized that all the windows were now gone. There was no way to get inside.

Terrified, she hurried back toward the man, but he'd disappeared. She was forced to stand and watch the house burn down. Kaely dropped to her knees and cried.

"Kaely. Kaely, are you all right?"

At first she wasn't sure who was talking, but when she opened her eyes she saw Jason leaning over her. "I heard you crying. Are you okay?"

The look of concern on his face touched her heart. "I'm sorry," she whispered. "Just a bad dream. I'm fine."

"You're still having those dreams?"

Kaely shook her head. "No, not like the ones I had when I was a kid. This was just a standard rotten dream. The kind we all have."

Jason straightened up. "Are you sure?"

"I am."

Jason patted her shoulder and stood up. He grabbed some clothes from the closet and went into the bathroom. Kaely lay on her back, staring up at the ceiling. Was she right? Was that really a standard rotten dream? What did it mean? Why did the arsonist have two faces? And why did he say she had the wrong man? Was it confirmation that Sam wasn't the arsonist? Could the arsonist really be Jack Lucas?

She fell back into a restless sleep, but thankfully there were no more dreams.

THIRTY-EIGHT

When Kaely woke up, she could see light streaming into the room from under the curtains. She checked her watch, which was lying on the nightstand. A little after seven. She got out of bed and padded softly over to the small coffeepot on top of the dresser. She opened the bag that held the coffee inside a filter and put it in the top of the machine. After getting some water from the sink outside of the bathroom, she poured it into the coffeemaker. A couple of minutes later, she was sitting on the edge of the bed, drinking a cup of hot coffee. She was surprised to find out it was pretty good. She wanted to turn on the TV and check the weather, but she was afraid she'd wake Jason up. As she sipped her coffee, an alarm on his phone went off. It only took a few seconds for him to reach over and turn it off. He flipped over toward Kaely and smiled.

"Good morning," he said.

"Good morning. Wasn't sure how long you were going to sleep."

He sat up and yawned. "Man, I'm still tired, but I need to get to the hospital." He sighed and pushed himself up, swinging his legs over the side of the bed. "I've been trying to witness to Mom, but losing her house hasn't helped. She told me yesterday that she thinks God burned her house down."

"You know that's not true."

Jason nodded. "I told her that. Not sure she heard me."

Kaely scooted closer to the edge of the bed and took his hand. "You know, Jason, some people find God through adversity. Maybe that will happen to Mom. We need to pray that God will help her through this. Show her how much He loves her. This could actually work out better than you think. I mean, what else can she do but call out for help? We know He'll respond."

Jason exhaled slowly. "I don't know, Kaely. I have to admit she's been more laid-back than I thought she'd be. But she still shuts me down when I bring up God."

"I think you're the one to help her. She trusts you, but she doesn't have much faith in me." Kaely shrugged. "That will take time, I guess. Trust is something we'll have to build." Kaely laughed lightly. "To be honest, I'm not sure Mom even likes me."

Jason squeezed her hand. "You might be right about the trust thing. But I know she likes you, Kaely."

Kaely shook her head. "I think you're wrong. She quit liking me when I was a teenager. I was too much trouble. She was relieved when I moved out."

"You weren't that bad. I knew kids who behaved a lot worse than you did."

"Maybe so, but I wish I'd been easier on her. She was having her own problems. I certainly didn't help by acting out." Kaely sighed. "And now I'm responsible for her house burning down. That should really help her opinion of me."

"You didn't burn down her house," Jason said, looking surprised.

"If I hadn't been here, her house would still be standing. Don't think she won't figure that out."

"Okay, maybe she will blame you," Jason said. "But after

the fire, her first reaction was relief that you were all right. That doesn't sound like someone who doesn't like you. Besides, whether she likes us or not . . . tough. We're what she has. She needs to get over it. I like who I am . . . now. And I like you too, if it makes any difference."

Kaely smiled. "It makes a big difference. I'm so grateful to have you back in my life. I love you, Jason."

"And I love you too." He sniffed a couple of times. Kaely was touched to see his reaction. "Now, let's talk about what's really important," he said, pointing at her cup of coffee. "I want some of that."

"I think that can be arranged, but after I make you a cup, we're out. So I'll only do it if you'll go to the office and get more of these packets."

Jason's eyes widened. "That's blackmail. You're a federal agent. Is that legal?"

Kaely stood up. "Yeah, it's under the Irritating Brother Statute."

Jason burst out laughing. "Okay. You've got me. Make me a cup while I get dressed, and I'll run down and ask for some more."

"Deal." As Kaely made another cup of coffee, she thought about her and Tuck's meeting with Dr. Roberson later that morning. Would they finally get some answers, or would he only add to their confusion?

After a quick breakfast in the small community kitchen downstairs, Jason left for the hospital. Kaely hung around for a while, drinking coffee and waiting for their room to be cleaned. A little after nine she went back to the room, and around nine thirty she got dressed to go out. She realized her coat smelled like smoke too, but there wasn't anything she could do about it.

It was too cold to go outside without it. She squared her shoulders and sighed. Hopefully, Tuck and Dr. Roberson wouldn't notice.

As she stepped outside, she could almost swear the temperature had dropped even more since they'd gotten back from breakfast. How was that possible? The past few winters had been pretty mild in St. Louis. Adjusting to these Nebraskan temperatures was hard. Kaely loved winter weather but only when she was inside with a book and a cup of coffee. Trying to get around town in this stuff wasn't her idea of fun. At least it wasn't snowing. Before getting into the car, she looked up at the sky. The clouds were dark and heavy-looking. They promised more precipitation. Great.

She walked over to her car. Something else she had the fire department to thank for. They'd protected her vehicle before the fire from the house reached it. It hadn't occurred to Kaely that her car was in danger, but the firefighters knew that surrounding structures and even vehicles were at risk.

When she got inside her car, she opened up her text message from Tuck and entered the ME's address into her GPS. A few minutes later, she was winding her way through the streets of Darkwater. She wondered if media interest in the fires would put Tuck and Josh under more pressure. It was possible public concern would alert the state fire marshal. She was pretty sure Tuck wouldn't appreciate anyone else stepping in, as Tuck seemed rather possessive when it came to his department.

It took her about fifteen minutes to reach Dr. Roberson's house. It reminded Kaely of her mother's house. Almost all the houses in town were small and boxlike. This place was no different, except it looked as if it hadn't been updated or painted in quite some time. Also, the pine tree in the front yard was huge and needed a good trimming.

Would she learn something that would bring her closer to catching the arsonist, or was this going to be a huge waste of time? Kaely felt like she was in a race against time. When would the arsonist strike again?

THIRTY-NINE

Tuck's Jeep was already in the driveway when she pulled in behind him. After she got out of her car, she checked his vehicle to see if he was waiting inside, but it was empty. She walked up the steps leading to the front porch and rang the doorbell.

A few seconds later, the front door, covered with peeling green paint, swung open. Tuck ushered her in.

"I just got here," he said softly. "Haven't asked him anything yet, but I did tell him we have questions about an old case. He seems willing to talk to us."

Kaely nodded. "Good."

Tuck led her into a living room that showed the same lack of care that the outside of the house displayed. Although everything was in its place, the area rug that covered most of the floor was frayed and in need of a good cleaning. The furniture, which was dated, could certainly use some attention.

"Kaely Quinn, this is Dr. Marvin Roberson," Tuck said, gesturing to a man sitting in a wheelchair.

Kaely stepped forward to shake Marvin's hand. The retired medical examiner looked to be in his late fifties or early sixties. His handshake was firm and his hazel eyes clear. Although his body was lean, his face reminded Kaely of a bulldog. When he nodded, his jowls bounced. His hair was cut in a style not many men wore anymore, unless they were in the army. Shaved on the sides, short on the top.

"I'm glad to meet you," Kaely said. "Thank you for seeing us."

Marvin nodded. "So you're the profiler," he said in a gravelly voice.

Kaely glanced at Tuck, who noticed the look Kaely shot him and gave her a slight shrug. Maybe he'd felt he didn't have a choice but to tell him.

"I was trained as a behavioral analyst with the FBI," Kaely said with an even smile.

Marvin swept his hand toward a dilapidated couch. "Why don't you have a seat? Tell me what brings you here today."

She and Tuck sat down. The couch dipped down in the middle and wasn't very comfortable. Kaely slid over to the side, where she felt a little more secure.

"Marvin, we want to ask you about an autopsy," Tuck said. "It happened a long time ago. I'm hoping that talking about it might help you remember it, but I did bring copies of the records with me. Do you mind looking at them?"

Marvin appeared to study Tuck for a moment. Kaely wasn't sure he was going to take the file, but finally he reached out for it. Marvin was wearing a T-shirt, and Kaely noticed the muscles in his arm. Very well developed for a man his age, which wasn't surprising since he was in a wheelchair, but his legs looked strong as well.

Marvin put the file on his lap and then slowly opened it. He scanned it for a few seconds before saying, "What do you want to know? Everything seems pretty clear to me."

"Do you remember this autopsy, Marvin?" Tuck asked.

Marvin sighed and began looking closer at the file. Kaely could tell by the tautness in his face that he was upset. His hands clenched the file as if he were hanging on to it for dear life.

As she waited, Kaely gazed around the room, trying to get a quick sense of the man. This room had once been lovely. She could tell that the furnishings had originally been selected with care. On the fireplace mantel, she noticed several framed photos of a woman who appeared to be in her early fifties. She had a friendly face and a nice smile. She looked like someone Kaely would like to know. There were more pictures of the same woman with a boy with dark hair and eyes who smiled for the camera. But a later photo of the boy when he was much older, maybe in his early twenties, showed a sneer of contempt. The friendly child was gone, replaced by a discontented young man.

Kaely assumed Marvin's wife had passed away. If they'd divorced, the photos wouldn't be here. She was probably the one who had originally decorated the home. She must have died years ago for the house to be this neglected. Marvin also seemed to be estranged from their son. If not, there would be more recent photos. From the young man's hairstyle and clothing, she figured the picture must be at least fifteen years old.

"I know it may sound crazy, Marvin," Tuck said. "But someone told us that this autopsy might have been pushed through a little too fast. That the body identified as Jack Lucas could have been someone else." He looked carefully at the retired medical examiner. "Whatever you tell us will stay here," Tuck said. "It won't leave this house. You have my word."

Kaely was alarmed by Tuck's reassurance. If Marvin revealed a crime, how could they stay quiet? She had no jurisdiction to arrest anyone unless it was a federal crime or a crime that occurred in their presence. But they could still file a complaint as individuals if they had sufficient probable cause. As a law enforcement officer, Kaely felt it was her duty to expose crime, not cover it up.

Tuck, who was obviously tired of sitting in the middle of the drooping couch, got up and moved over to a chair next to Marvin. Almost immediately the retired medical examiner's face turned red. "Don't sit there," he barked out. "That's Essie's chair."

"I'm sorry," Tuck said, standing up, but Marvin had already motioned for him to sit back down.

"I . . . I'm sorry," Marvin choked out. "It's silly for me to try to keep people out of her chair. It's not like she's going to walk back into the house and want to sit there."

Kaely felt a surge of compassion for the man. Somewhere in the back of his mind, he probably held out hope that someday his wife would do just that. Facing reality was heartbreaking.

"Are you sure?" Tuck asked. "I can move."

"Nah," Marvin said, shaking his head. "It's fine." He closed the file. His head dropped to his chest, and he stared down at his hands. They were clasped together, and the knuckles were white with pressure. No one said a word. Kaely waited expectantly, hoping he had something helpful to tell them. Finally, Marvin raised his head and fixed his gaze on Tuck. "Do you remember about eighteen years ago when that grain elevator on the edge of town exploded?"

"Sure. Six men died. Everyone in town who was alive back then remembers."

Marvin nodded slowly. "We were a small department with not a lot of experienced help. We did the best we could. The Lucas fire happened the next day. We were still processing bodies from the explosion. Besides another ME, I also had a couple medical students assisting us. One of them . . ." He took a deep breath and let it out slowly, as if trying to steady himself. "One of them released Jack Lucas's body before we'd done the official ID. By the time I found out, Jack had already been cremated."

FORTY

That was almost exactly the story Turner had told her. Kaely was shocked to hear it confirmed. "You can't be sure that body belonged to Jack Lucas?" Tuck asked, incredulity in his tone.

Marvin shifted in his wheelchair. "Even though I knew I should have said something at the time, I let it go. I mean, who else could it be? Jack and his parents lived in that house. We had the remains of two adults and a teenager. The teenager had to be Jack. Oh, and we found a bracelet on the body that belonged to Jack. Made of silver with two snakes intertwined. It was very distinctive. Sam verified it was Jack's. I was so certain it was him." He rubbed his forehead. "At the time I felt confident our identification was right. That no harm had been done. But it's bothered me for all these years. It's a loose thread, something that wasn't done quite right." He scowled at them. "Why are you asking about this now?"

Tuck cleared his throat. "I'm going to tell you something you need to keep to yourself."

Kaely started to stop him. He shouldn't give out information about an unsolved case to anyone—not even to Marvin. Although it was against her better judgment Kaely clamped her lips together. She hoped this wasn't a terrible mistake. What if Marvin spread the word around town that they were accusing a ghost of setting fires?

"You know we've had several house fires in Darkwater," Tuck continued, "and we're trying to figure out who's behind it."

"Wait a minute," Marvin said. "Do you think Jack Lucas is still alive?"

"I'm not saying that," Tuck replied. "We're just following up on every lead."

Marvin looked at Tuck like he'd lost his mind. "First of all, the body we accidentally released was most likely Jack. I wouldn't have signed the death certificate if I wasn't pretty confident about that. Secondly, if he is alive, why in heaven's name would he suddenly show up in Darkwater and start burning down houses? He lost his family in a fire. That would be the last thing he'd want to do."

"I'm not saying it's Jack," Tuck said. "Like I said, we're just eliminating all possibilities. You remember how it works." He stood to his feet. "Thanks for seeing us, Marvin. And thank you for being honest with me." He nodded at Kaely. "We need to be going." He turned his attention back to Marvin. "Is there anything you need?" he asked softly. "All you gotta do is ask, you know."

"Well, I'd like to walk again, but that's not gonna happen." He peered at Kaely. "So what did you learn by looking at my pictures, young lady?"

Kaely started to deny she'd been studying them, but instead she decided to be straight with him. He'd done the same for them.

"Well, you loved your wife very much," she said, standing up. "You're estranged from your son. And I think you're very lonely. But it doesn't take any special training to see that."

"It's that obvious, huh?"

"Yes," Kaely said. "Maybe you're afraid to reach out to your friends because of the wheelchair. Perhaps you think it makes you seem weak or that you'll be seen as an object of pity. But it's not true. Your real friends don't care about that chair. They care about you." She walked over to a small side table. She picked up a brochure from a local animal shelter. "You're thinking about adopting a pet. Probably a dog. But you're worried. Can you take care of it properly? Is it fair to the dog?" She came over and handed him the brochure. "I think it's a marvelous idea. Not only for you but for the dog you rescue. You'll be a great dog owner. No doubt about it."

Marvin's eyes grew wet, and he reached out and took Kaely's hand. "Thank you, young lady. I appreciate that." He stroked the brochure with one hand. "I will call." Then he looked over at Tuck. "And I'll call my friends more often. Maybe you can pick me up one night and we can go to Gannon's for a beer. Like we used to."

"You got it," Tuck said. "I know the other guys would love to see you."

For the first time since they'd entered the house, Marvin smiled. "Thanks, Tuck. I appreciate it."

"We'd better get going, but I'll call you," Tuck said. "We'll give old Gannon a run for his money."

"Sounds wonderful."

They said good-bye to Marvin and stepped out onto the porch.

"There's a good burger joint about a mile from here. We can talk about what Marvin said. And I have something I want to show you."

"Okay, but I can't stay too long. I need to get to the hospital."

"You'll be on your way as soon as you finish your lunch," Tuck promised. He stepped down off the porch. "Follow me to the burger place." With that, he got into his car.

Kaely slid into the front seat of her SUV, started it up, and shivered at the cold air that came out of the vents. After dialing Noah, she clicked the speaker button and slid the phone into the hands-free holder clipped to her dash. He picked up on the first ring. "About time. I've been waiting to hear from you."

Kaely quickly brought Noah up to speed on her concerns about Jack Lucas and her visit with Marvin. Since it now seemed remotely possible that Jack was alive, she realized she had to tell Noah the truth. He would be furious if she kept something like this from him. As long as it seemed impossible Kaely didn't have a problem keeping Noah out of the loop. But after talking to Marvin, things had changed.

"What does that mean?" Noah asked, clearly astonished.

"It means it's possible Jack Lucas started the fire that burned down his house and killed his parents. And now he's back for some reason—hiding in Darkwater, setting fires, and getting away with it."

FORTY-ONE

Are you sure about this?" Noah asked.

"No, but it makes a strange kind of sense," Kaely said as she wove through the streets of Darkwater, following Tuck's Jeep. "He got some other kid to stay the night and then took off after the fire."

"Or the house just caught fire and Jack Lucas died with his mother and father," Noah said. "How can you seriously believe this? It's so farfetched."

"I know it sounds ludicrous. But it would explain a lot."

"Maybe," Noah said. Kaely could hear his skepticism. She didn't blame him.

"Let's say you're right," Noah said suddenly. "Then why is he back? What does he want?"

"I'm not sure," Kaely said. She flashed back to the look of contempt on the face of Marvin's son. There were kids who despised their parents, blamed them for all the failures in their own lives. What if Jack hated his parents enough to kill them, along with an innocent teenage boy, then left town almost twenty years ago? But, as Noah asked, why would he return now? He certainly couldn't hurt his parents anymore. Was he really here to exact revenge on his brother? "Look, I need more information before I can give a logical answer to your question. Right now all I can do is guess. Let's put this idea on the shelf for a while."

"We need solid leads," Noah said, frustration in his tone. "Not fanciful fairy tales."

"I'm meeting Tuck for lunch, and we're going to talk more about it," she said. She could sense that part of Noah's annoyance was at being stuck in the hospital instead of being able to help her work the case. "I'll come to the hospital after that and fill you in, okay?"

"Sure. Sorry. I guess this situation is starting to get on my nerves." A heavy sigh came through the phone. "Can I tell you that the food they have in the cafeteria is *not* what they serve to patients? I want a nice big juicy cheeseburger with fried onions. Can you smuggle one in?"

Kaely laughed. "Not unless your doctor says it's okay. I have no intention of causing you any more harm."

"I thought you were my friend," Noah grumbled.

"I am. That's why you're not getting a greasy, artery-clogging cheeseburger."

"Traitor."

"Sorry," Kaely said.

"What's your read on the medical examiner?" Noah asked.

"He's a very lonely man. I like him, but I got the feeling he wasn't telling us everything."

"Is he a suspect?"

"No. I doubt if a man in a wheelchair is capable of setting these fires, especially in the winter," Kaely said. "Besides, what's his motive?"

"Yeah, you're probably right."

"Hey, how are you feeling this morning?" Kaely asked.

"Sore. Trying to back off the pain meds, but it's not as easy as I'd hoped. At least I'm not talking to people who aren't there anymore. That morphine is something else."

Kaely laughed. "Well, I'll be there in a little while, okay?"

"Okay. See you soon."

Noah had just hung up when Kaely's phone rang. It was the agent she'd asked to search ViCAP for the MO they were seeing in Darkwater. Unfortunately, it was a dead end. She hadn't been able to find anything that seemed connected to the man who called himself Jack.

Kaely thanked the agent for her help and hung up. She noticed Tuck turning off the road and followed him. She pulled into the parking lot of a plain white building labeled Bucky's Burgers. This was the place where Noah had picked up cheeseburgers when he first got to town.

Unfortunately, it seemed Bucky didn't believe in clearing his parking lot. Tuck parked his car and went inside. It took Kaely a few minutes to find another parking space, and she ended up on the other side of the lot. She had to walk carefully to keep from falling.

Once she was inside, she gazed around the crowded room until she saw Tuck waving her over. Forgiving Bucky's parking lot was easy as the aroma of hamburger, fried onions, and cheese wafted through the air. She felt a little guilty since this was exactly the kind of food Noah was currently craving.

As she tried to make her way toward Tuck, she ran into someone. She started to apologize when she realized it was Aaron Pollard, the man she'd met the night of the Mayfield fire.

"Fancy running into you," he said with a smile.

Kaely laughed. "Sorry. Too many people in a small place."

He nodded. "Bucky's burgers are worth the aggravation, though. I've been living on his food. Probably not the healthiest choice."

"Probably not. How's your mom?"

"Getting better," he said. "Hopefully she'll be home soon."

"That's great. Nice to see you again."

"You too."

Kaely began pushing her way through the crowd waiting to order until she finally was clear and made her way to where Tuck waited.

"Who's your friend?" Tuck asked when she sat down.

"Not a friend. I met him the night of that fire over on Mayfield. Aaron Pollard. He's staying at his mom's house while she's out of town. Nice guy."

"I assume you checked him out," Tuck said.

"Of course. Yeah, he's okay."

"Well, I hope you're not one of those healthy eaters," Tuck said. "If so, maybe they can toss some lettuce and tomato in a bowl for you."

"You're nuts," Kaely said with a grin. "Double cheeseburger, please."

"Good for you. Why don't you keep our table while I order? If we both get up, we'll probably lose it."

"Sure." Kaely told him what she wanted on her burger. She also ordered onion rings and a soda.

As Tuck walked to the counter, she noticed Aaron picking up a bag of food he'd ordered ahead. As he walked toward the front door, he turned and waved at her. Kaely smiled and raised her hand.

Tuck's table was in a corner of the restaurant, near a side door. Cold seeped in from the gap underneath the door. Kaely shivered and kept her coat buttoned. Normally she'd suggest they move, but there weren't any other empty tables.

Tuck hung around the counter, talking amiably with someone until their order was ready. He brought the food to the table, then fetched napkins and condiments. Once they were situated and had started eating, Tuck picked up a small folder he'd carried with him into the restaurant. He opened it and took out a picture. "This is a blown-up photo from that video Greg gave me. I think you'll find it interesting."

"Josh showed me this yesterday," Kaely said, carefully wiping her hands.

"I know, but I have a friend who cleaned it up even more."

Kaely took the photo. It was the same picture she'd seen except, as Tuck had said, it was clearer. She stared at the man in the photo, who was wearing a hoodie. Again, it looked like Sam. "The photo is still grainy. I can't tell for sure who this is. Only part of his face is showing."

"Look closer. That's a scar on his cheek."

She peered closer at the picture. "I don't know. Maybe."

"You're being too cautious," Tuck insisted. He reached into the folder again and took out another photo. "This is a copy of a picture taken of Sam and Jack not long before the fire."

Kaely took the photo from Tuck and stared at it. Two teenage boys stood together on a basketball court. They were so alike it was startling—except for one thing. One of them had a scar on his right cheek. The placement and the texture looked remarkably like the photo from the video. Kaely looked down at the caption below the picture. It read "Darkwater High's Twin Tornados. Sam and Jack Lucas celebrating their state basketball championship."

But the thing that really shook her was Jack's eyes. They looked dead. Like shark eyes.

FORTY-TWO

Noah woke up around one in the afternoon. He hadn't meant to fall asleep again. He wanted to be awake when Kaely got there. He was still trying to wean himself off his medication, but his pain level was pretty bad. His doctor was encouraging him to "stay in front of it," whatever that meant, but Noah wanted out of the hospital as soon as possible. He wasn't fully convinced the arsonist was done targeting Kaely, and he needed to be by her side. He was wriggling around in the bed, trying to get comfortable, when the door to his room opened and Kaely came in.

"Hey, you look pretty good. Still talking to your invisible friends?"

Noah realized the irony of her question but kept a straight face. "No, I seem to be alone now. At least most of the time. There have been a few others in my room, but they claim to be doctors or nurses. I'm pretty sure they're telling the truth."

Kaely laughed. Noah had missed that sound. It did more for him than the morphine they'd given him the first few hours out of surgery.

"You're very entertaining." Kaely walked up next to the bed. "But no more hospital visits for a while, okay? I've got better things to do."

"Well, stay out of the path of bullets and out of burning houses. Then I'll do the same."

Any amusement in Kaely's expression melted away. "You saved my life. Twice."

"Aren't you going to chew me out and tell me you don't need me to protect you?"

"Would it do any good?"

"Nah. Probably not."

Kaely didn't say anything. She just stared at him in a way that made him feel uncomfortable. But in a good way. Feeling he needed to interject something to fill the emotionally charged silence, he said, "You know, I may have gotten you out of the house, but Sam pulled us both to safety. If it wasn't for him . . ."

"I know. I'm sorry I couldn't help you. The smoke practically knocked me out."

"Not your fault. I'm just glad Sam got you into the yard, away from the danger. We owe him a lot."

"Yes, we do."

"Is he okay?"

"Doing fine. He hasn't come to see you?"

Noah shook his head. "Not yet. I suspect he will when he can."

"I'm sure you're right."

Kaely exhaled softly. She looked frustrated. And tired. "Talking to Marvin confused me."

"But you told me on the phone you were almost convinced Jack Lucas was behind everything, that it was listening to Marvin that led you to that conclusion. Did I misunderstand?"

Kaely walked over to a chair a few feet from Noah's bed and plopped down. "Are you talking about my fanciful fairy tale?"

"Sorry," Noah said. "It's just frustrating being stuck in here."

"I know. It's okay." She looked away for a minute before saying, "I had a thought."

"Uh-oh."

"Uh-oh might be right. There's one person we haven't considered."

He frowned at her. "Who's that?"

She leaned back and crossed her legs. "If Jack died in that fire, who's missing?"

Noah had to think for a moment. His mind was still a little fuzzy. "Raymond Berger?"

Kaely nodded.

"But what reason would he have to come back to Darkwater and start these fires? And why would he go after you?"

She sighed. "I have no idea, but I'm going to meet his family later this afternoon. I doubt our UNSUB is Raymond, but he's a loose end I need to tie up."

"What are you hoping to discover?"

"I'm not sure," Kaely said. "But I need to find out if his family or anyone else has heard from him since that night. I'd also like to know if there's a reason he'd want to leave town. Sounds like he was close to Sam's family. They cared for him in ways his own parents didn't. If he didn't die in the fire, I'm sure losing them devastated him."

Noah considered what she'd said. "That makes some sense. I mean, I can see why he'd run away. I just can't understand why he'd return now. And what he's so angry about."

"Maybe he's like any other psychopath. Something set him off. Something we don't understand yet."

"Is someone going with you to the Bergers'?"

She nodded. "I called Josh on the way over here. He knows them and set up our meeting."

"Jason was with you last night, right?"

"Yes. We shared a room, and I'm moving into the room next

door this afternoon. It's got connecting doors. Don't worry about me. I'm being careful. You have nothing to worry about except getting well."

"The doctor says I have to stay here at least two more days—that's if everything goes well. And when I do get out, he wants me to take it easy."

"You'll obey the doctor's orders, or I'll rat you out. I mean it, Noah."

"You'd snitch on me?"

"In a second. Without hesitation."

Noah scowled at her, but he was touched by her concern for him.

Kaely leaned forward. "Noah, please just concentrate on getting well. Our UNSUB is probably scouting out his next target. I don't think he's concerned about me. Besides, I keep my gun with me at all times. Seriously, I'll be fine."

"Why do I want to add 'famous last words' after that?"

"Oh, don't be silly." She straightened up and pointed at him. "You be good."

"Okay," he said with a sigh. "But call me after you see the Bergers, okay? I'm curious."

She nodded. "It may not lead to much, but you never know. Just trying to chase down every lead."

"You must have really impressed SSA Turner."

"What do you mean?" Kaely asked.

Noah grinned and gestured toward the window with his right hand. There was a huge bouquet of colorful carnations on the windowsill. "From the North Platte office," he said.

"Will wonders never cease." Kaely got up and came over to the bed. "He really is a nice guy. I hope everything goes well for him." She reached over and picked up Noah's hand, squeezed it, and then let go. "I need to head out of here. I'll be back as soon as I can." She reached down and brushed a stray lock of hair off his forehead. She'd done it before and he liked it.

They said good-bye and Kaely left. After the door closed behind her, an odd memory stirred in his brain. Was it real? He could almost swear that Kaely Quinn had kissed him. Noah entertained the thought for a moment but then dismissed it. It had to be the drugs. That was something she'd never do.

When Kaely reached her mother's room, she found the door closed. She knocked, and a nurse poked her head out.

"We're giving your mother a sponge bath. Can you give us a few minutes?"

"A sponge bath?"

The nurse nodded. "She had a setback last night. Nothing to worry about. Just a reaction to her treatment." The nurse smiled. "She's okay. Just tired. We decided to let her rest this morning."

Kaely breathed a sigh of relief. "Thank you. I'll be in the waiting room. Will you let me know when I can see her?"

The nurse promised to get her when they were done, so Kaely headed down the hall. When she got to the waiting room, she pulled out her phone and called Josh. Her call went to voice-mail, so she left a message confirming she'd meet him at the Bergers' at three o'clock. After she hung up, she checked her notes for the address and directions to the Bergers' house. She glanced up at the clock on the wall. A little after one thirty. She had some time, but she was also grateful she had a reason to leave. She hated feeling that way, but she couldn't seem to help it.

"Hey, there you are," a voice called out. "When did you get here?"

"Just a little while ago," she said as her brother walked into the waiting room. "Stopped by to see Noah and then came to visit Mom."

"Yeah, I saw Noah this morning. He keeps reminding me that I need to stay near you."

"I'm fine."

"Regardless, I'd like to know where you're going today," Jason said. "You promised to keep in touch."

"I was with Tuck this morning, and I'm going to be with Josh Brotton the rest of the afternoon." She smiled at him. "I couldn't be safer than being with the sheriff. I should get back to the motel around four o'clock. Maybe a little later."

Jason nodded. "Okay. I'll try to make it there around the same time." He sat down next to her and put his hand on her shoulder. "I realize letting me know where you are is a pain, but if you don't, Noah might check himself out of the hospital before he should."

"You're right. I'll do my best. Deal?"

Jason nodded. "Deal." He withdrew his hand from her shoulder and stuck it out. "Should we spit on our palms first like we used to when we were kids?"

Kaely couldn't help but laugh. "No," she said. "I think it's okay to leave that part out. It's certainly more hygienic."

Jason grinned at her. "I agree."

"The nurse said they're giving Mom a sponge bath," Kaely said. "I guess she had a reaction to her last treatment."

"Yeah, I stopped by her room before I came looking for you. Those treatments are rough."

The nurse she'd talked to earlier came into the room and

told them Marcie was ready to see them. When they entered her room, they found her sitting up. Although the nurse had said she was weak, she looked pretty good.

"Hi, Mom," Jason said, going right over to her bed and kissing her on the cheek. Marcie reached up and hugged him.

"You didn't need to come back so soon," she told him. "I don't want you to wear yourself out."

"I'm fine. Let's just worry about you, okay?"

Marcie glanced at Kaely. "Both of my children at once? What have I done to deserve this?"

"We've been here together before, Mom," Kaely said.

Marcie didn't respond, just pointed at the two chairs sitting against the wall. "Have a seat. Have you eaten? I could ask the nurse to bring a couple of trays."

"Thanks, Mom, but I'm not hungry," Kaely said. "I . . . I can't stay long. I have to meet Sheriff Brotton in a little bit."

"Oh." Marcie straightened up in the bed and reached for the glass of water on her tray. "I appreciate you working me into your busy schedule, Jessica."

"Mom, I didn't mean . . . I'll come back when I have more time. We're trying to find the person who burned down your house."

"Thank you," Marcie said curtly. "But I'd rather spend time with you than worry about that silly house."

Kaely released an annoyed sigh. "I want to spend time with you too. But then this morning—"

"Why don't you leave now, Kaely?" Marcie said sharply. "I wouldn't want you to be late."

"Fine." Kaely stood up, grabbed her purse, and made a hasty retreat. Was this the way it would always be between her and her mother?

FORTY-THREE

Kaely got to the Bergers' house early, thanks to her quick departure from her mother's bedside. She prayed as she sat in the car. "God, will you please help me? I don't know what to do anymore. My mother is so bitter that I can't seem to find a way to reach her."

As soon as she said the words, she began to replay the interaction between her and her mother in her mind. It wasn't just what her mother had said and done. It was Kaely. What *she'd* said. How *she'd* acted. She knew she wasn't perfect, but until she actually saw herself through fresh eyes, she hadn't realized how unapproachable she'd been. Before she knew it, tears were sliding down her face. It wasn't just her mother's fault they weren't getting along. It was hers as well. She'd been telling herself that she couldn't help the way she responded to Marcie, but that wasn't the truth. Kaely could draw from the kindness, gentleness, and self-control God had put inside of her—the fruit of the Spirit. Even when she didn't really feel like it, she knew those gifts were there for her.

"Thank you, God," she whispered, "for showing me I can't change my mother, but I can approach her differently and change myself. Help me to walk in love and forgiveness. I can't do it by myself. I need you to make me into the person you want me to be. You've brought me so far. I'm sorry there's still such a long way to go."

She had no sooner finished her prayer than she noticed that

Josh's car had pulled up in front of the Bergers'. Kaely quickly wiped her face and took a deep breath to calm herself. Then she got out of the car and walked over to where Josh waited.

He smiled as she approached. "I called Mrs. Berger. She's expecting us."

"Is there a Mr. Berger?" Kaely asked.

"There was," Josh said, "but he ran out on the family when Raymond was thirteen. There are two brothers and a sister, but I have no idea where they are. They were all older than Raymond, so I assume they've moved out."

Kaely gave the house a quick assessment. This seemed to be the older part of town. The tiny blue-and-white house had seen better days. The windows on the front were covered with plastic. There weren't any storm windows. The steps leading to the front door were broken and cracked. Kaely remembered what Josh had said about Raymond, that he hadn't been cared for properly.

As they walked toward the porch, Kaely noticed the side-walks were still covered with snow, a sign that Mrs. Berger didn't get out much. Kaely walked carefully, trying not to slip. The steps were not only dangerous because of the ice, but they were crumbling as well. Frankly, they were a hazard.

When Josh knocked on the door, there wasn't any response at first. Then a woman's voice called out, "Just a minute." A few seconds later, the door swung open. A woman stood there, smiling. She was rather plain, but she had a pleasant face.

"Mary Louise?" Josh said, surprise etched in his voice. "I thought you'd moved away a long time ago."

"Josh. Good to see you. Come on in." As she swung the rickety door open, it squeaked loudly.

Kaely and Josh stepped into a small living room with furniture designed to be functional, not attractive. Mary Louise gestured toward a well-used couch pushed up against the wall. When Josh and Kaely sat down, Kaely could have sworn the couch groaned.

"I moved to South Carolina after college and started teaching," Mary Louise told Josh. "My brothers live out-of-state as well. We come home when we can, but I haven't been back for a little over a year. I'm here now to take care of Mama." She swung her eyes toward Kaely.

"I'm sorry, Mary Louise," Josh said quickly. "I was so surprised to see you I forgot my manners. This is my friend Kaely Quinn. She's helping me investigate the fires we've been having."

Kaely put her hand out, and Mary Louise shook it firmly. Kaely was relieved that Josh didn't mention that Kaely was with the FBI.

"Nice to meet you, Kaely," she said. "Josh and I went to school together. I was two grades above him, but he knew my brother Raymond."

"I'm glad to meet you too," Kaely said, smiling. "Maybe you can tell me the truth about Josh. What was he really like in school?"

Mary Louise laughed. "Let's just say none of us would have believed he'd become the sheriff someday."

"Hey," Josh said good-naturedly. "Don't ruin my reputation. What little there is left of it."

"Sorry about the election," Mary Louise said. "Mama voted for you."

"So that's who it was?" Josh joked.

Mary Louise chuckled and sat down across from them in a chair with sagging springs.

"You said you came home to take care of your mother," Josh said. "Is Agnes ill?"

Mary Louise nodded. "The doctor thinks it's Alzheimer's. We're still awaiting test results. She was capable of taking care of herself for a while, but lately she's really slipped. When I got here, I found the house a mess. I've been cleaning for the last week." She waved her hand around. "As you can see, the place wasn't in good shape anyway, but it was really awful when I arrived. I feel so bad about it. My brothers and I should have kept a closer eye on her, but she kept telling us everything was fine. A friend of hers finally called me to let me know she had some concerns. When I go back to South Carolina, I'll be taking her with me. There's a nice Alzheimer's facility near our house." She frowned at Josh. "When you called, you said you wanted to talk about Raymond?"

"I didn't realize that was you on the phone," Josh said. "I assumed it was your mom."

"I felt it would be better to explain things when you got here," she said.

Josh hesitated a moment before saying, "I know this seems strange, Mary Louise, but what can you tell us about the time when your brother went missing?"

Mary Louise sank back into the cushions of her chair. "Wow. That was a long time ago. Can I ask why you're interested?"

"It's really hard to explain," Josh said. "Let's just say that we're wondering if there's any connection between the fire that burned down the Lucases' home and the fires we're dealing with now."

Mary Louise's forehead creased. "I don't understand. How could they possibly be connected?"

Kaely glanced over at Josh. How would he handle this?

274

Without missing a beat, he said, "I really can't say much about that, but since it was about the same time Raymond went missing, I thought you might have more reason to remember that night than most people. Can you think back? Tell me everything you can recall? It could be very important."

For several seconds Mary Louise stared at Josh as though she were trying to read his mind. Finally, she said, "I . . . I don't know. I mean, I remember Raymond didn't come home from school that afternoon on the day of the fire. It wasn't completely unprecedented. He didn't really have many friends, except for Jack Lucas, who I never trusted. I felt he was using my brother. For what, I couldn't say." She paused a moment. "But I will tell you that Raymond was a lot happier after Jack came into his life." She shrugged. "Maybe I should have been kinder to Jack. Especially since he's gone now."

If he really is, Kaely thought.

"Back to the night of the fire, Mary Louise," Josh said. "Is there anything that sticks out in your mind? Something Raymond said that day that seemed strange? Or in the days before he went missing?"

Raymond's sister frowned, her eyes looking past Kaely and Josh as if trying to pull up an old, stale memory. Probably one she didn't really want to recall. "You know, there was something." She sighed and clasped her hands together. "My father had left several years earlier. Mom never recovered from it. She went into a very deep depression. Some days she wouldn't even get out of bed. I tried to help my brothers, but I was just a kid myself. There wasn't much I could do. Jack and Sam's mother was so kind to us. Gave all of us clothes. Came to visit my mom many times. She brought food, even cleaned the house from time to time. She was a good woman. Raymond adored her. But he was never really sure about Jack. He could be kind, but then he'd suddenly turn on Raymond, you know? Call him names. Say cruel things. It hurt my brother very much. Then a few days before Raymond disappeared, Jack gave him something that seemed to change everything."

Kaely's inner radar sprung to life. "A silver bracelet with two snakes clutching each other?"

Mary Louise's eyes widened in surprise. "Yes. How did you know that?"

Kaely looked at Josh, who looked shocked by the revelation.

"Jack loved that bracelet," Josh said slowly. "Never took it off. I can't believe he gave it away."

"But that's the point," Mary Louise said. "Raymond knew how important the bracelet was to Jack. To him, it was a symbol that Jack really was his friend."

"Mary Louise, where do you think Raymond is?" Josh asked gently.

She rubbed her hands together as if she were cold. "I think he ran away from home because Jack did something to him. I believe he broke Raymond's heart. With that and everything going on at home . . . Well, I think it just got to be too much for him."

"In all these years have you ever heard from him?"

She sighed again. "No. Not once. Honestly? I truly believe he would have contacted us at some point . . . if he could." She wiped away a tear than ran down the side of her face. "I'm convinced my brother is dead."

"That's not true."

Kaely turned her head to see a woman who'd stepped into

the living room from the hallway. She wore a nightgown and a robe. Her hair was mussed, her eyes wild.

"That's not true," she said again. "I saw him. Raymond is back. I saw him. He came to see me yesterday while you were gone." The woman's gaze latched on to Kaely and Josh. "You've got to believe me. My son is alive, and he's come home."

FORTY-FOUR

After leaving the Bergers' house, Josh suggested he and Kaely get coffee and discuss their visit. He mentioned a coffee shop that was on the way back to the motel.

Kaely followed him to a cute little café that served desserts and coffee. She was still full from lunch, so she passed on the delicious-looking baked goods and ordered a caramel latte.

"So, what do you think?" Kaely asked once they were seated and had their coffee.

Josh took a bite of the cheese Danish he'd ordered, then he wiped his mouth and frowned at Kaely. "I'm not convinced that that Raymond died in that fire," he said, "or that Jack gave him the bracelet"

"What about his mother's claim that she saw Raymond? That he came by to see her?"

Josh's eyebrows knit together. "She has dementia, Kaely. Alzheimer's."

"According to Mary Louise."

This time his eyebrows shot up. "You don't believe her?"

Kaely scooted her chair closer to the table. "I don't know. Maybe Jack did give Raymond that bracelet. But Mary Louise said she thinks Jack did something to hurt her brother. Could Jack have taken it back? It's possible that's what pushed Raymond over the edge and made him leave town."

Josh shook his head. "Look, if we could prove Raymond was wearing it at the time of the fire, then I might accept the possibility that Jack Lucas survived that night. But like you, I worry that we're going down a slippery slope with conspiracy theories and scenarios that belong in a mystery novel."

"There's the video," Kaely said slowly.

"You know that video means next to nothing. It's a distraction. We've all agreed it's not clear enough to use as evidence. It could be anyone. It could be me."

Kaely had no plan to tell him she'd actually considered that possibility.

"We have the note, but there aren't any fingerprints. Nothing to tie us to a suspect."

"So what do you think really happened eighteen years ago, Josh?" Kaely asked.

He exhaled slowly. "I think Jack Lucas and his family died that night. As far as the bracelet, I'd rather believe Jack took it back than think he killed his family and an innocent kid, and then disappeared for all these years."

"You believe Raymond started a new life somewhere else?"

"Maybe, but I think the odds are higher that he's dead." Josh took another bite of his Danish and frowned at her. "You and Tuck visited Marvin Roberson earlier today?"

Kaely nodded.

"Did you find out anything helpful?"

"Not sure, but he's certainly an interesting man."

Josh nodded. "He was a great medical examiner. His department helped us close quite a few cases over the years. Of course, I'm sure our numbers aren't anything like what you see in St. Louis. But here . . . Well, we all know one another, so each case is important."

"I can understand that," Kaely said. She hesitated a moment. "What can you tell me about Marvin? He seems so alone."

"He is alone. His wife died a few years back. He was close with his son until Brad became a teenager. Brad had trouble at school. You know, bullying, that kind of thing. Most of it was because of Marvin's job. Kids made fun of him because his father worked with dead people."

"Didn't the school intervene?"

"Marvin met with the principal several times but couldn't get help for Brad. Seems some adults also had a negative view of what he did for a living."

"That's ridiculous. Without good MEs, law enforcement couldn't possibly get convictions in a lot of important criminal cases."

"I know that and you know that," Josh said, "but some people aren't that smart. Especially kids." He gazed out the window at the snow-covered ground. "Marvin blamed the town for causing Brad to leave. Of course, that's not the complete truth. If Marvin's relationship with Brad had been better, they might have been able to overcome the problems at school."

"That's really sad. Maybe Brad will come back someday and fix things with his dad."

Josh shook his head. "Unfortunately, he won't. He's dead."

Kaely stared at him in surprise. "Marvin didn't mention that."

"He doesn't talk about it, and I'd appreciate it if you'd keep it to yourself. It happened about six months ago. He was found in a cheap motel in Kansas. He'd shot himself."

"Oh no."

"Yeah. Marvin took it really badly. He still had hope, you know? He loved that kid."

Kaely felt tremendous sympathy for the retired medical examiner. "Why is Marvin in a wheelchair?"

"He suffered an injury not long before he retired. He was

called out on a case during the winter." Josh grunted. "Right around this time of year. Slipped and fell on the ice. The doctor hoped he'd recover, but he didn't. The city granted him his entire pension, even though he was a few years away from receiving it. Since the ice was on a city street, they also paid him a nice settlement." Josh shook his head. "He may be okay financially, but it certainly doesn't make up for his disability. "

"He can't walk at all?"

"No, not really. He told me once he can at least take care of his personal business—you know, bathroom, shower, dressing. Things like that. Not sure how much mobility that takes, but his bathroom has been remodeled to make it handicap accessible, and he has a cleaning lady who comes in once a week." He frowned at her. "Can I ask why you're interested?"

Kaely shrugged. "Just curious. It's my personality. I'm nosy."

Josh chuckled. "Don't I know it." His eyes met hers. "Look, Kaely. I'm glad you're here. And I appreciate what you're trying to do. But I think you need to admit that you haven't made any progress in finding our arsonist."

"Don't give up on me, Josh," Kaely said. "I feel like we're close."

"I hope so," Josh said, "but we're running out of time. I heard the new sheriff could be ready to take office sooner than expected, and he may not want to work with you. If that's the case, we'll all have to walk away and let the dead rest in peace."

When Kaely got back to the motel, she didn't see Jason's car in the parking lot. She was rather relieved. She needed to think about her visit to the Bergers' and her discussion with Josh. He was right. They still didn't have any evidence. Just possibilities.

She needed to find this UNSUB sooner rather than later. She was frustrated. Why couldn't she get a solid lead? What was it she wasn't seeing?

She wondered if she should add Marvin to her list of suspects. Although it didn't seem likely, she had to consider him. Did he believe Darkwater was responsible for his son's death? But there was no way a man who was paralyzed could have set these fires. One thing that stuck in Kaely's mind was that his legs looked strong. She'd expected his limbs to be atrophied after all this time, but they weren't.

Ever since her visit with Josh, something else had been bothering her. Troubling her mind. She felt like she'd missed something. Something really important. She kept going over things Marvin and Mary Louise had said, but she couldn't figure out what it was. It was driving her crazy.

When she got back to her new motel room, she grabbed her tote bag and took out her files. Then she sat down at the table and began looking through them again. She felt like the truth was somewhere in front of her, and it was trying to get her attention. Georgie's voice echoed in her head.

"Perhaps what you're missing is right in front of you. You've got to eliminate the impossible. Once you do that . . ."

But what, exactly, was impossible? The lines between the impossible and the improbable were getting more and more blurred.

FORTY-FIVE

It was almost six o'clock before Kaely made it back to the hospital to see Noah. He had great insight, and she could really use that right now.

She'd called Jason, who was getting ready to leave the hospital, and told him to stay put since she was coming down.

When she got there, she went to Noah's room first. He was looking great. More like his old self.

"I can't wait to get out of here," he grumbled. "I feel like life is passing me by."

Kaely laughed. "It's been two days, Noah. I don't think you need to worry too much about life as a whole."

"Well, maybe not, but I don't like you being out there without me. I know you're taking precautions, but I still worry."

Kaely sighed, trying to be patient with him. "Someone's with me almost every minute of the day. I even called the motel manager and asked him to keep an eye out for anyone hanging around the complex who doesn't belong. He assured me he'd call if he had any concerns. Everything's fine. Really."

"I guess there's not much I can do about it from here."

At that moment, Jason walked into the room and greeted them.

"Kaely says you're keeping an eye on her?" Noah said as soon as he saw Jason.

Jason threw his hands up in the air. "No, 'hello'? No, 'I'm so glad you came to see me'?"

"Funny." Noah glared at him. "I'm serious about you staying close to your sister."

Jason walked over and gave Kaely a hug, then he looked over at Noah and sighed loudly. "I'm doing my very best. Just remember I also have to be here for my mother. And I like to stop by once in a while just to make sure you're still breathing."

"I appreciate that."

"You're welcome."

"If you two are finished, can I ask how Mom's doing?" Kaely asked her brother.

Jason smiled. "She's doing better, Kaely. Her numbers are improving." He swiped at his eyes, which were moist. "The doctor said he thinks the trial treatment is working. He said it's too early to declare it a success, but he likes what he's seeing, even with the minor setback."

Kaely fought back tears. "Oh, Jason. That's wonderful. I'm so happy."

"And Mom's insurance company found a nice condo where she can stay while they rebuild the house. They're also giving her money for new furniture and whatever else she might need. She can move in whenever she's ready. She's feeling pretty good about it. You plan to see her before you leave, right?"

"After our visit earlier? Are you sure she wants to see me?"

"Yeah, I'm absolutely certain. She's asked about you several times. I told her you were coming back to the hospital today."

Kaely wanted to see her mother, but she feared another confrontation.

As if he knew what she was thinking, Jason took her arm. "You need to let anything hurtful she says roll off your back," he said gently. "She's been fighting for her life. She lost her home and her belongings. We're the only family she has. Sometimes people going through a rough time take out their frustration on those they love the most. Usually, they're the only ones still hanging around. It doesn't mean anything. She feels awful when it happens, and that makes her feel worse physically."

Kaely knew he was right, but this wasn't a temporary thing. Marcie had treated her this way for years. Still, she had no choice, especially after what God had shown her earlier. She had to ignore Marcie's harsh comments. Even if it was hard. "I'll try, Jason. I really will."

She turned her attention back to Noah. "Any news on when you get out of here?"

"The doc's gonna take out this chest tube sometime tomorrow. He thinks my lung is healing nicely. Then he'll make a decision."

"Good. You need to relax. Take this time to catch up on your sleep. Read. Watch TV."

"I'm not used to doing nothing."

Kaely smiled. "You don't have a choice, you know."

Noah pointed at a stack of books on the stand next to the bed. "One of the nurses dropped those off. Some James Patterson. Grisham. I would probably enjoy them."

"I think you would too," Kaely said. "Give them a try, okay?"

Although he didn't look happy about it, Noah nodded. "Okay." He frowned at Kaely. "When are you bringing me a cheeseburger?"

"Take it slow. Your body's been through a lot."

"So has my stomach," he growled. "And it wants cheeseburgers."

"I think we need to talk to your doctor first and see if he has any instructions about food."

"When you get out," Jason said, "we'll go to Bucky's. Best burgers in Nebraska, am I right?"

"I've been dreaming about those cheeseburgers," Noah said with a sigh.

Kaely's phone buzzed, and she took it out of her pocket. She didn't recognize the number. She walked a few feet away from Noah and Jason and answered. She was surprised to find it was Sam Lucas.

"How's Noah doing?" Sam asked once she answered.

"Great," she said. "Except for an incessant craving for cheeseburgers."

Sam laughed. "I was thinking you might need a break from all your sleuthing." She could hear a note of nervousness in his voice.

"Uh, maybe. Not sure I have much time for a break."

"Can you find a couple of hours tonight?"

"For what?" Kaely asked, thinking it had something to do with the investigation. She'd just let the words out of her mouth when she realized what he was suggesting. She felt herself flush. "I mean, did you have something in mind?"

"Dinner? With me?"

Kaely turned her back to Noah and Jason so they couldn't see her smile. "I think I could work that out. What time?"

"How about I pick you up at your motel at eight?"

"Sounds good. I'll see you then."

"Great. Bye."

The relief in his voice was evident. It tickled her to know that asking her to dinner made him nervous. Sam was still on her suspect list, but her gut told her he wasn't their UNSUB. Besides, maybe she could pick his brain about Jack. He might be more willing to talk if they were relaxed, having dinner. Be less defensive. She didn't want to use his request for a date as a chance to work the case, but she could really use his help.

When she walked back over to Noah's bed, he was complaining to Jason about the hospital food again.

Noah lowered his voice. "All I'm asking for is a double cheeseburger and fries. I'll even agree to a single burger, if it helps. You could just sneak it in."

"Don't you like our food, Mr. Hunter?" A rather severe-looking nurse walked into the room. She stared at Kaely and Jason over her bifocals. "The doctor is coming by to check on your friend. I'll need you both to wait outside."

"I'm going to see Mom anyway," Jason said. "Are you coming, Kaely?"

She nodded, but she tensed at the thought of seeing Marcie again. Kaely took Noah's hand. "I'll be back in the morning. Don't cause your nurses any more trouble, you hear me?"

"Now that *would* be a miracle," the nurse said. Clearly Noah's charm was lost on her. Kaely found it funny.

He made a face at the nurse, who chuckled as she left the room. "Who called?" he asked Kaely.

"It was nothing important."

Noah's eyes narrowed. "Are you sure?"

"I'm certain." She let go of his hand. "You rest, mind the doctor, and eat all the watery gelatin they serve you."

Kaely heard Jason laugh from behind them. She said goodbye and followed Jason out the door. As they headed upstairs, Kaely felt a little guilty about not telling Noah that she was going out with Sam tonight. She felt it would upset him, and she didn't want to think of him lying in bed worrying the whole time she was having dinner.

He smiles as he assembles everything he'll need for his final act. It feels so good to make fools of the authorities. The police, the fire department, and those idiots from out of town. No one is close to finding him. No one knows who he is. He's got them right where he wants them. His next move will leave them breathless—literally, in at least one case. He laughs at his cleverness.

The beast is getting ready to rise one more time. The last fire. The most important one of all.

FORTY-SIX

Kaely's visit with her mother was tense but polite. She was relieved when the nurse brought Marcie's supper in and used that as an excuse to leave.

When she got back to the motel, she immediately went to her closet to see what she had to wear. She looked through the new clothes she'd picked up at the department store. Eventually, she chose the black slacks that had been in her Go Bag and a green sweater with gold threads she'd bought. With her black jacket, she felt she'd fit in anywhere. She carefully checked the pants and jacket. No signs of being rolled up tightly to fit into her bag.

She put on some makeup and brushed her hair. Once she was ready, she made a cup of coffee in the one-cup coffee dispenser in the room. She heard Jason moving around next door. She'd told him about her date with Sam and promised to check in at least once during dinner.

"You're still not seeing it," a voice said.

Kaely jumped. She turned to see Georgie sitting on the bed. "You frightened me."

Georgie looked at her with raised eyebrows. "How could I frighten you? I am you."

"Yeah, yeah." Kaely sat down at the small table near the window. She pulled the heavy curtain back. It was still snowing. Even though she was in a motel room, sitting here with a cup of coffee while it snowed outside felt really cozy. "What do you want?"

"I said you're still not seeing it."

"I know that. Trust me, I'm as frustrated as you are." Kaely chuckled at her joke. "There's something I saw. I can't figure out what it was, but it's important. And I still can't figure out who our UNSUB is. It's like the answer is close, but a piece of the puzzle is missing."

"It will all come to you," Georgie said. "Just relax. You're so tense. It's making it harder for you."

"I need facts," Kaely said. "Hard evidence. Without it, all I have are a lot of these stupid puzzle pieces that don't seem to fit together."

"But they do." Georgie's gaze was piercing. "It's time to try it again."

Kaely looked at the empty chair across from her. "I . . . can't do it. Last time . . ."

"It will be okay. Try it again. Trust me."

Kaely shook her head. "You want me to trust myself?"

"That's exactly it. You have to remember that you're in control." She frowned. "Use your authority. You know where that comes from."

Kaely got up from her chair. She just couldn't use the table this time. She grabbed her files and spread everything out in front of her. Then she grabbed a chair and pulled it up near the bed. She sat down on the edge of the bed with the chair in front of her. She took a deep breath and began.

"You're a white male in your twenties or thirties. You're organized and you know what you're doing. You're exacting some kind of revenge. But revenge for what? You go after families. What is it about families that you hate? Is it because you didn't have one?" As she continued to shift through the information on the table, Raymond's school picture appeared in front of her. He'd had a terrible childhood, but why destroy a family that cared about him? It didn't make sense.

"Keep trying. Don't give up," Georgie whispered.

Kaely squared her shoulders and started again. As she stared at the information next to her on the bed, a figure began to form in the chair in front of her. Although she wasn't completely surprised, she was still unsure. Was this really the person she was looking for?

He looked like Sam but instead of kindness in his eyes, malevolence poured out in waves. Kaely felt sick.

She took a deep breath. "Hello, Jack," she said quietly.

"Hello," he said, his voice as smooth as silk.

Kaely leaned toward him. "It all fits," she said. "Except . . ." She struggled to find the reason why she kept going back and forth about him. This had never happened before.

"Except you can't figure out why. What is so important that it would bring me back here? Why am I so angry?" His malicious eyes bore into hers. "When you figure that out, you'll understand everything."

As she stared at him, she suddenly realized what she'd forgotten. She should have seen it before. A chill ran through her. "Blue," she said. "They were blue."

As Jack disappeared, Kaely picked up the phone and made a call.

By the time Sam arrived to pick her up, Kaely was ready. She looked at herself one more time in the mirror. The green sweater was a good choice. She pulled on her black coat. Then she checked her sweater and jacket, making sure everything was in place. She looked out the window as Sam pulled into the parking lot. She stepped outside the room and started toward Sam's car. Before she got far, he got out and walked slowly toward her. Although the motel had put ice melt on the parking lot, there were still slick spots.

"I'll be okay," she said as he approached. At that very moment, she felt her feet go out from under her. Sam reached out and grabbed her before she fell. She was already a little anxious about being around him, but suddenly she found herself in his arms.

"I don't think you're supposed to say you'll be okay out loud," he said with a grin. "It's just asking for trouble."

Kaely laughed nervously. He hooked his arm through hers and helped her to his car. At one point Sam slipped, and she reached out, steadying him. When they got to the car, he opened her door. When she was safely inside, he went around to the driver's side.

"Sorry about the weather. It wasn't supposed to snow tonight. The roads are pretty good though."

"It's not a problem," Kaely said. "A little snow won't hurt us."

"A little? It seems to be snowing every day," he said as he started the car. "But it is beautiful, isn't it? I've always loved the snow. Reminds me of times with my family. When it snowed Mom would make popcorn and hot chocolate." He smiled. "She taught me her hot chocolate recipe. If you're interested, after dinner we could go to my place. I'll make it for you."

Kaely looked at him in surprise, and Sam's eyes widened. "I . . . I . . . didn't mean that as some kind of come-on," he said, looking embarrassed. "I was just talking about hot chocolate."

Kaely smiled. "I believe you, Sam. Please don't worry about it."

He put the car in gear and headed toward the street. "Thank you. Boy, I've started out really great here, haven't I?"

"You're fine. Hey, you saved my life. You don't have to worry about offending me."

He turned to look at her, his forehead wrinkled. "You don't need anyone to save you. You're the most capable person I've ever met."

"Thank you. I appreciate that. My partner and my brother seem to think I can't make it through the day without their help."

"I think I'd feel the same way if I had a sister."

"Maybe," Kaely said. "But it can get annoying."

"I imagine it could." Sam turned to look at her. "I thought we'd go to the Twisted Tree Tavern. It's a lovely old house on the edge of town that's been turned into a restaurant. They have the best steaks in this part of the country. Does that sound okay? Or we could go somewhere else if you'd rather."

She smiled at him. "It sounds perfect. To be honest, I haven't had a good steak in a long time."

"Great. They have a lot of other incredible dishes too. I think you'll find something you'll like."

"I'm sure I will."

A few minutes later, they pulled into a circle driveway in front of a large Victorian house. It was painted a deep red and had white trim and a wraparound porch. In the snow, the house was breathtaking. It was the kind of home Kaely had always wanted for herself someday. There was a large sign outside painted with the name *Twisted Tree Tavern*. Sam parked the car in the adjoining lot. He got out of the car and opened Kaely's door. Then he took her arm and led her up the stairs to the entrance of the restaurant. The snow swirled around them, and the tiny tea lights outlining the huge front porch created a romantic atmosphere that made Kaely wish she could truly enjoy it.

When they got inside, a hostess showed them to a table. The lights were lowered and candles dotted the white linen tablecloths. The dining room was absolutely gorgeous. After taking their drink orders, the hostess left.

"Oh, Sam," Kaely said. "This place is really special. I'm glad I got to see it while I'm in town."

His eyebrows shot up. "You're not ready to go yet, are you?"

"Not until we find our arsonist and the police make an arrest."

The waitress approached them to take their orders. Sam recommended the dry-aged prime rib with cognac pepper cream sauce. Kaely ordered that with a side of roasted asparagus and a wedge salad with blue cheese.

"Two of the same," Sam said with a smile at the young waitress, who didn't seem to want to leave the table. Kaely was afraid she was going to pull a muscle trying to lean closer to Sam. He didn't even seem to notice.

"So, how's Noah doing?" he asked when she finally walked away.

"Better. He should be out in a couple of days."

"He'll be going back to St. Louis?"

"At some point. Frankly, I think Noah got injured just so I would do the driving."

Sam laughed. "I'm kind of surprised you drove all the way here. Why not fly?"

"I hate flying. I have ever since I was a kid. Sometimes I don't have a choice, but this time I was able to take my car since I wasn't originally on assignment."

Sam's eyebrows shot up again. "I'm shocked. I can't see you being afraid of anything."

"You're wrong. I'm human. Everyone has phobias."

He nodded slowly and gave her an incredible smile. She felt her heart thud in her chest. She took a steadying breath in an effort to calm herself.

"You might be surprised by this, but I hated fire for years after I lost my family. One more reason I wanted to join the fire department. I was tired of being afraid. I was determined to overcome my fear."

"That's impressive, Sam. It seems to have worked."

He shrugged. "I still feel some panic when we get called out, but I can deal with it now." He cleared his throat. "There's only one other thing that scares me. Well, more like haunts me, I guess."

"What's that?"

Sam looked down at the table. "You might think this is nuts, but I've held on to what's left of our old house all these years. I just couldn't get rid of it, you know? I realize people think I'm crazy for keeping it this long, but I . . . I just couldn't . . . Well, there's a developer who wants the land in that area. Our property is the only thing he needs to acquire so he can build some kind of shopping mall. It would be a good deal for Darkwater. Lots of people from other small towns would come here to shop. He offered me a great deal of money. I said yes." Tears sprang to his eyes. "I'm sorry," he said, dabbing them with his linen napkin. "You'd think after all these years . . ."

"Don't be ridiculous. You suffered a major loss. I can't even imagine what it was like for you."

"It was terrible. If it hadn't been for Josh and Tuck, I don't know what I would have done."

"I'm glad they were there for you."

"Me too." He reached over and took her hand. "I hope we'll be friends too. I really like you, Kaely. You're not like any other woman I've ever met."

Kaely smiled as he held her hand. Getting through tonight was going to be tougher than she'd thought.

FORTY-SEVEN

Kaely and Sam had a pleasant, easy conversation as they ate. Sam told her stories about his life in Darkwater when he was a kid. He even talked about his parents.

"Dad was a great guy. He headed the fire department like it was a paid position. His men respected him." He chuckled. "And yes, back then all firefighters were men. I think there were female firefighters in other places but not in Darkwater. We seem to run about ten years behind the rest of the country. In the nineties we still thought Olivia Newton-John was cool. Hadn't heard about Michael Jackson's comeback." He lowered his voice and looked around. "To be honest, I still like Olivia. Have several of her CDs. Don't tell anyone."

"I'll keep your secret if you don't tell anyone I have the soundtrack to *Grease* and play it at home whenever I clean. Gets me going."

"I have that CD too," he said, grinning. "Now we have to keep each other's secrets. We could destroy our chances of meaningful social lives with this kind of information."

Kaely laughed as she finished the last bite of her steak. It was delicious. She told Sam how much she'd enjoyed it.

"Good," he said with a wide smile. "Let's share one more treat that will keep you from having to come to my house. Hopefully, it will make up for my faux pas." He waved the waitress to the table. "Two of your Aztec hot chocolates, please."

She nodded and scurried away.

"Trust me, you'll love it. It's made with actual dark chocolate chunks, milk, cinnamon, and just a touch of cayenne. I know that sounds odd, but it's out of this world."

"I'll trust you. Hot chocolate sounds great right now."

Sam frowned and looked down at the table.

"Is something wrong?" Kaely asked.

"No. I just . . . Well, I'd like to ask you a question. A favor, really."

Kaely downed the last of her coffee and put the cup down. "Sure. What can I do for you?"

"I rarely go by the old house. It's out on the edge of town, and I never go that way. No one lives out there anymore. All the neighboring houses were sold and torn down. I haven't actually gotten out and looked around for years. Too many bad memories. But we're so close, so maybe before I turn it over . . ."

"You want to see it again?"

He nodded.

"Do you want me to go with you, Sam?"

His blue eyes peered into hers. "Is that asking too much?"

"Of course not. I'd be honored." She studied him closely. "Are you sure it won't be too emotional? Maybe you should just let them tear it down. Stay away."

"You might be right, but I guess I need some closure, you know? I just can't let it go without walking through it one more time. We were happy there once."

The waitress came up to the table with two large mugs topped with whipped cream. Kaely gasped softly. "Oh my. How am I going to finish that?"

"Trust me, you will. It's easier than you think."

She thanked the waitress, who didn't even seem to know Kaely was sitting at the table. It wasn't until Sam offered the same word of thanks that she smiled and said, "You're welcome. Enjoy your Aztec."

Once she left, Kaely picked up the cup and took a sip. It was incredible. She'd been sure cayenne and chocolate would be an awful combination, but it turned out she was wrong. It was like they were made for each other. She'd just taken a second sip when Sam chuckled. She realized her upper lip was white with whipped cream. Embarrassed, she wiped her mouth and smiled at him.

"You have no business laughing at me," she said, grinning.

He touched his upper lip with his fingertip and pulled back whipped cream. They both laughed.

"Do you like it?" he asked.

"I love it. My mother made great hot chocolate, but she wasn't this inventive."

"My mom stuck to regular hot chocolate, but it was delicious. The secret is to use real sugar, cocoa powder, milk, and a touch of vanilla. And the whipped cream should be the real thing."

At that moment, Kaely's phone rang. She picked up her purse and pulled out her phone. It was Noah. She looked up at Sam. "I need to take this. Will you excuse me a moment?"

Sam waved his hand at her. "Of course."

In an effort to not disturb the other patrons, Kaely got up and went out the front door of the restaurant. She stood on the freezing patio, wishing she'd grabbed her coat, and answered the phone.

"Just wanted to know what you're doing tonight," he said in a bored tone. "The TV in my room only gets one channel, so I'm watching *Big Brother*. I have an overwhelming urge to find my gun and blow the TV set out of the wall. Of course, the rubbery chicken and cold mashed potatoes I had for dinner helped my mood immensely."

"Oh, you poor baby," Kaely cooed. "No one has it worse than you do."

"You might laugh now, but when I get out of here I'm eating whatever I want, whenever I want."

"We'll see what the doctor says."

"Don't fight me, woman. My mind's made up." He paused for a moment. "Your voice is shaking. You sound cold."

"Probably because I am. I'm standing outside."

There was a brief silence from the other end of the phone. "You may not realize this," Noah said, "but it's winter here. Staying inside is much better."

"Ha ha. I decided to grab some supper. I came outside to take your goofy call."

"Goofy call? Is that what you think of my scintillating conversation?"

"I don't know," Kaely teased. "When will I hear that?"

"You're incredibly humorous, you know?"

"Yes, I do. Look, why don't you go back to your TV program? I'm going inside."

"You really do hate me, don't you?" Noah said with a sigh. "Is Jason with you?"

Kaely hesitated. She wasn't going to tell him she was with Sam, but she didn't want to lie to him.

"No, but I'm staying in touch."

"I don't like you being out alone, Kaely," he said.

"I'm actually finishing up. I'll be back at the motel soon. Would you feel better if I call you when I get to my room?"

"I would."

"Okay. Done. Now let me get back inside. I'm freezing."

"You left your coat in the restaurant, didn't you?" Noah said.

"You're starting to bug me."

"Because I'm starting to know you. You don't like that."

"That goes two ways, my friend. I'll talk to you in a little while." She hung up. Noah wouldn't like it when he found out she hadn't told him about her date with Sam, but for now, it was something she couldn't share with him.

She slid her phone into her pocket, then she gazed out at the parking lot for a moment before going back inside. It was still snowing. She hoped they wouldn't have any problems getting to Sam's old house.

Once she was back at the table, she apologized for stepping away. "Noah's not very happy with his accommodations. He's ready to get out."

"I hear that. Sounds kinda good at first: bed, TV, and food served to you. But then a nurse walks in with a needle the size of a soda straw."

Kaely laughed and picked up her hot chocolate. The whipped cream had melted while she was gone, but that only made the drink creamier. She stirred it a few times and drank it down.

"We're not in that much of a hurry," Sam said with a grin. "You could have taken your time."

"I know," Kaely said, "but it was so good I didn't want it to get cold." She sighed. "The entire dinner was wonderful, Sam. Thank you."

"You're very welcome. Are you ready to go?"

Kaely looked around. "Don't we need to pay our bill?"

"I've already taken care of it."

"I didn't expect you to pay for everything," Kaely said, not sure she should let him pick up the entire tab.

"Look, I asked you to dinner. Besides, I wanted to thank you for everything you've been doing. Trying to stop our arsonist, I mean. Darkwater is a great town. It doesn't deserve to be burned down."

"You're right." Kaely took a deep breath. "Before we go, could I ask you a few questions?"

Sam's expression darkened. "About Jack?"

She nodded.

"Why don't we talk in the car, if you're ready to go? I'm uncomfortable speaking about him in public."

Kaely nodded. "I understand. Let's go."

Sam got up, came around, and took Kaely's coat from the empty chair between them. He held it out so she could slip it on. "We won't be outside at my house for long. You should be warm enough with a coat and a sweater," he said.

Kaely nodded. "Believe me, I've learned my lesson. I'm bundling."

"Smart."

He took her arm, and they headed to the door. The women in the restaurant all turned to look at Sam as they walked out. Kaely tightened her grip on his arm, praying that tonight would turn out the way she hoped.

FORTY-EIGHT

By the time they were in the car, Kaely felt more relaxed. In fact, she was calmer than she thought she would be tonight.

"How far is your house from here?" she asked.

"About six miles. Darkwater isn't that big. It doesn't take long to get anywhere."

"I've noticed that." Kaely looked out the window next to her. "You know, it's not a bad little town. If it weren't for the fires, I think I'd find it rather charming."

"It is," Sam said. "There are a lot of good things about this place. Good place to raise a family."

"Why haven't you ever married, Sam?" Kaely asked. She surprised herself by asking that question. Although she'd wondered why he was still single, it didn't really matter now. But for some reason, the question just slipped out.

"I don't know," he said, drawing out his response. "I think when you have a loss, you tend to shelter yourself from future pain. It's . . . scary. You don't want to hurt like that again. I've dated, of course, but when it gets too serious, I pull out. I'll take the step someday, I guess. When I'm ready."

Kaely searched his face and saw sincerity there. Surprising.

"I'm sorry," he said. "I didn't mean to spill my guts like that. I hope it didn't make you uncomfortable."

She shook her head. "No, I was just thinking about how similar we are."

"I'm sorry, Kaely. I didn't know you'd suffered a loss."

"More a loss of trust," she answered. "Fortunately, I still have a chance to get my family back. I'm sorry you've lost so much. I really am."

"Thank you," he said. "I appreciate that."

Kaely turned away again and looked out the window. The silvery-white snowflakes drifted lazily from the sky. They seemed so free. So peaceful. But that was stupid. Soon they would melt and be gone. Their existence was so short. Still, she couldn't help but envy them a little. Right now, she wished she could drift with them.

A wave of dizziness washed over her. "Was there alcohol in that hot chocolate?" she asked. Her tongue felt a little too large for her mouth.

"Yeah, some," he said. "I thought I mentioned that."

"No. I don't drink."

"Oh, Kaely. I apologize."

"No reason you should," she said. "I'm sure I'll be okay in a little bit."

Sam didn't say anything as he took a turn off the main road. The lights that had lined their path faded into the background. At one point, the car fishtailed, but Sam brought it under control.

A few minutes later, he pulled into a long driveway. At the end was the shell of a large house. "319 Harbor Lane," Sam said. "All that's left of it, anyway." He sighed. "Time to end this." He got out of the car, came around, and pulled Kaely out. The only light they had was from his car headlights.

"Stop," she said, but he dragged her through the snow until they stood in front of the forlorn structure. "Please don't do this." Her words came out slowly, and she found it difficult to speak.

"Seriously, Kaely, I only put four sleeping pills in your cocoa. You have a really low tolerance."

"I don't take prescription medicine. My mom . . ." She realized she didn't need to explain anything to him. She pulled up all the strength she could muster and wrestled out of his grasp. She stumbled back a few feet and turned to face him. The headlights illuminated him from behind, hiding his face, but that was okay. He'd been hiding his face for a long time.

"So we meet officially, Jack," she said, taking a deep breath of fresh icy air. It helped clear her mind a little.

He was quiet for several seconds. "How did you know?" he asked finally.

"It had to be you. I needed to suspend my disbelief to figure it out. When you eliminate the impossible, whatever remains, no matter how improbable, must be the truth."

"Sherlock Holmes? I don't get it."

"It means I had to eliminate everyone who couldn't be the arsonist." She fought the light-headedness that battled her determination to see this through. "It had to be someone who knew who I was. Marvin Roberson didn't meet me until after my mother's house was set on fire. It couldn't be Josh. Losing the election didn't bother him at all. He didn't want to continue being sheriff. From everything I've learned about Sam, he wasn't the type of person to hurt anyone. That left one person. The improbable one."

"You think you're pretty smart," Jack said, his smile more of a sneer.

"What happened to your scar?"

Jack leaned down and picked up some snow, then he rubbed it on his right cheek. The scar became visible. It had been covered up with makeup.

"All conjecture. What was it that finally convinced you it was me? What actual evidence could you possibly uncover?"

"I suspected it for a while. But then I saw you at Bucky's today. You had blue eyes. Aaron Pollard had brown eyes when I met him. You forgot to put your contacts in."

Jack laughed out loud. "I wasn't planning to run into you," he said, overemphasizing the southern drawl he'd used when he was Aaron. "But I didn't think you'd notice. I underestimated you."

"I assume the real Aaron Pollard is dead."

"As a doornail. I met him in a bar when I came into town. He told me about staying at his mother's. And that he'd never been here before. It was the perfect place for me to hide. I followed him home . . . and the rest, as they say, is history. Good ol' Aaron is in the basement."

Kaely heard a sound from behind them. She stepped to the right of Jack and saw someone on the ground behind them, tied to a large piece of rebar coming out of the ground. "Sam?" she called out. "Are you okay?" She almost cried with relief when she heard his voice.

"I'm all right, Kaely," he said. "But I think he plans to kill us."

"Ding, ding, ding, brother! You win the prize!"

"Why did you come back to Darkwater?" Kaely mumbled, hoping he could understand her. "Why set those fires? Why do you have to kill us?"

Jack pulled a gun from underneath his coat and pointed it at her. "You're the profiler. You tell me."

Kaely gathered all the strength she could find to say, "You hated your family. You wanted them all dead, including your brother. You believed your parents loved him more than you.

You killed poor Raymond Berger, hoping everyone would think he was you. That's why you gave him your bracelet. Your brother escaped, so you're back to finish what you started."

Jack sighed dramatically. "You're partially right, you know. I got tired of my parents treating Sam like the good son. I was always the bad seed. They sent me away once, did you know that? To a mental hospital. They hoped the doctors would straighten me out. Didn't work, obviously. Just made me angry. I came home and pretended to be *fixed*. That's why they didn't see it coming." He grinned as if remembering something funny. "I asked nerdy Raymond Berger to stay the night. That dumb kid would have done anything for me. It was embarrassing, really. I hated giving him my bracelet. That was the hardest part of my whole plan."

Kaely felt a chill run through her that had nothing to do with the cold. Jack killed his parents and an innocent boy but the only regret he had was losing a bracelet?

"How . . . how did you do it?" Kaely needed to get Jack to admit to everything, but a wave of fatigue crashed over her entire body. It took everything she had to get the words out. All she wanted was to sink down into the soft snow and sleep.

He grinned at her, the headlights from the car highlighting only half his face. The half with the scar. He looked frightening, like Heath Ledger as the Joker in *The Dark Knight*. Gone was the handsome Sam Lucas. In his place stood madness. Unrestrained lunacy.

Jack sighed, as if tiring of her questions. His eyes burned into hers. "I offered to make hot chocolate for everyone that night. I put my mother's sleeping pills into the chocolate, just like I did to you tonight. After the five started, I left town." He sighed. "We made one mistake. We didn't realize they could identify bodies with dental records. Thankfully, we lucked out. Raymond was cremated before anyone knew the truth. We got away scot-free. It's easy to hide when you're dead. No one looked for me."

"You said *we*. I don't understand."

He walked closer, until he was inches away from her face. "The great Kaely Quinn who thought she had it all figured out. You made a mistake, profiler. I didn't set the fire."

As Kaely stared into his eyes, she believed him. "Who . . ." She gasped, breathing in more cold air. It reenergized her a little. She turned around and looked at Sam. "It . . . it was you?"

Sam broke into sobs. "My parents planned to send Jack back to the hospital. He said he'd kill himself if they did that. I didn't know what to do. Jack came up with the plan. I . . . I don't know what made me go through with it. Jack had a way of manipulating me back then. He said that after our parents were gone we'd inherit everything, including the insurance money from the fire. We were only months away from turning eighteen. I didn't do it for the money, I really didn't. I did it because I wanted my brother to live, and I was angry that Mom and Dad were going to send him away again. I shouldn't have gone along with it. I've regretted it every day of my life."

"You were so smitten by the great Sam Lucas, you couldn't see the truth, could you?" Jack said with a sneer. "You made a major mistake and here we are. I won and you lost. Big-time."

Kaely fought to ignore Jack's accusation. There was more truth there than she wanted to admit. "The s-s-space . . ." It took all the strength Kaely had to get out the questions she had to ask him.

"That's how I started the fire," Sam said through his tears. "We used space heaters in the winter because my mother turned down the heat every night. She thought it saved money. So I tipped one of them over. I set it up and went to my friend's place. It took a while for the fire to engulf the house. Everyone thought I was gone when the fire started."

"I stayed and watched for a while," Jack said. "They all slept through it, you know. The smoke killed them before the fire consumed everything. Sam didn't want them to suffer. He was always such a thoughtful person, you know. Caring about people and animals." He laughed, but it wasn't joyous. It was sick. Kaely swallowed the sour bile that rose up from her stomach.

"But . . . but why come back? Why start these fires now?" Kaely choked out. She stepped back a few feet from Jack, not wanting to be so close to him.

Jack swore loudly. "Questions, questions, questions. You're a real pain. It will be a relief to shut you up for good." He sighed. "It's a boring story, really. Bar fight. Killed a guy. Went to prison. Under another name, of course. I contacted my brother. Asked for help. Told him I expected to get my share of the money. He never answered. Never tried to contact me. I knew he had no plans to give me my half. So I had a friend in prison write him a letter a few months ago. Told him I was dead. Gave me time to plan my revenge. Sam thought I was gone for good. He could have stopped this, you know. All he had to do was write to me. Tell me he planned to give me what was due me. My father had a small pension from being the fire chief, but he had a tidy inheritance from his parents. And there was the insurance money. Altogether it was quite a substantial amount. Enough to give me a better life than what I've had."

"I spent it all," Sam said. "Bought the veterinary practice. It wasn't as lucrative as I thought it would be. I was sure I could earn back what I'd spent and pay Jack his share of the money.

When I thought he was dead . . . well, I guess I was relieved in a way. I'm so sorry."

Kaely turned once more to look at Sam, but she was overcome by the pills and slumped down into the snow. "You didn't think it was Jack because you thought he was dead. That's why I never picked up signs you were lying."

"I didn't believe it until I saw the note. I would have done anything to stop him. You've got to believe me."

"Sorry, dear brother." Jack's voice came from behind Kaely. "I spent the last several months planning my return to Darkwater. I wanted to ruin my brother's reputation. Frame him for setting the fires, and then kill him. That way I could take everything away from him. Just like he did to me." He sighed dramatically. "But I made one mistake. Forgot to hide my scar the night of the fire on Mayfield. I'm so used to it, I didn't think about it." He laughed. "Oh, sorry. Two mistakes. Forgot about those stupid contacts.

"I started out using space heaters here. You know, to re-create that night. I figured my brother would get the hint. It was important to me that he realize he was finally paying for what he'd done to me. I followed people home from the store where they bought them, picked the families that way. But then the town got spooked. I actually had to purchase one myself and bring it into the house on Mayfield. I *needed* to set that fire. Twin boys. Just like Sam and me. Now *that* was my pièce de résistance. A clear message to Sam. But in the end, the space heaters were too much trouble."

"Then you wrote . . . wrote the le-le . . ."

"The letter?" he finished for her, laughing. "Yeah. I decided to show my hand, let Sam know for certain I was back, if he wasn't already convinced. Then I switched to good ol' gasoline. You can make a much bigger fire that way, you know." He stared at Kaely. "Sure thought I'd taken care of you the night of the fire at your mother's house, but just in case you made it, I walked past the window. I hoped you'd suspect Sam might have set the fire. But still, nothing. You kept him out of trouble. Just like everyone has all these years. Just like my parents did." He stopped and sighed loudly. "I'm tired of talking, and I don't have a lot of time to kill." He laughed hysterically at his choice of words and went back to his car.

Kaely could only watch as he removed two large containers and carried them back. He unscrewed the lids. Kaely could smell the gasoline. He swept his arm toward the shell of the house behind them. "Tonight this evil house finally comes down. You're my last victim, Kaely Quinn. And my brother will finally die. This is delayed justice, brother. You betrayed me. I've hated you all these years. Tonight I get my revenge."

Jack came over and grabbed Kaely, pulling her to her feet. Then he ran his hands up and down her body, searching for her holster. She tried to fight him off, but she could barely move her arms. They had no strength. It was like hitting him with limp noodles. He pulled out her gun, then he tucked it into his waistband. Jack reached down and scooped her up in his arms, carrying her over to the house. As they approached it, Kaely could only pray.

Jack stepped through the doorway of the ramshackle structure. The door was long gone. He carried Kaely over to where Sam was tied up. Then he pulled a piece of cord out of his pocket and tied her to a nearby beam. He stepped back, clearly admiring his work.

"This will be the most glorious fire of all," he said, his breath like smoke. Snowflakes swirled around him in a mad waltz, as if becoming a part of his insanity.

FORTY-NINE

Although she knew she had to stay conscious, Kaely began to drift away. She was startled awake by someone whispering in her ear. She turned to see Georgie crouched down next to her.

"Wake up," she said. Then she whispered again. At first Kaely couldn't understand her, but her words became sharper. Louder. Kaely prayed that God would give her strength for what she needed to do next.

"Time to see this monstrosity come down once and for all," Jack was saying. "In case you're wondering, Kaely, the ropes holding Sam to that rebar will burn away. There won't be anything left of your corpses except bones. I'm leaving these canisters right next to my brother. Everyone will think he started this fire. Killed you and did away with himself. Overcome with grief for what he'd done. Good plan, huh?"

Kaely could punch several holes in Jack's plan, but this wasn't the time to make him angrier. All she could do was pray and try to hold on to consciousness.

Jack picked up the canisters and took a step toward them. Kaely could hear him chanting, "'Jack be nimble, Jack be quick, Jack jump over the candlestick. Jack jump high, Jack jump low, Jack jumped over and burned his toe.'" His high singsong voice made the old nursery rhyme sound ominous.

"Don't do this," Sam said. "Please, Jack. I'm your brother. I never meant to use all the money. It was a mistake. Let us go. I'll make sure you get everything you're owed. I promise. I should have come to you when you were in trouble. I . . . was afraid. Afraid that if I was connected to you in some way, people would figure out what we'd done." His voice broke. "I've always loved you, Jack. I never stopped. We . . . we can leave here. Start over. Just you and me. Please . . . please don't hurt us." He looked at Kaely. "Or just punish me and let her go. I'm begging you."

"Oh, stop it," Jack spit out. "Although I do like to hear you beg." He shook his head. "You never liked me. And you certainly didn't love me. The only thing I ever saw in your eyes was fear."

"You need help, Jack," Kaely said, her voice breaking. "Let us help you."

"No one can help me. Nor do I want it. When I'm done here, I'll start a new life. No ghosts. No one looking down on me."

"But you'll still be sick."

Jack walked over and slapped Kaely in the face. "I may be sick, but you're going to be dead."

"I can't believe you think I wouldn't do anything after I realized who you are. If you're so smart, why didn't you figure that out? Seems pretty obvious to me." She took a deep breath, trying to revive herself once more before losing consciousness. "I feel sorry for you, Jack. I really do." Kaely gulped in one more large breath, sucking in as much cold air as she could. Then she said, "9-1-1."

Suddenly, lights flicked on from the police cars that surrounded them, filled with officers just waiting to hear her call for help.

"What's going on?" Jack said. His face was locked in an expression of shock and rage.

Kaely, who was barely hanging on, said, "I'm wired. They've heard everything we've said."

Jack took several steps back, the gas canisters still in his hands. He put one down and reached into his pocket, pulling out a lighter.

Josh walked slowly into the ring of light. "Jack, put the lighter down. You're not going to use it."

"I burn people," Jack said. "It's what I do. It's what I have to do."

"We're going to get you some help, and I'll be with you every step of the way."

"I'll be there too." Tuck came walking up next to Josh. "Put it down, Jack. Let's get out of here. It's cold and we need to get inside, okay?"

"It is cold." Jack's voice was tinged with madness. Before anyone could stop him, he poured the gasoline on his head and clicked the lighter.

A week later, Kaely and Noah met Tuck and Josh at another diner Tuck recommended. Tuck was better than an app when it came to finding good places to eat. The Washington Street Grill was packed with locals who liked to meet and gab.

Kaely and Noah were heading back to St. Louis right after breakfast. She'd had dinner with her mother and Jason the night before in the nice condo the insurance company had found while Marcie's house was being rebuilt. The doctors couldn't have been more encouraged about her condition, and Kaely was convinced her mother was going to recover. She still had treatments ahead, but her attitude was great, and she was looking forward to overseeing the rebuilding of her house.

Before she left last night, Kaely and her mother sat down and talked. Really talked. Although they still had a lot of things to work on, at least they were finally communicating—and trying to forgive each other. Kaely apologized for her role in their problems. She'd realized that since God had forgiven her a great debt, she had no business holding on to the past, trying to make her mother pay for her mistakes. Her mother's debt was nothing compared to hers.

After her apology, Kaely's mother had taken her hands. "It goes two ways, Jessie," she'd said. Her mother's eyes had filled with tears. "When your father was arrested, it shocked me to the core. I . . . I tried to carry on for you kids, but to be honest, I felt like a robot. It was hard just trying to put one foot in front of the other. I didn't want to break down in front of you. But the truth is, it probably would have been better." She shook her head slowly as a tear ran down her cheek. "I cut you off emotionally because I . . . I couldn't deal with my hurt and my anger." Her eyes searched Kaely's. "It was the only way I could keep living. Keep moving. But it wasn't fair to you. I'm so sorry."

Kaely tried to respond, let her mother know how much her confession meant, but she couldn't find the words. They felt stuck in her throat, almost choking her. Finally, she'd simply put her arms around Marcie and they both cried together. Before she left, Kaely promised to stay in touch and come back for a visit as soon as she could.

Jason had decided to stay a bit longer, but he and Kaely hired a woman to help Marcie until she could get by on her own. Jason wanted to make sure the arrangement was working before he left, and he'd arranged for Audrey to come to Darkwater before he headed home. Thankfully, this time Marcie accepted the help without complaint. It was a huge relief to both her children.

Saying good-bye to her brother had been hard. Kaely felt closer to him now than she ever had, even when they were kids. She was really going to miss him.

"What do you recommend I order?" Kaely asked Tuck.

"The chocolate pancakes are off the chain," he said. "You'd love them."

Kaely laughed. "Chocolate for breakfast? I'll pass. How about the pecan pancakes? I think I can handle that."

"They're great too," he said with a grin. "Coward."

"I call it being smart," she said, returning his smile.

The waitress came over with coffee and filled their mugs, then they all ordered. Kaely picked up her mug and took a sip. It was delicious. Right now she wanted coffee more than anything else. It had taken her days to get the aftereffects of those sleeping pills out of her system.

"Well, I can't say this turned out the way I thought it would," Josh said with a deep sigh. "I really didn't believe Jack was in Darkwater, setting those fires. And finding out Sam was the one who set his house on fire? I still don't completely understand that. It's just not like him."

"I'm not a psychiatrist," Kaely said, "so all I can tell you is that it seems Jack was born without the ability to relate to others or to care for anyone except himself. Every slight, every rebuke from his parents, no matter how small, made him furious. That anger built up into hatred. He finally decided to get rid of his family. I don't think Sam would have been involved if he wasn't so afraid of his brother. Jack is obviously a great manipulator. He was the strong twin and Sam was the weaker one. My guess is that Sam felt he had no choice. We have to remember that he was just a kid."

She shrugged. "The authorities will have to figure all that out. I expect at some point Sam will be charged in the death of his parents. I believe he became a firefighter to try to make restitution for what he'd done."

"That's why he took so many chances," Tuck said quietly. "Trying to make things right."

Kaely nodded. She could tell that Tuck was still devastated by Sam's confession. "Sam tried hard to put the past behind him. He really thought Jack was dead. He didn't get suspicious until he saw the letter."

"It's still hard to fathom," Josh said, " that Jack has so much hate inside of him."

"Yes, he does and it won't go away overnight. At least he has a chance to get help. Your quick thinking saved his life, you know. Pushing him down into the snow and putting out the fire kept his injuries to a minimum."

"After he recovers physically, the hospital is going to transfer him to a mental facility in Omaha," Josh said. "It doesn't mean he won't face charges. Getting off by pleading insanity is getting harder and harder in this country."

"He was very clever," Kaely said, "and showed great planning. I don't think his lawyers will get away with an insanity plea, but you never know."

"What he did is monstrous," Tuck said. "People are dead. I just can't forgive him. But Sam is at the hospital every day, trying to help him. Jack doesn't want him there, but Sam won't leave. After everything . . . I just don't understand why he would do that."

"Sam and Jack are brothers, Tuck," Kaely said. "No matter what, that will never change."

"We both promised to stick by him, Tuck," Josh said. "We need to keep that promise."

"I know I told Jack I'd be there for him," Tuck said. "I'll try, I really will. But only because I made a promise."

"Monsters may not deserve compassion," Kaely said softly. "But everyone gets forgiveness from God if they want it."

"I'm not God," Tuck mumbled.

"Why did he burn down your mom's house?" Josh asked, changing the subject. "And how did he even know who you were?"

Kaely sighed. "It's a good question. One I don't have the answer for. I can only guess." She took a sip of coffee before responding. Trying to understand the mind of a madman wasn't easy. "Somehow he found out about me. I was looking for the arsonist the night of the fire on Mayfield, and I believe he was watching me." She shook her head. "I wanted information from some people watching the fire, so I showed them my creds. I shouldn't have done it. I think he asked those people about me after I left."

No one said anything in response to her admission, but Kaely knew she'd made a mistake. Nothing she could do about it now.

"Maybe that's how he found out you were FBI," Tuck said, "but why burn down your mother's house? And why try to kill you the other night?"

"Again, I just have guesses. I think he felt I was challenging him. And Jack doesn't like being challenged. His ego wouldn't allow it. He wanted to beat me. Win whatever game he thought we were playing." She looked at them. "It doesn't make sense. Neither does his reasoning when he wanted to destroy the remainder of his house with Sam and me inside. The evidence wouldn't have supported his strategy. But by that point, he just wanted us gone. He was devolving, falling apart. The scary thing is that he might have gotten away with it if I hadn't realized that Aaron Pollard was Jack. Not wearing his contacts gave him away." She felt a shiver run down her spine. If Jack had murdered her and Sam and taken off, would anyone have thought to look for him since no one believed he was alive? The thought of another psychopath unleashed in the world was frightening. How many other people would have died?

"You waited too long to send us your 9-1-1, you know," Josh said accusingly. "I was getting ready to call it off several minutes before you signaled us."

"I'm glad you didn't," Kaely said. "Of course I wanted to summon you sooner, but we needed Jack's full confession. I have to admit that finding out what Sam had done took me by surprise. There was always something about this case that bothered me. As much as I tried to understand Jack's motivation, I always felt as if something was missing. Sam's involvement was it." She smiled at Josh. "I wanted to make sure we had everything. Even Sam's confession."

"You know that getting a confession wasn't the reason we went along with this plan in the first place," Josh said. "Locating Sam was more important. Once you knew who Jack was, we realized Sam was missing and figured that Jack had to have him. We were afraid Jack would kill him before we could find him."

"I have to agree with Josh," Noah chimed in. "You could have died, Kaely. Waiting so long was extremely reckless."

"It was my call," she said. "I'm not sorry about my decision. I still feel it was the right thing to do." She looked over at Noah, but he wouldn't meet her gaze. She knew he was upset with her. He'd been quiet, uncommunicative ever since the night they arrested Jack.

"It might have taken us a while to get to the truth," Josh

said. "But we would have. You shouldn't have taken a chance like that."

"Maybe you're right. But it was mine to take." Kaely took another drink of her coffee. "Yes, finding Sam was the top priority, but getting a full confession from Jack was icing on the cake."

"Well, no matter what, thanks for everything," Josh said to Kaely and Noah. "Without your help, I don't think we could have stopped Jack."

"So maybe the FBI isn't so bad after all?" Kaely asked with a grin.

"Yeah, maybe not." Josh raised his coffee cup, and all of them tapped their cups together in a gesture of victory.

FIFTY

About an hour later, after Noah and Kaely had said their good-byes, they were on their way. The roads were clear, so they didn't anticipate any problems getting home.

Kaely noticed Noah swallow two pain pills with the cappuccino he'd purchased at a convenience store.

"You better be careful with those things," Kaely warned.

"If your arm hurt as much as mine does, you'd take them too."

"Definitely not. I'm done with being drugged. It's getting old." Kaely sighed. "Next case let's do something easy."

Noah was quiet for a moment. Then he said, "I have a couple of questions."

"Go for it," Kaely said.

"You told me you felt Dr. Roberson was hiding something. Did you ever figure out what it was?"

Kaely nodded. "I'd noticed that his legs looked stronger than they should have. Once I had time to think about it, it came together. There were footprints on the carpet, and the bottoms of his slippers were worn. Things in the kitchen were too far back on the counter to be reached by someone in a wheelchair."

"He can walk."

"Right. He's probably afraid he'll lose his benefits if he admits to it. I doubt seriously that would happen, since I assume he still has significant pain, but when you're in his situation, you protect yourself."

"You didn't tell anyone?" Noah said.

"No. It's none of my business. I was in Darkwater to see my family and try to stop an arsonist, not to ruin the life of a man already broken by tragedy."

"He may have committed fraud."

"I doubt it. My guess is he couldn't walk after the accident. He may be getting better, but that doesn't mean he can work. Besides, it's only conjecture on my part. I don't have any proof. No reason to turn him in. What's your other question?"

"When did you set up the plan to catch Jack? I know some of it, but we haven't had much time to talk, since you needed to spend time with your family before we left."

"I called Josh when I realized the truth about Jack. The police went to the Pollard house and found Aaron's body. Then Josh tried to contact Sam but couldn't locate him. He was supposed to be at the fire station, but he never showed up, which was when we suspected Jack had him. Since 'Sam'"—she made air quotes with her fingers—"had already called me, asking for a date, we figured Jack was ready for his end game. I was certain he was going to take me to Sam. We were the two people who'd escaped his attempts to kill us."

She sighed. "I kept feeling like I had overlooked something. Something important. But it never occurred to me that Sam was involved. A friend tried to tell me I'd failed to see a major clue, but I just couldn't figure it out."

"That's when you and Josh came up with the idea for you to wear a wire?"

"Exactly. And thank God we did. They heard Jack say he wanted to go to his old house, so the police drove there ahead of us. There's a dirt road that runs behind the trees on the property. Josh and his deputies arrived before we did and waited with their lights off."

"Why didn't Josh just get Sam out of there?"

Kaely shook her head. "We didn't want to set Jack off. If we got there and Sam was gone, who knows what he would have done?"

"Did Sam know they were there?"

"No. We were afraid he might accidentally give away our plan. We couldn't take that chance. We needed a confession."

Noah was quiet, and Kaely snuck another look at him. His expression was taut and his lips were thinned.

"You're really hurting, aren't you?"

"It's not that, Kaely."

"Then what is it?"

"You did it again. You put yourself in danger."

She was startled by the anger in his voice. "Like I said, I wanted to make sure Jack incriminated himself. Then when Sam started to confess—"

"Stop it," Noah barked. "Just stop it."

"I don't understand."

"Yes, you do. We've been over this and over this. You're reckless with your life. You take chances you don't have to. Josh said the same thing, that you should have signaled him earlier. I blame him too. He was in charge. He should have gotten you out of there before things went so far, but in the end, the fault lies with you."

Kaely didn't know what to say. Noah had never been this angry with her before.

"I don't know if I can work with you anymore."

Kaely couldn't believe her ears. "What? What are you saying?"

"I'm saying that I care about you. I can't stand by and watch you kill yourself. I won't."

Kaely felt as if her whole body had suddenly grown cold.

"Noah, please. We can work this out. You're the only person in the world I trust."

"Trust?" His laugh was bitter and shocked her.

"Yes, I trust you."

"Okay, Kaely. Who is the friend who helped you? The one who tried to steer you in the right direction? As far as I know, the only people who knew what was going on besides me were Josh, Jason, and Tuck. Oh, and Sam, but it couldn't have been him."

Kaely hesitated as she wrestled with what to say. Suddenly the image of the kiss she gave Noah in the hospital popped into her mind. She couldn't lose him. She just couldn't.

"Don't do it." Georgie's voice came from the back seat. "You told one other person about me. He's gone. Noah will leave too."

Was Georgie right? Would she lose him if he knew who she really was? Frankly, she felt she could explain Georgie. What really frightened her were the UNSUBs who had begun to talk back. The last time she'd used her profiling technique she'd been threatened. The dark words she'd heard drifted through her head like slow-acting poison, taking over the rest of her body, causing her to tremble. "*You're going to die. It will not happen here, in Darkwater, but it will happen. And soon.*"

"Kaely, please. Listen to me." The pleading tone in Georgie's voice caught her attention. Would Noah think she was crazy and walk away?

She glanced over at him. "The truth might be hard to believe," she said finally, unable to keep her voice from shaking.

"Try me."

Kaely glanced in the rearview mirror. Georgie was gone. She took a deep breath and sent up a silent prayer. "I . . . I've never told you about my friend named Georgie, have I?"

ACKNOWLEDGMENTS

My heartfelt thanks to one of my heroes, Supervisory Special Agent Drucilla L. Wells (retired), Federal Bureau of Investigation (Behavioral Analysis Unit). This series wouldn't exist without you. Thanks, Dru. I'm incredibly grateful.

Thank you to retired Battalion Chief William S. Farmer, Clayton County Fire & Emergency Services, Clayton County, Georgia. Your help was invaluable. And thanks for stopping me from blowing up one of my main characters!

My special thanks to Dr. Andrea McCarty in Wichita, Kansas, for stepping in when I needed her. You're such a blessing.

My sincere appreciation to USCG-licensed Captain Randall J. Davis, BBA, NR-PARAMEDIC S/V PAINKILLER. You never know who you'll meet sitting in a doctor's waiting room! Although I didn't have time to use all the great information you provided me, I hope you'll hang in there with me. I think we have more work ahead of us!

Once again, thank you to Raela Schoenherr for her help with *Fire Storm* and for giving me the chance to introduce Special Agent Kaely Quinn to my readers.

Nancy Mehl is the author of more than thirty books, including the Road to Kingdom, Finding Sanctuary, and Defenders of Justice series. She received the ACFW Mystery Book of the Year Award in 2009. Nancy has a background in social work and is a member of ACFW. She writes from her home in Missouri, where she lives with her husband, Norman, and their puggle, Watson. To learn more, visit www.nancymehl.com.

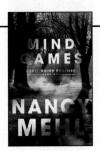

More Gripping Suspense from Bethany House

When a Coast Guard officer is found dead and another goes missing, special agent Finn Walker faces his most dangerous assignment yet. Complicating matters is the arrival of investigative reporter Gabby Rowley, who's on a mission to discover the truth. Can they ignore the sparks between them and track down this elusive killer?

The Killing Tide by Dani Pettrey, COASTAL GUARDIANS #1
danipettrey.com

When corporate litigator Mia Shaw finds her colleague brutally murdered, she vows to make the killer pay. The accused is a friend of Noah Ramirez, who knows something doesn't add up. As Mia takes on a case of corporate espionage, Noah becomes her only ally. But can he convince her that the killer is still on the loose—and protect her from growing threats?

Breach of Trust by Rachel Dylan, ATLANTA JUSTICE #3
racheldylan.com

Once lost to history, the Book of the Wars has resurfaced, and its pages hold ancient secrets—and dangers. Former Navy SEAL Leif Metcalfe has been tasked with capturing the ancient text, but a Bulgarian operative snatches it, determined to secure her freedom. When a series of strange storms erupt, they must form an alliance to thwart impending disaster.

Storm Rising by Ronie Kendig, THE BOOK OF THE WARS #1
roniekendig.com

◆ BETHANYHOUSE

You May Also Like . . .

A century apart, two women seek their mothers in Pleasant Valley, Wisconsin. In 1908, Thea's search leads her to an insane asylum with dark secrets. In modern-day Wisconsin, Heidi Lane answers the call of a mother battling dementia. Both confront the legendary curse of Misty Wayfair—and are entangled in a web of danger that entwines them across time.

The Curse of Misty Wayfair by Jaime Jo Wright
jaimewrightbooks.com

Three bestselling Christian romantic suspense authors team up in this intense novella collection. In Dee Henderson's "Betrayed," a woman cleared of a murder she didn't commit faces another deadly betrayal. In Dani Pettrey's "Deadly Isle," a couple is trapped on an island with a murderer. And in Lynette Eason's "Code of Ethics," two people must outrun the killers hunting them.

The Cost of Betrayal
by Dee Henderson, Dani Pettrey, and Lynette Eason
deehenderson.com; danipettrey.com; lynetteeason.com

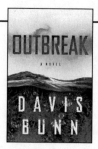

Along the coast of West Africa, strange algae is growing and mysterious deaths are rising—until suddenly, with the sea currents' shift, the deaths stop. Professor Theo Bishop and biological researcher Avery Madison are the only ones who know the truth. Will the authorities heed their warning before it happens again?

Outbreak by Davis Bunn
davisbunn.com

◊ BETHANYHOUSE